Bonds of Aggar

by Skye Montague

set in a universe by

Chris Anne Wolfe

Blue Forge Press
Port Orchard * Washington

First Print Edition May 2016
Second Print Edition January 2023

ISBN 978-1-59092-932-2

For information about film, reprint or other subsidiary rights, contact: blueforgegroup@gmail.com

Blue Forge Press is the print division of the volunteer-run, federal 501(c)3 nonprofit company, Blue Forge Group, founded in 1989 and dedicated to bringing light to the shadows and voice to the silence. We strive to empower storytellers across all walks of life with our four divisions: Blue Forge Press, Blue Forge Films, Blue Forge Gaming, and Blue Forge Records. Find out more at www.BlueForgeGroup.org

Blue Forge Press
7419 Ebbert Drive Southeast
Port Orchard, Washington 98367
blueforgepress@gmail.com
360-550-2071 ph.txt

Before her death from cancer in July 1997, beloved lesbian-feminist author Chris Anne Wolfe published two of her four classic Amazon adventure novels — *Shadows of Aggar* and *Fires of Aggar*.

Wolfe left her literary estate to friend and publisher, Jennifer DiMarco. After releasing Chris Anne's *Sands of Aggar* and *Oceans of Aggar*, as well as *Roses & Thorns: Beauty and the Beast Retold, Annabel & I, Talismans & Temptations*, and the *Amazons Across Aggar* card game, Jennifer finally opened the world to authors passionate about Aggar who want to help continue Chris Anne's legacy.

Bonds of Aggar is the first of this new generation of adventures.

To become a writer for Amazons of Aggar, write to Jennifer at blueforgepress@gmail.com

More by Chris Anne Wolfe

Amazons of Aggar

Book 1: Shadows of Aggar
Book 2: Fires of Aggar
Book 3: Sands of Aggar
Book 4: Oceans of Aggar
Book 5: Bonds of Aggar
Book 6: Wilds of Aggar

Annabel and I

Roses and Thorns

Talismans & Temptations

www.BlueForgePress.com

Bonds of Aggar

by Skye Montague

set in a universe by
Chris Anne Wolfe

PART ONE

KIN

CHAPTER ONE

The sun rose high in the sky, the last of the twin moons dipping low behind the horizon. Elana hugged her arms close to her chest, the softness of Di'Nay's shirt a warm whisper against her skin. She closed her eyes as the rising sun lit against her cheeks and a gentle breeze fluttered through the window, tousling wisps of her long, thick ebony hair.

She could hear Di'Nay's gentle breathing from the bed, her Amazon buried in a nest of blankets and pillows. A gentle smile rose to her lips. She could still smell the pine soap mingled with her lover's skin from their bath the night before. She could still feel Di'Nay's arms, hear the gentle beat of her heart beneath her chest. Every sensation had been like sunlight to flowers, bringing Elana back to life after being separated for far too long.

Elana glanced over her shoulder at the roaring fire leaping and dancing in the hearth. It was a careful balance, keeping the fire stoked high enough to offset the cold from the open window before it could wake Di'Nay. The Amazon couldn't rest when she was chilled. Her blood ran hotter than the people of Aggar. Elana had gotten used to the warmth of their shared room, but sometimes, when her mind was spinning and her Sight felt muddled and clouded, she missed the cold.

She ran her fingers over the icy stones of the windowsill. She had spent most of her life within the walls of the Keep, studying with would-be seers and guides to both hone her Blue Sight abilities and become a Shadow – a bonded guide – for someone worthy of such a formidable companion.

She knew every line of the building, every stone and ridge. The cold of the stones – it was such a familiar sensation. The faint ghosts of amarin – spirit and emotion entwined – and memory buzzed through every crevice of the Keep. Generations of study, dreaming, reaching out for the stars and destiny coalesced under her fingertips. She could taste it in her mouth, feel the warmth of the seers and shadows that came before her nestling around her, forever entwined with her soul. She was woven into a web of the past, present, and future. A Blue Sight. A Shadow of the Keep.

And today she would leave Aggar forever.

It made sense that she would feel so ill at ease. Her Sight made her sensitive to the moods of others, but it made her own emotions difficult to control. It had taken her entire life to learn to set herself aside. To become a true Shadow. But even with all her lessons and meditation, exhaustion could still cloud her mind.

The back of her neck tingled and her breath quickened as she felt Di'Nay slowly sit up, her amarin still heavy with sleep. Between her Sight and their Shadowbond, Elana's heart, her breath, every function of her body was synced to her lover. When they weren't close, her body fell into its own rhythm but sometimes, with Di'Nay near, especially after they'd been separated for so long, her body seemed desperate to bond with her partner.

"I didn't mean to wake you," Elana called as Di'Nay glanced at the empty bed in confusion.

Di'Nay's bare feet were soft on the stone floors as she slid out of bed and crossed the distance between them in three long strides. She wrapped her arms around Elana's waist, her forehead resting heavily on the Blue Sight's shoulder.

"I thought you'd sleep longer." Di'Nay's normally low voice was husky with exhaustion. Her grip on Elana's waist was desperate. Elana could feel a lingering fear darkening her Shadowmate's thoughts. She smiled and gently laid her hands over Di'Nay's.

"I'm all right. I already feel stronger with you by my side."

"You should be sleeping. I felt how tired you are. You were near death."

Elana shook her head slowly and turned to face her lover, laying a gentle kiss on her lips. "I'll sleep enough on your ship. You said the journey takes a quarter of a tenmoon?"

"Roughly. We'll be in hypersleep, but the process isn't particularly restful."

"Tell me about it."

Di'Nay's eyes were steadily growing sharper as she woke, no longer misted with sleep. Elana held her tighter as she felt her Shadowmate's amarin darken with unease. "Is something wrong, Soroi n'ti Mee? Are you rethinking your decision?"

Elana shook her head. "No, not at all. I told you I wouldn't hide anything from you anymore. I'm just still in recovery. And I'm curious about the journey."

Di'Nay let out a nervous breath, still so careful with her young lover. Elana felt the shift in her amarin as she became suddenly protective and Elana fixed her with a knowing glare. She didn't need to be handled with care.

Di'Nay laughed aloud at Elana's incredulous glare and kissed her. "Forgive me, Ona."

Elana laughed at Di'Nay's use of her childhood name. "Answer my question."

"We'll be laid to rest in hypersleep chambers. Our bodies will be frozen, stopping even cell growth. We'll be locked in time until we're awakened on Shekhina."

"So you meant it literally. There will be no rest, as our bodies can't restore themselves while we travel."

"We'll arrive exactly as we left."

Elana suppressed a shudder, carefully guarding her fear. To be so far from life, frozen in a metal ship... Elana kissed Di'Nay once more and shut the window. It would be worth it. A life with her Amazon, her Shadowmate, a life of adventure on a new world – all of it was worth the journey.

She stretched her arms over her head. Perhaps she should try to sleep again. "When is Cleis coming with the shuttle?"

Di'Nay sat on the bed. "At dusk. I assumed you would want time to say your goodbyes."

"I made my decision. I'm a Shadow. No one will expect me to bid them farewell."

Di'Nay leaned back on her hands, her brow furrowed. The light of the fire left sharp shadows across her angular face and the narrow swath of skin exposed by her unlaced sleep shirt. "Are you sure? That sounds so... cold."

Elana smiled. "They're very happy for me. Not every Shadow finds someone to bond with, and even fewer make such a happy match. They knew I would leave. They hoped I would."

Di'Nay shook her head. "I've been here for years. I pride myself on my ability to assimilate and respect other cultures. But I still don't understand this. Forgive me if I'm being insensitive."

Elana glanced over her shoulder, her blue eyes flashing. "You're not. I didn't choose a gentle life. I chose a life that would be mine. But that doesn't mean there's no joy."

Di'Nay hesitated. "Will you miss it?"

Elana crept toward her, leaning over her, their eyes meeting as Elana flooded her partner with her certainty. "It's a chapter of my life that's come to an end. My future is with you. And I choose it with all my heart."

Di'Nay gently caressed her face and guided her down to the bed, her strong hands cupping her cheeks and drawing her into a tender kiss. Elana pressed her hands under Di'Nay's shirt, her skin warm and smooth.

Di'Nay grunted as her transmitter emitted three low rings.

Elana glanced at it on the other side of the room with Di'Nay's pack. "Do you need to get that?"

Di'Nay shook her head and pulled Elana into another kiss. "I'm busy."

The transmitter started ringing once more, the sound insistent. Elana glanced at it again and Di'Nay sighed. "I'll answer it."

Di'Nay climbed out of bed and grabbed the communicator, her eyes flicking across the screen. Her lips pressed into a hard line. "It's Cleis."

"Is everything all right?" Elana questioned.

Di'Nay nodded. "I should return her call."

Elana settled back into bed. "Talk to her. I'll try to get more sleep. Wake me when you're done?"

Di'Nay nodded as the transmitter started to ring again. "This is Diana n'Athena..." Di'Nay's voice faded as she stepped out of the room to give Elana peace.

Elana leaned back in the bed and pressed her face against the pillows, savoring the scent of her Shadowmate infused in every stitch. Just a few moments with Di'Nay had brought her back to herself. It had made her aware of her repairing body. She was exhausted.

She curled under the blankets and held a pillow that smelled of Di'Nay close to her chest. Within moments she'd drifted into the oblivion of a dreamless sleep.

Elana stirred and slowly woke. She felt heavy with sleep and better rested than she expected. Her eyes flew open as she realized how late it was. It was already past nightfall.

She sat up with a gasp, looking around with wide eyes. Why had she slept so long? Hadn't the ship arrived? "Di'Nay?"

Elana couldn't feel her lover near. She slowly slid out of bed and padded on bare feet across the cool stone floors. Di'Nay's bags were gone, as was her transmitter. Elana felt a flash of fear. Di'Nay wouldn't leave her? She shook her head at her own foolishness. Di'Nay would never leave her again. And after nearly dying from being apart, Elana would feel if her Shadowmate was dangerously far from her side.

Elana pulled on breeches and tall boots. She slipped out off the room into the long, narrow hallways of the Keep.

The click of Elana's boots rang through the empty passage, bouncing off the gray stone walls. Something felt off. There was a darkness about the Keep that had nothing to do with nightfall. She reached out with her Sight, trying to interpret the offending sensation, but nothing seemed abnormal. The Seers, bound with their hive-mind, drifted through nonlinear time. The Council went about their various tasks as the students finished their chores and began their late-night studies.

There wasn't a panic in the air. Elana was sure if something had happened, either to the Keep or to Di'Nay, there would be more chaos. But she couldn't shake the darkness that settled around her.

Elana ran her long, tapered fingers through her thick hair, her curls twining and tugging gently at her hands. The physicality of the motion was centering, pulling her out of her own mind.

Perhaps it was a bad dream she couldn't remember. It wouldn't be the first time she'd been unsettled just after a nightmare, and she had certainly been sleeping deep enough to forget dreaming. Still, she thought she was beyond such foolishness. She hadn't been afraid of imaginary things since she was a child.

"Elana."

Elana turned as she passed a small study, a fire burning in the hearth. A gentle smile rose to her lips. The old Mistress of the Keep stood from a cushioned chair and smoothed her long, black robe. Her hands were gnarled with age, her body frail, but her eyes were still as sharp as her mind.

Elana had learned recently that the old woman was her grandmother. It mattered little to two women who had taken the vows of a Shadow. Familial sentimentality was a quirk, something to be cast aside or kept as an amusement, but nothing to be loyal to. Nothing that should tie them down. Still, knowing their genetic bond, Elana couldn't stop herself from studying her face a little more closely whenever they met, searching for similarities.

The Mistress of the Keep smiled, instantly interpreting Elana's gaze. Elana cleared her mind with a faint blush. “Mistress?”

The Mistress welcomed her into the room and gestured to a chair. The rope that bound her robe closed swayed, the tawny fibers catching the firelight and seeming to glisten gold.

“You're looking better, Elana. Healthier. How are you feeling?”

Elana took a seat as the Mistress poured her a cup of tea. “Much better with Di'Nay returned. But Mistress, I thought the Amazon ship would have arrived by now. Did something go wrong? Is Di'Nay--”

The Mistress raised her hand. “Fine. She's fine. I believe there was a delay. Your Amazon didn't want to wake you while you rested so well.” Elana shifted uncomfortably. “Something still troubles you?”

Elana leaned back, drawing on the comfort her mentor had always given her. “I think it was a dream.”

“Another vision?”

Elana shook her head. “No, nothing like that. Just a feeling. Like a child who wakes and thinks she sees something moving in the shadows. It will pass.”

The old Mistress considered her words carefully. “You are not my student anymore, Elana. You are bonded and destined to leave this world. But if you'll indulge me?”

Elana nodded. “Of course.”

“You know the strength of your skills. You know you See as well as any adept Seer and if you were not bonded, you would still be our Eldest Prepared. You inspired the trainees by surviving without your Shadowmate for so long. They still whisper in the halls about how you triumphed over the bond. You took their fear.”

“You know as well as I do that I had less than a day left in me when Di'Nay returned. If she'd been delayed, it would have been too long.”

“I have my doubts, but that isn't the point. You are powerful. Stronger than you realize. You should trust your instincts.”

Elana shot a sardonic grin. “I'm a bit old to be letting my nightmares guide me. My Sight shows nothing out of the ordinary. I'd be lying if I said my senses weren't still recovering from Di'Nay's separation. I'll trust my instincts when I'm sure they're rooted in reality."

The Mistress bowed her head, raising a single hand in acquiescence. "Again, I don't presume to instruct you. I can only advise."

"I'll take your advice to heart."

A twinkle of humor lit the old woman's eyes. "No you won't. But that is your right."

They shared a smile. The sound of boots striking the stone floors echoed through the hall and Elana closed her eyes, drawing a deep, warming breath. Di'Nay.

"Elana? You're awake?"

Elana turned to the door and reached one hand out to her love. "Mistress told me Cleis was delayed. Thank you for letting me rest."

Di'Nay strode forward and took her hand, her eyes warm as she saw the color returning to Elana's cheeks and the strength growing in her grip. She would be back to her full strength in less than a day.

"Politics. Senior Terrans scrutinizing our paperwork. I'm afraid there are those among the Empire who enjoy making my life difficult."

Elana's brow furrowed in concern. "Will they discover I'm not really a Sister? They won't let me leave if they realize I'm of Aggar."

Di'Nay held her hand tighter. "You are a Sister. And you don't have to worry about the immigration laws. There are Sisters hidden throughout the Empire who will make sure our documentation clears. We just have to wait a bit longer. I admit I'd rather you be at full strength before we leave anyway. I may delay the journey entirely until I hear back about my request to shorten your assimilation. I don't think our metal moonbase will be safe for you after so long in space."

Elana nodded. "I trust you, Di'Nay."

"You're both welcome here until you leave," the Mistress offered.

"Thank you, Mistress."

"Of course, Elana. This is always your home when you have need of it."

The old Mistress leaned over her hand, a rough cough ripping from her throat. A spot of blood appeared on the back of her hand. Elana leaned forward in concern. "Mistress?"

The old Mistress waved her off. "It is nothing. Just over the mantle is a box. Medicine." Elana pulled a vial of deep green liquid from the box. "Mix it in my tea? Just a couple drops."

Elana did as she was asked. The new brew emitted a foul, pungent odor that curled Elana's lips in disgust and surprise. The old Mistress laughed. Elana's expression quirked into a mischievous smile. "I don't have to drink it."

The Mistress took her tea and emptied the cup in a single gulp. "The privilege of youth."

Elana knelt beside her Mistress and took her hand. Her grandmother's skin was silken and paper-thin, so fragile for a woman with such inner strength. "What's wrong, Mistress?"

"A bad cold. A flu."

Elana ran a finger over her hand, smudging the spot of blood. "This isn't common."

"Elana, my dear. In a Keep full of the greatest seers, Blue Sights, and healers in the world, you think I wouldn't know if there was something more?"

Elana squeezed her hand. "I suppose you would."

"Now." The Mistress's eyes sharpened, her voice losing any sign of illness. "There's no reason for you to push yourself today. Night has fallen. I recommend you both get to sleep."

Elana shook her head. "I've slept all day. I'm not tired anymore."

The old Mistress touched the dark circles under Elana's eyes. "You should know by now I can tell when you're lying, Dear." She glanced around Elana at Di'Nay. "And if your pride insists that you stay awake, I'm sure you can find a way to fill your time."

Di'Nay blushed, and hid a cough behind her hand.

Elana stood with a teasing glare, knowing a dismissal when she heard one. "You're too perceptive."

"Proof I'm not terribly ill."

"Still. Call for me if you need me."

"I'm sure I'll be perfectly fine."

Elana joined Di'Nay. "Good night, Mistress."

"Good night, Elana."

Elana and Di'Nay walked together out of the study back to their room. Despite her insistence that she had slept enough, Elana caught herself yawning behind her hand. Di'Nay wrapped a steadying arm around her waist and shot her a teasing smile. "Your

Mistress was right?"

Elana leaned on her shoulder, savoring any closeness with her Shadowmate. Even innocent touches seemed to flood her with new strength. "You're just as smug as she is."

"A compliment if ever I heard one."

"You like her?"

"I do."

Elana smiled gently to herself, unexpectedly pleased with the praise. The old Mistress had been a mother to Elana in many ways. While the Mistress would call her foolish for clinging to such sentimentality even subconsciously, it warmed her heart that her partner and her family approved of each other.

"What did you do today?"

Di'Nay tensed, a gentle blush coming once again to her tanned cheeks. "I was communicating with the Empire most of the day, trying to get our paperwork cleared."

Elana laughed, reading the truth in her amarin. "You lost your temper?"

"A few times," she admitted.

"You're so patient with them. You deserve to lose your temper every now and then."

Di'Nay kissed the top of her head. "It's still not becoming of a diplomat."

Elana glanced up at her. "You were afraid they'd learn the truth about me and I wouldn't be allowed to leave with you."

Di'Nay shook her head. "No matter what happens, Elana, I'll be with you. Either here on Aggar or at home. Many in Dey Sorormin wouldn't be above smuggling you out."

Elana grinned at the thought of subverting the Empire. "I love you."

They reached their room and dressed for bed. Elana entertained notions of doing something more, but the moment her head hit the pillow her eyes started to close. How could she be so tired after a day of rest?

Di'Nay wrapped Elana in her arms and laid a gentle kiss on her long neck. "I'm glad you're finally getting sleep."

Elana could only muster a gentle sound of agreement as she nestled deeper into her lover's embrace, surrounding herself with Di'Nay's strength, her scent, and softness as she drifted into dreams.

"Elana."

Elana woke with a start as Di'Nay grabbed her shoulder. Her heart leapt in her chest at her Shadowmate's urgency. For a moment she was transported to the mountains further north, traveling with Di'Nay once more into the hazardous lands of the Maltar.

Di'Nay released her with a silent apology. "I didn't mean to scare you."

Elana shook her head. "I'm fine. What's wrong?"

Di'Nay hesitated and Elana's breath caught in her throat. "It's the old Mistress."

Elana leapt from bed and ran out into the hall. Her night dress whipped around her legs as she moved, her heart pounding in her chest. Di'Nay kept stride with her. "She's still alive. She slipped into unconsciousness in the night."

"Her cough? This can't be normal."

"The healers are running tests."

Elana burst into her Mistress's room, startling two healers standing over her bed. The wizened old head healer of the Keep stepped forward. "Elana, you can't be in here."

Elana took a step forward, her eyes wide. The old Mistress was pale. She seemed impossibly frail in her sleep, her breathing labored. "Miriam --"

Miriam shook her head and guided Elana out. Her grip was weak, but Elana didn't fight her. "Elana, I know this is hard, but we don't know what's wrong with her. If it's contagious, you could be in danger."

"I don't care about me," Elana argued.

"Then care for her. Her immune system has weakened. If you have even a breath of a disease in you, your presence could make her worse."

Elana grasped her own hands behind her back, holding them in tight fists to keep them from trembling. "She just had a cough. She was taking medicine. You don't know what's wrong anymore?"

Miriam's lips folded into a frown. "She didn't have a cough, but we were treating her illness. We thought we knew what was wrong, but her previous diagnosis wouldn't account for this. We're doing the best we can for her."

Elana's stomach turned and soured. The darkness she'd felt

the day before returned. She shook her head. “Something else is wrong. She's not just sick.”

Miriam let out a gentle breath of surprise. “You've had a vision?”

“No, but I can feel it.”

Miriam took Elana's shoulders. “You've been under a lot of pressure lately. You're just recovering from your own brush with death. We'll take care of the Mistress.”

Elana shrugged out of her grip. “This isn't anxiety. There's... darkness surrounding the Keep. Something is off.”

“Wouldn't the seers sense something like that?”

Elana frowned. “Seers can be deceived.”

“You should rest. We'll send for you when the Mistress wakes.”

Elana grit her teeth, carefully burying her rising frustration. There was no use talking to her anymore. “Thank you.”

She stormed away. Her gaze flicked to Di'Nay's mouth, getting her attention without meeting her eyes as she passed. She didn't need her lover to feel her rage.

Di'Nay followed her back to their room. “Are you all right?”

Elana leaned back against the wall, her arms crossed and her nails digging into her skin. “Something's wrong. They won't listen to me.”

“She made a good point. Could your fear be --”

“I'm not wrong.” Di'Nay leaned back in surprise at the acid in Elana's voice. Elana instantly softened her tone. Di'Nay didn't deserve her anger. “I'm sorry.”

“I've never seen you so riled.”

Elana rolled her shoulders, trying to ease her own tension. “She's important to me. My family. I want to help her.”

“Is there anyone you can talk to? Anyone who will listen?”

Elana considered potential allies. “Yes, but without the seers sensing danger, they'll be wary. I'm powerful, but I can't see the future.”

“What *do* you feel?”

Elana close her eyes, opening her Sight and her heart to the energies around her. “Darkness. Ill intent. It seems to be everywhere, dusting every bit of the Keep.”

“Like a plot? Do you think someone is trying to hurt the Mistress?”

Elana grunted in frustration. “I can't feel anything in particular. It's not like I feel the presence of an assassin or saboteur. Just something wrong. Something that isn't natural.”

“What could be blocking the seers from feeling what you are?”

Elana's shoulders sank. “I have no idea, but if the Maltar proved anything, it's that the seers aren't infallible.”

“Should we wait a while? Maybe the healers will be able to discover what's wrong with her.”

Elana turned, staring at the ground as her mind spun. “I don't know what else we can do. I just... I don't like doing nothing. I don't like feeling helpless.”

Di'Nay wrapped Elana in her arms. Elana closed her eyes, breathing in Di'Nay's scent and relaxing in her warmth. She felt a flash of Di'Nay's memory, a night spent alone in the forest, fearing for Elana when she'd been imprisoned by the Maltar. “I know how you feel.”

Elana returned her embrace. “I know.”

“What will make you feel better? Do you need sleep?”

Elana shook her head. “I'd rather work. With the Mistress ill, training will be disrupted. I used to teach fighting and riding.”

Di'Nay tensed. “Are you sure?”

Elana glanced up at her Amazon and smiled. “I'm not so fragile.”

Di'Nay shook her head. “I never meant to imply--”

Elana silenced her with a gentle kiss. “I'll be careful. I just want to run. I want to be useful.”

Di'Nay nodded. “Then you should. Whatever makes you happy.”

“Help me?”

“Is that allowed? I'm not a Shadow. I don't want to impose or offend anyone.”

“The students are fascinated with you. A real sister of Yemaya. An Amazon. They could learn much from you.”

Di'Nay smiled. “All right then. We'll teach together.”

They headed toward the practice courts, still holding hands. Elana tried to draw comfort from her lover, but she couldn't push aside her fear. There was more coming. Complications. Pain. Hardship. She could feel it. But if it saved her Mistress, her Keep, she was willing to meet it.

CHAPTER TWO

Diana n'Athena crouched low to the ground and retrieved a fallen arrow. She could hear Elana's voice, sure and steady, as she corrected the young Shadow trainee's form. Diana paused, appreciating her lover's strength and certainty. She hadn't spent enough time with Elana in peacetime. She had only had a handful of days with her before their journey north when they first met. Watching Elana in her element, going about her old duties with a practiced rhythm and confidence, was enthralling.

Still, Diana had to remind herself that it wasn't peacetime. Not really. Even now just under Elana's calm exterior, Diana could sense her frustration and fear. Pain that went beyond the Mistress's sickness. Diana gripped the arrow hard. She had always been uncomfortable with how readily Elana agreed to leave her homeworld behind. Elana insisted coming with Diana to Yemaya would be an adventure, that their love would keep her strong, but the fear in Elana's eyes betrayed deeper uncertainty. She was afraid of leaving her home in trouble. She was still linked to the people she loved. People she would probably never see again if she let Aggar. Was it really responsible for Diana to take her away? Was it selfish?

As if she could read Diana's mind, Elana looked up from the archery range, meeting her eyes. Diana didn't need Elana's Sight to interpret the glance. Elana had never played the victim or done anything simply to please Diana. She wouldn't appreciate Diana's fears.

Diana sighed. She couldn't pretend she didn't want her Shadowmate with her. That she didn't want to see Elana standing in the fields of home, cast in the faint tint from the lavender sky or clad in the garb of the healing Shae crones. Elana would be safe on Yemaya in a way she never could be on Aggar. She could learn and grow without prejudice or fear. It wasn't unfair of Diana to want that for her.

And no matter what Diana thought or wanted, at the end of the day it was Elana's choice.

Diana jogged back to the range and placed the arrow in the young trainee's quiver.

"Thank you, Di'Nay," the student muttered, her cheeks dark with embarrassment.

Diana ruffled her hair with a chuckle. "You were close. Just aim a bit higher. No one gets it right at first. I'm sure even Elana struggled in the past."

Elana shook her head, her eyes teasing. "Never."

"Really?" the young trainee questioned, unsure.

Elana smiled softly. "I couldn't even pull back the string on the practice bow when I started. You're doing very well, Aleid."

Aleid smiled wider and notched another arrow.

"Thank you for your help," Elana muttered as the dozen trainees she was teaching shot as one at the targets a hundred paces away.

"It's been a pleasure. You're a good teacher. The scholars in House Minona would value you."

Elana smirked. "I thought you said I belonged in House Shae?"

"You belong in the House you choose. You would be accepted in many of them, but you'll only excel where your heart lies."

"Did you always know you were going to be n'Athena?"

Diana nodded. "Always. My mother was of Athena, as was her mother before her. I was drawn to adventure. To the idea of protecting my sisters. It was always n'Athena."

Elana nodded slowly. "That's how I felt about being a Shadow. The thought of becoming a seer, of merging minds and souls with the other seers... I didn't find it peaceful. I found it terrifying. I wasn't going to join their ranks just because I have blue eyes."

Diana kissed her cheek, keeping the motion quick and chaste in front of the children. "I'm glad you made the choice you did. I wouldn't have met you otherwise."

"I often make good choices." Elana smiled warmly.

Diana shifted uncomfortably. "Can you always see my

thoughts?"

"You're not hard to read, even without my Sight."

"There's an empire of Terrans that would disagree."

Elana shook her head. "You set such a low bar."

Diana laughed aloud. "I like this. I like being with you with nothing to do but live."

Elana corrected a trainee's grip and helped another notch an arrow. "It won't last long."

Diana lifted a brow. "You've Seen it?"

"It's the nature of things."

"I suppose."

Elana stood as the trainees aimed again. She rested her head on Diana's shoulder. The weight of her was already familiar, already home. Diana smiled softly as Elana touched her hand. "I like this, too. Thank you for being here."

"Of course, Soroi n'ti Mee."

"I don't just mean by my side. I mean here for me. With the Mistress sick, I appreciate having someone at my back. I've never had that."

Diana's smile faded as she felt the weight of Elana's pain. "You shouldn't have to go through this alone." Elana tensed and pulled away. "Elana?"

The Blue Sight turned toward the Keep, her eyes flitting cross the stones. "It's all right."

"That didn't look all right."

Elana shook her head and returned to her class. "I was just surprised."

Diana caught her eyes, hoping her Shadowmate felt her concern. "What happened?"

"It's the Seers. They're combining forces. Searching. It's rather loud."

"Is that common?"

"Not with this kind of intensity."

"What are they looking for?"

"An answer to the old Mistress's condition."

"The healers still don't know what's making her ill?"

Elana's lips were tight and her shoulders square. "Apparently not."

"That's good, though, yes? Your seers are famous for discerning truth. We had to travel North because it was so rare the seers couldn't find what they were looking for."

Elana shifted uncomfortably. "You aren't wrong."

"You question their abilities?"

Elana glanced at the students. She clearly didn't want to say more. "I know the seers' abilities."

"We can talk later."

Diana watched in silence as Elana finished her lesson, only interacting when Elana needed help. Diana could tell her lover's thoughts were elsewhere, but she never once faltered or lost concentration. She was a good teacher. Diana wondered what else she might discover about her young love.

"Do you want to tell me what you're really worried about now?" Diana questioned as they watched the trainees run back to the Keep.

"You know what I'm worried about."

"You don't seem to trust your Keep."

Elana paused as she lifted a dropped bow. "I trust my Keep. I trust my Council. But they aren't infallible."

Diana studied her. "A moment of trouble doesn't negate generations of ability and guidance."

Elana's shoulders drooped and her face fell in a rare moment of vulnerability. For a moment, her heart was laid bare. "She's my family."

Diana rushed to her side and wrapped her in her arms. Warm drops of Elana's tears dampened Diana's cotton shirt and she held her mate tighter. "We can search for answers. I'll contact Cleis. She'll be able to reach home, counsel with the crones n'Shae. They might have suggestions."

"They don't know Aggar, and whatever is happening to the Mistress is from here."

"You still think it's not natural?"

"I know it's not. Your crones are mighty healers. Maybe even mystics. But this problem is closer to home."

Diana held her tighter, but Elana's words stung. "My crones? Elana, if you're coming with me back to Yemaya, they're your sisters, too."

Elana looked up. "I didn't mean it that way."

"I know, but you feel that way."

"Di'Nay."

Diana kissed her. "I didn't mean to make you feel guilty. I just want you to really consider your choice."

"I've already told you --"

"I know. And I'm not questioning you. I just want you to be happy."

A bell rang in the distance, its deep, metallic tone calling everyone in the Keep to dinner.

Elana pulled away from Diana and wiped her eyes with the back of her hand. "Let's go. I want to commune with the Seers before bed."

Diana took her hand. "Of course."

They walked in silence back to dinner.

Diana leaned forward, her elbows on her knees and her hands clasped as she waited. Elana had disappeared behind the large stone doors to the Seer's vault hours ago. Diana wondered once again if she should follow, but Elana had warned that being too close to a gathering of Seers could be hazardous to one without the Sight or training to shield her mind.

Diana grunted and stood, pacing the entryway. The echo of her boots tapping across the floor rang through the empty hall, reverberating off the walls into the distance. It was hard to ignore how far underground she was or the stifling energy of dozens of mystics communing together. She could almost feel the weight of the soil above her, bringing back memories of rescuing Elana from the Seer's prison not long ago.

Diana grasped her wrist, drawing comfort from the steady warmth of her lifestone, assuring her that Elana was well. She knew they were both safe in the Keep, but Diana felt uneasy being separated from her Shadowmate by magic, especially at a time when Elana was so sure there was foul play in the Keep.

She turned sharply as the doors opened and Elana stepped outside. Her cheeks were dark with a worried flush.

"What happened?" Diana questioned. "Did they find what they were looking for?"

Elana nodded, her eyes sharp and focused. "She's not sick, Di'Nay. She was poisoned."

Diana's face paled in shock. "Poison?"

"By way of her medication. The medicine I gave her."

Diana reached out to Elana. "You can't blame yourself."

Elana barely acknowledged Diana's touch. "I don't. But I won't let her die. And I will see her attacker brought to justice."

Diana's breath caught in her throat at Elana's intensity. She was like a goddess of vengeance risen from the Fates' Cellar. Diana knew what Elana was capable of when she was focused. What would happen if she lost her emotional control? "Do the healers have an antidote?"

Elana pressed a piece of paper into Diana's hand. "There's a recipe, but they're missing a key ingredient. We leave in the morning."

Diana looked down at the list as Elana walked away, disappearing down the twisting halls as she returned to their room. She unfolded the paper to reveal a sketch of a purple flower with long, slender petals and a woody stalk. She ran her thumb over the series of location coordinates. She immediately recognized the area. She'd traveled the deserts of the southern continent many times since arriving on Aggar, but she didn't remember seeing this flower. It couldn't be particularly common and its marked location was far from the Keep. Even with Elana's Sight, it wouldn't be an easy find.

Diana folded the paper and tucked it into the pouch at her hip, her mind spinning through the list of traders she'd met over the years who might carry the medicinal plant. There was a lot of preparations to make before morning.

The sun rose slowly, its light reflecting off the last glimmers of the second moon. Diana pulled her hood lower over her face, skimming the horizon as her breath escaped her lips in steamy puffs. The Keep was just coming to life behind her, the students rising with the sun to prepare for the day. The warm scents of porridge and eggs drifted from the kitchens.

Diana blinked hard and yawned behind her hand. "Did you sleep at all last night?"

Diana turned as Elana stepped up behind her. She smiled at the familiar sight of the green cloak and soft, travel-worn leather gloves. Elana pushed her long, thick braid back over her shoulder. "No. You?"

"A little," she admitted. "But it wasn't restful."

Elana walked up beside her and took her hand. Her anger from the night before hadn't settled. Her energy was hot, almost suffocating, but Diana didn't know how to bring it up naturally.

"It's a cold morning. You must be looking forward to the desert heat."

Diana held her cloak tighter around her shoulders. "Nights in the desert can be just as cold. The Council Speaker mentioned the snows would come early this year."

Elana nodded. "I heard you were up talking with him most of the night."

"While you were sitting up with the Mistress?"

"Miriam couldn't turn me away. She isn't contagious. I couldn't... I couldn't leave her alone."

"I understand, Soroi."

"What were you speaking with the Master about?"

"I was planning for our trip. The desert is far away and navigating it is very different from the wastelands of the North. We're going to have to get supplies on the way. I can call in a few favors farther south, maybe even find a merchant who carries the herb, but it will take a while to get to the desert, even on horseback, and we'll have to convince my old contacts that we're traveling merchants."

Elana lifted her hood, disappearing into its darkness with all the skill of a professional Shadow. She was ready to leave. "That won't be a problem. I know where we can get what we need."

Diana lifted a single brow. "You care to share your plan?"

Elana only smiled. "We should ready our horses."

She strode across the grassy courtyard toward the stables. The frost-covered ground crunched gently beneath her weight. Diana settled back, watching her go. At least she still had enough humor to tease.

Diana rushed forward to catch up with Elana. Elana pushed open the stable door. A wave of heat from the resting horses engulfed Diana. The scent of hay and animal musk filled the air. Elana went immediately to her mare, Leggings, named for the black markings on her legs. She nuzzled the bay's neck, her tapered fingers lingering in the bay's fine mane.

Diana turned to her chestnut stallion, Kaing. He shuffled in his stall, recognizing his mistress with a welcoming snort. Diana laid a steady hand on his neck, watching Elana with her horse, Leggings. "Can you at least tell me what direction we're heading?"

Elana patted Leggings once more. "North a ways. To Black Falls."

Diana's eyes widened in recognition. “To your parent's home?”

“If anyone can help us with the supplies we need, it's my father.”

“Your family would have so much to spare?” Diana questioned, her stomach turning uncomfortably at the thought of taking from her Shadowmate's parents.

Elana laughed. “Of course they would. They love you.”

The off-hand statement brought a warm smile to Diana's lips. “Perhaps not when they learn of our plans to leave Aggar.”

“Don't be foolish. My family knows I'm a bonded Shadow. They would thank you for bringing me on such an adventure.”

Diana nodded. She could understand that. Her mothers and cousins on Yemaya had been overjoyed when she had been assigned a position off-world, not because she'd be leaving, but because she would be doing what she loved. “It would be nice to see them again. And good for you to see them as well.”

Elana didn't respond, only nodded slightly as she ran a brush through Leggings's mane. There was something weighing on her mind. Something heavier than her fears for the Mistress. But the weight of her emotion demanded silence. Instead, Diana focused on preparing Kaing.

After a time, Diana carefully broke the quiet. “Do you think Sy will be angry that his sword was destroyed? Your father worked so hard on it.”

Elana shook her head. “He will be proud that it served you so well. That it kept us both alive. It was made for a particular purpose. It served that purpose.”

“Still, it was a piece of art.”

“A challenge for him to best in the future.” Elana paused as she passed Diana's stall. She paused and looked her over. “We're not being followed or tracked. You don't need to dress as a man anymore.”

Diana glanced down at her men's breeches and vest. “It's a habit. People will stare at two women traveling together.”

Elana leaned forward, her eyes never leaving Diana's as her hands found the laces of her vest and swiftly loosened them, unbinding the weight of Diana's breasts. Diana watched her fiery Shadowmate in shock, her desire rising in her chest, burning away the morning's cold.

“Elana...”

Elana's hands found the curve of her breasts, lingering over her heart. "I like you better as a woman, Di'Nay. I don't care what anyone else thinks."

Before Di'Nay could answer, Elana turned. She cinched the last strap of Leggings's saddle and led her out of her stall to the courtyard.

"Are you coming, Di'Nay?" Elana questioned. The light of dawn streamed around her through the door, casting a fiery aura around the Shadow.

"Mae n'pour," Diana muttered in breathless, prayerful wonderment at the woman.

Elana glanced over her shoulder with a playful smile. "Your goddesses don't rule here, Amazon."

Diana took Kaing's reigns and moved to join her, her vest still hanging open. "My goddesses follow me everywhere, Soroi. You're evidence of that."

Diana helped Elana secure the saddle bags prepared by the trainees the day before. There was enough food for a few days travel and enough gold to purchase more along the way. The farther south they traveled, the more Diana would be comfortable scavenging as well. Diana just hoped the Mistress would hold out long enough for them to return.

"I don't want to draw too much attention in leaving. The trainees think we're going away on a holiday. The nature of the Mistress's condition isn't public," Elana warned, moving smoothly from flirtation to business.

"A holiday? Are Shadows prone to leaving on vacations?"

Elana smiled gently. "No. But they're also not prone to being away from their shadowmates for so long."

"They think you're still sick?"

"Better me than a member of the Council. The Mistress is adored. Her passing would be devastating, both for the people and the daily functions of the Keep."

"I heard her condition was stable?"

Elana shook her head. "She's deteriorating very slowly, but she's still deteriorating. The healers may be able to stabilize her, but they haven't had any luck so far."

Diana mounted Kaing with an easy swing of her leg, slipping up into the stirrup-less saddle. "Then we'll move quickly. She'll be all right, Elana. We'll help her. And then I'll take you on a holiday for real."

Elana mounted Leggings with a solemn expression. "You don't have to lie to me. We'll do our best, but you can't know she'll be safe."

She rode out into the orchard and Diana followed close behind, lost for the words to help her love.

Elana and Diana rode in silence as the sun rose high in the sky. Daybreak did little to chase away the chill and Diana found herself rubbing her hands together even through her gloves. She let out a heavy breath, the steam rising from her mouth and the taste of pine slipping past her lips. It was fast becoming familiar on her tongue, linked with her memories of Elana.

The forest was thick, but the path well-traveled. They didn't have to worry about traveling unseen this time, so they traded the wild route they'd taken to Black Falls the first time for a shorter, more manageable caravan trail.

Elana rode ahead, barely glancing back. It felt off, having Elana ride ahead so confidently. Diana was happy to see her taking charge, but it was so unlike the Shadow. Elana usually preferred to hang back, to blend with the darkness, to remain unseen. The woman who urged her mare forward, her hood falling back in her haste, wasn't pure Shadow. She was Amazon. But Elana's silence hinted at a source other than internal strength driving her forward.

Elana hesitated, and a moment later a silvery gray Eitteh leapt into the air out of a nearby tree. With a great heave of her ebony wings, she escaped the forest canopy. Diana watched it go with a smile.

"A good omen, maybe?" she called. "Another mission beginning with a flying cat."

Elana studied the Eitteh as it disappeared into the clouds. "At least this Eitteh wasn't hurt."

Diana rode forward. "The journey has been going smoothly so far."

"Our mission is a matter of time, not security. It isn't inherently dangerous," Elana pointed out.

"That never stopped us from finding trouble." Diana frowned. Her quip didn't earn the smile she'd hoped for. "Elana?"

"I'm fine, Di'Nay. I'll be better when we have the antidote."

"Are you certain?"

Elana turned, her eyes narrowed into a fierce glare, but the anger subsided unspoken. “I'm certain.”

“Because you seem equally as intent on vengeance.”

“Is that so terrible? Someone invaded my Keep. Poisoned my Mistress. My grandmother.”

“I just worry about you.”

Elana urged her horse forward. “I appreciate it, but I'll be all right.”

Diana squared her shoulders and clenched her jaw, torn between the urge to press her point and not to fight. A sour ache formed in the pit of her stomach. She liked to think of herself as rational. Diplomatic. But there was something about Elana. Something about the mysterious woman who fluctuated between so open her Sight could knock Diana unconscious and so enigmatic Diana couldn't even begin to understand her thoughts. It drove the Diana insane.

“I feel like there's something unspoken between us.”

“I'm not pulling away from you,” Elana promised, but her words were hollow. “I'm angry. What would you do if someone poisoned your kin?”

“I understand that, but I feel like there's more.”

“You're over-analyzing.”

Diana bit back a sharp retort, her cheeks coloring in frustration. Aggar women were so guarded. “Perhaps. Just tell me if there's ever anything I can do for you?”

Elana rode in silence for a long moment before sighing, her shoulders falling. “I'm sorry for being so sharp. I'll let you know if I need anything. I promise.”

Diana settled back in her saddle. It was better than nothing, but it did little to reassure her heart. In the grand scheme of things, they had known each other for such a short time. There would be a lot of moments like this. They were no strangers to arguing. But still, Diana feared the day her Shadowmate would wake and find her lacking.

Even more than that, Diana feared what anger and vengeance would do to her focused, protective lover. Was this a normal part of her? Or was it awakened by the situation? The irony of worrying about Elana's closed-off nature wasn't lost on her. Elana had battled against Diana's emotional walls for most of the time they'd known each other.

Diana sighed aloud. Even her own worries had become a jumbled mass of confusion and frustration. "How long do you suspect it will take us to reach Black Falls?"

"A few days if we don't camp long and aren't waylaid. I'm hoping my parents will have a spare caravan we can borrow. We'll travel much faster with a cart and stronger horses. We'll need the caravan space and shade to move through the desert potentially long-term. We'll also put up a more convincing front as traders."

"And if they don't have such supplies available?"

Elana tensed, her silence once more wrapped in her own thoughts and intentions. "We just have to hope they will."

Diana grit her teeth. She rarely envied Elana her Sight, but she couldn't help but wish she had a stronger ability to interpret her feelings.

Elana paused and hung her head. She reached her hand back and Diana rode forward to take it, comforted by Elana's touch. "Just be patient with me, Di'Nay? Please?"

Diana leaned to the side, bracing herself against Kaing's back as she kissed her partner. "Always. I promise. Just don't pull away from me. We spent so long hiding from each other."

Elana smiled softly. The expression was as complex as the Blue Sight, full of appreciation, compassion, and around her eyes a heat that made Diana's breath catch in her throat. "I was never hiding from you."

A sly smirk reached Diana's lips. "I remember."

Elana brushed a stray strand of short, golden hair from Diana's face, her touch feather-light. "I can't hide from you. We're Shadowmates. But I know what my Sight can do. I need to deal with my feelings on my own until I can control them again. I don't want to hurt you."

Diana caught her hand, her brow furrowed in concern. "It's not good to repress everything you feel."

Elana laughed, the sound easing some of Diana's fear. "You have much to learn about my Sight, Soroi."

Diana's cheeks burned with a blush at Elana's use of her language. The word sounded so right on her tongue.

"You're using Amazon language to distract me."

Elana kissed her once more, slow and teasing. She parted just enough to speak, her breath hot on Diana's cheeks, her lips brushing Diana's skin as she spoke. "And it's working."

Elana nudged Leggings forward once more, leaving Diana to stare after her in shock. Kaing huffed, glancing back at his mistress, awaiting her command. She grunted and nudged him forward with her heels. “Don't judge me.”

She raced forward to join Elana as they continued down the trail.

CHAPTER THREE

Elana stoked the fire higher, the blast of heat warming her arms through her leather bracers. The sound of Di'Nay laying out the bedmats while the horses settled down for the night brought a swell of mixed emotions. What was happening to the Mistress? Was she alive? Was she getting better or worse?

We shouldn't be stopping. We should be riding through the night. The thought raced through her mind, tugging at her heart. She knew it would be irresponsible to push the horses so hard in such an environment. They were already riding through most of the night, stopping for only a few hours to rest. Everyone needed sleep – herself possibly most of all – but she knew if the Mistress passed while she was away, she would regret every moment she hadn't been riding, every night she had slept.

She closed her eyes, squeezing them hard. She didn't need Di'Nay feeling her erratic emotions again. It was clear the Amazon was disconcerted by her anger and her silence. She didn't need Di'Nay to close herself off again. But she knew her Love couldn't handle the full brunt of her pain. She had only allowed Di'Nay to feel the full brunt of her frustration once before and she'd passed out just from meeting her eyes.

Her path was clear. She had studied for years to control her power. She needed to pull the emotions tighter inside her heart, needed to snuff out their intensity. She could let them turn cold. Her vengeance didn't need to burn. It could simmer.

"Are you hungry?" Di'Nay's voice drifted over the sounds of the fire and Elana's intense thoughts. "Or maybe some tea?"

Elana shook her head. "I'm fine. We should sleep. The sooner we rest, the sooner we can ride again."

She felt the heavy warmth of Di'Nay's hand on her shoulder. For a woman so strong and tall she moved with the quiet grace of an eitteh. "Are you feeling well?"

Elana covered Di'Nay's hand and nodded. "I'm just anxious to continue."

"Then come to bed."

Elana stood and followed Di'Nay, sliding down to rest on the wide sleeping mat the Amazon had prepared. Di'Nay wrapped her in her arms and instantly fell asleep. Elana closed her eyes and tried to draw comfort from her firm embrace.

Despite her exhaustion, her mind wouldn't settle. As she began to drift off, the thoughts and memories jumbled into a tangled blur. She thought of her Mistress, unconscious in bed, the poison slowly eating away at her fragile body. She thought of the complications of the journey, of everything that could go wrong.

As she slipped even further into sleep, she thought of her parents. She had made it clear the last time she'd visited that she probably wouldn't return. She had said her goodbyes. She'd been so ready to leave them behind. Why was she so intent on returning now?

I want to make sure they're safe. The thought shocked Elana enough to wake her. She had left behind such cares as a child before coming to the Keep. It wasn't her place to worry about her parents. Still, she found herself wondering just how much her insistence on traveling north actually hinged on the supplies her father could provide.

Elana turned, waking Di'Nay just enough for her to ease her grip on Elana's waist. Elana felt a flash of emotion from the Amazon – the fear that she was holding Elana too tightly – before she fell asleep once more. Elana smiled. It was such a simple concern. Delightfully mundane. Elana had never cared for the mundane, but with Di'Nay it was comforting.

She frowned as she wondered if she would ever be able to enjoy a truly quiet moment with her love. Her stomach twisted. She settled tighter back against her Shadowmate and closed her eyes again, fighting hard to return to sleep. It wasn't the time to think of the future. She had to stay focused on the present.

Elana's head bobbed suddenly, waking her with a jolt. She gripped the reigns tighter, settling back in her saddle. She sighed and rubbed her eyes with one hand, suppressing a yawn.

"Didn't sleep again last night?" Di'Nay questioned.

Elana blinked hard, trying to focus her exhausted mind. "Only a little," she admitted.

"We'll stay a couple days with your parents. You'll be able to sleep in a real bed. Should be more restful than icy dirt and roots."

"No, I want to keep our speed."

Di'Nay didn't respond. Elana could read in her amarin a determination to convince her later, but Elana knew she couldn't be swayed. She would find a way to sleep again once she saw her family. She wasn't sick, she was anxious. There was no reason for her to be treated like an invalid while the Mistress suffered.

The trees parted in the distance, revealing the town of Black Falls. The village filled a valley basin at the foot of the mountains, the houses close-packed and the town protected by the hills and sheer cliff sides. A silver column of water, the towering falls that fed the village, sparkled in the dimming daylight.

Elana's heart warmed at the sight. Before her recent journey with Di'Nay, she hadn't been home since she was a small child. Still, the sound of the falls and the comfort of the tight-packed houses and shops brought back old memories of comfort. Of safety. Of a time before training and the Keep.

Di'Nay glanced back over her shoulder, a smile lighting her face. "That's the first genuine smile I've seen in a long time."

Elana smiled wider. "I shouldn't be so pleased to return. This isn't my life anymore. Isn't my home."

"But it's a part of you. Moving on doesn't invalidate the places and people that were once precious to us."

Elana glanced back at the village. Di'Nay had such a strange way of looking at things. Any other family would have parted ways when their child became a Shadow, not from shame, but from necessity. Elana hadn't been raised with Di'Nay's sentimentality for home and the past.

Then again, her parents had never stopped communicating with her. Her grandmother had eventually revealed herself despite the fact that she should have abandoned family when she became Mistress of the Keep. And now Elana herself was insisting on returning, feeling joy at the sight of her childhood home. Perhaps the sentimentality Di'Nay held so dear was a part of her as well.

"Are you worried about seeing them again? With me?"

Elana turned to her in surprise. "Why would I? They've already met you."

Di'Nay shifted, her face uncertain. Elana's lips curled into a smile as she sensed the truth in her bondmate's amarin. "Not like we are now, sae? I presented as a man when they met me."

"They knew you are a woman."

"Knowing and seeing are different things sometimes. Will I discomfort them?"

"They know you as my Shadowmate."

"But we're more now. You're coming home with me. My mate. We could have a family someday."

"There isn't a difference between Shadowmate and mate for a Shadow of Aggar. I'm bound to you for the rest of my life. When you die, I will die. Where you live, I will live. My parents know this."

"You know what I mean."

Elana reached out and squeezed Di'Nay's knee. "I do. My parents won't be surprised." Di'Nay shifted again, her strong hands grasping at her reigns nervously. Elana chuckled. "They already like you."

Di'Nay looked up, meeting Elana's eyes. "Truly?"

Elana was shocked into silence. Di'Nay had met her eyes not out of fear or to make a point, but to seek comfort from Elana's abilities. No one had ever met her eyes like that before, not even Di'Nay. Looked into her eyes like she was special. Like her Sight was something useful and comforting.

Her heart pounded beneath her chest and her skin darkened. Di'Nay cocked her head to the side, recognizing the physical signs of pleasure and joy, but not understanding the source. Elana shook her head, her eyes still soft. "My father gave you a sword. He might like you more than he likes me."

Di'Nay laughed aloud and glanced out at Black Falls. The wind off the valley ruffled her short hair and tugged at her cloak. "Well then, let's go to them. Do you think your parents will let us join for dinner?"

Elana nudged her horse toward the familiar path into Black Falls. "My mother always expects company for dinner. You'll be lucky if she doesn't force second and third helpings on you."

Di'Nay nudged Kaing forward faster. "I wouldn't mind."

Elana's laugh rang through the valley, mingling with the

clatter of their horses' hooves.

Elana led her Shadowmate through the clusters of houses and shops, built into unofficial districts as Black Falls expanded. Every cobble and brick was familiar, recalling memories of running wild through the twisting streets and alleyways as a child. She could feel the textures of the stones under her fingers without touching them. She could smell the sweet rolls from her favorite bakery and the familiar soot of her father's smithy layered over the dust and pine scents of the street. She could feel the cobbles smoothed from use under her bare feet. She remembered looking out her window at the towering cliffsides and steep hills, feeling safe surrounded by the arms of Aggar.

She closed her eyes and she felt like she'd traveled back in time, before becoming a Shadow, even before arriving at the Keep. It was a sweet place to be.

"Lost?"

Elana didn't open her eyes, just let the softness of her smile answer Di'Nay's question. "I always forget how much I love this place until I return."

"I'm glad we got to come back."

"I am, too."

"Elana!"

Elana raised her arm as her foster brother, Alonz, spotted her out the door of their father's forge. A waft of heat blew through the open door of the stone building, the clang of hammers and heavy rush of the bellows mingling with the waterfall the town was named for was like a lullaby from Elana's childhood.

The youth raced across the street, his dusty hair swaying into his eyes. Elana reached down and clasped his arm. His taut forearms, chiseled from years at the forge, reminded Elana of her father. His skin was hot from the heat of the smithy. His hazel eyes sparkled with excitement.

"I didn't expect to see you again so soon. And not in disguise?"

"Fate is unpredictable. Is father here or in the house?"

"In his workshop, but we're almost done for the day. Do you want to speak with him?"

Elana shook her head. "I wouldn't want to disturb him. We'll stable our horses and head to the house. Is mother home?"

"Yes. We're not currently hosting visitors. You should be

alone. I won't tell anyone you're here."

Elana smiled, sensing his good intentions. She knew Alonz more through her parents' letters than through any time together. Her parents had adopted him after she left for the Keep. But he was sincere and welcoming. He was also learning fast what it meant to be related to a Shadow. "Thank you."

"I'll draw fresh water for your horses from the cooperative stores before dinner. There's feed in the back of the stable, along with brushes."

Elana breathed a soft sigh of relief. Her muscles were already sore from riding. It would be good to have someone else help care for the horses. "Thank you, Alonz.

"It's good to meet you again, Sister."

Elana nodded. "We'll see you at dinner?"

"Yes. I was going to sup with my betrothed's family, but I can delay to another day. This is more important."

Elana nodded and glanced at Di'Nay. "It'll be nice to have a hot meal and perhaps a bath?" Di'Nay let out a deep sigh of relief and excitement at the thought of bathing. Elana laughed. "I'll take that as a yes."

Alonz glanced between them, his eyes searching, but his amarin wasn't negative. "Mother will be happy to help."

"I'm sure she will. We'll see you soon."

Alonz scurried back into the smithy. Elana grinned and waved Di'Nay forward toward the courtyard that separated the forge from the main house.

They paused before Elana's childhood home, dismounted, and led their horses to the stable. Elana's family stable was larger than most in town. Elana's parents were regular hosts for traveling merchants, storytellers and even the occasional Shadow. Their reputations as good company, skilled craftsmen, and their familiarity with the Keep made them prime hosts for interesting people. Elana didn't doubt the stories from her parents' guests had been partially to blame for her ravenous desire for adventure and travel.

Elana's hand instantly found a brush and she ran it across Leggings' dusty neck. Both horses deserved a night of rest, fresh water and a thorough grooming. Leggings bumped her shoulder with her nose, her amarin grateful. Elana smiled gently.

"Is there a way I could take Leggings to Yemaya?" Elana

questioned, only half serious.

Di'Nay snorted as she filled both feed troughs. “Could you imagine? Cleis wouldn't appreciate me asking her to put a horse into cryogenic sleep on a spaceship.”

Elana sighed sadly as she worked a knot from Leggings' mane. “Not to mention the Terrans' strict biological contamination laws.”

“That, too.”

“There are horses on Yemaya?”

Elana grinned as she felt Di'Nay approach her from behind and wrap her arms around her slender waist. “Many. I'll find you a dozen horses.”

Elana leaned back against her shoulder. “I don't need a dozen horses. Just a mare who can run.”

“Broken?”

Elana glanced up at her lover. “I've trained many a horse. I don't need someone else to do it for me.”

“I don't doubt it.”

Di'Nay kissed her, her lips gentle, the touch full of a silent plea she hadn't dared to express since returning to Elana so sick and frail before the Mistress was poisoned. Elana instantly responded, her heart speeding faster, her body rhythms syncing with those of her Shadowmate. She reached up, wrapping an arm around Di'Nay's neck, her fingers curling in her hair.

“Of course, my Love.”

Di'Nay's hands tightened at Elana's waist as she deepened their kiss and Elana turned to face her Amazon, pressing tighter against her. She bathed in Di'Nay's loving, passionate amarin, basking in the heat the Amazon had withheld from her for so long. She could slowly feel her guilt at resting, at feeling joy while her Mistress suffered, dwindling. Her Mistress wasn't the only one who needed her. And she couldn't deny her Shadowmate.

Elana marveled once more at the feeling of entwining with Di'Nay, still clothed, and feeling the lines of her womanly body. For so long Di'Nay had dressed as a man, compressing her chest. Now Elana could feel every softness, every line. Her lover of dual natures. Chiseled muscle and silken curves. Masculine and feminine energies and shapes.

Elana gasped with need as Di'Nay pulled back reluctantly, glancing out the door. “Perhaps we should find somewhere else? I'm not sure you want your brother to learn of our relationship by walking in on us?"

Elana scowled. She kissed Di'Nay firmly. "Logic and will."

Di'Nay laughed affectionately. "Only the tiniest bit with you."

Elana took her hand and led her from the stable toward the courtyard. Perhaps they could find some private corner, some space nearby for a moment alone.

"Elana?"

Elana froze. Her breath caught in her throat and a burst of self-conscious anxiety spread from her heart throughout her body. Even now her mother's voice could unsettle her, take her back in time. Elana had been so young when she left home. She had only seen her mother once since she was less than five tenmoons. Her parents had left the Keep in their youth. Elana had chosen to stay. What did her mother really think of her adult Shadow daughter?

Di'Nay squeezed her hand, the message clear. *Don't be scared of her. She's already impressed by you.*

Elana turned. Her mother was like a specter of Elana's future self. She was willowy with a long cascade of curled black hair and deep brown, almost black eyes. Despite the darkness of her eyes, Rai Min Sym's expression was warm and full of shock and wonder. Elana glanced to the side, unable to even come close to meeting her mother's eyes for the intensity of her amarin.

"Hello, Mother," Elana greeted.

Rai rushed forward, scooping her daughter into a tight embrace. "I didn't think I'd see you again."

Elana held her close. How could she have doubted the love of this woman? "I'm afraid my visit isn't for pleasure," Elana whispered.

Rai tensed slightly, but nodded in acknowledgment. "You know you're safe here. We won't ask any questions."

Elana hesitated before leaning closer to her mother's shoulder and whispering, "The Mistress is very ill."

Rai pulled away, her eyes uncharacteristically hard and guarded. "What would the Mistress want with us?"

Elana's lips pressed into a tight line. Her mother and grandmother didn't get along. Rai had always felt abandoned by her mother. The Mistress had taken her place on the council after her husband's death, effectively rendering Rai an orphan despite providing a home and lessons for her. At the same time, the Mistress carried a grudge at her daughter for leaving her training.

Still, Elana knew their pain was rooted in care.

"She was poisoned."

Some of Rai's hardness faltered, pain bleeding across her amarin. "Who would do that?"

Elana fought to keep her own anger out of her voice. "I don't know. That's not my mission. Di'Nay and I are seeking necessary ingredients for her antidote."

Rai grit her teeth. A single thought shot through the tangle of her emotions, striking Elana hard through her Sight. "She's not awake. She couldn't have sent for you."

Rai shook her head. "It's fine, Elana. She wouldn't have sent for me even if she could. Thank you for telling me."

Rai forced a smile. She pushed thoughts of her ailing mother aside and clasped Elana's arms once more. "Are you hungry, Ona? I should feed you." She turned to Di'Nay. "Are you hungry, Min Di'Nay?"

Di'Nay nodded, shameless in her excited acceptance. "We've been riding hard, Min. I'd be appreciative of any comfort of home."

"Well you're staying with us for the night, of course."

Elana hesitated, but Di'Nay interrupted before Elana could argue. "Of course. Thank you."

Elana shot a slight glare at her Shadowmate, but she didn't protest.

"Then come inside. Sym and Alonz won't be home for dinner for a while, but I can come up with something now. Would you like baths?"

"I might die from happiness," Di'Nay announced.

Rai laughed. "As my daughter's Shadowmate, I'd ask you to fight that urge."

Rai led them deeper into the house, her stride confident, her fingers moving with a memorized precision as she tied an apron around her waist and tied back her thick hair. Rai had always seemed a goddess in the kitchen to Elana, owning her space with a confidence and dominance that reminded Elana of the Mistress.

Rai regarded her pantry. "I have fresh bread and jam. Roast lexion and fruit. I could also make eggs or a bread pudding."

"Di'Nay doesn't care for lexion," Elana explained, the words slipping from her lips with more ease and care than she intended. Rai glanced over her shoulder and eyed her curiously. Sometimes Elana wondered if her Mother had a touch of the Sight despite her dark eyes. Elana carefully tried to redirect the conversation. "I would love bread. I've never found a match for your recipe."

"Of course. And Di'Nay?"

"The same. I trust Elana's judgment."

Rai made a short sound of smug understanding as she sliced bread and applied a hearty layer of fruity jam to each piece. "Will that be two baths or one?" she questioned as she sat a plate before each woman.

Di'Nay choked in surprise, her Terran skin blushing red beneath her tan as she glanced away from the suddenly-frank Rai. Rai's eyes narrowed in knowing glee.

"One will do fine," Elana admitted.

"I thought it might. Are you all right, Di'Nay?" Rai teased.

"Fine, Min. Just surprised."

"You are Shadowmates. It's not uncommon for such a close bond to become romantic," Rai admitted. "Though unconventional, I admit, I'm not surprised my daughter's heart could be swayed by such a handsome Amazon."

"I thank you for your understanding."

Rai waved her hand dismissively. "There's nothing for me to understand. I'm just pleased my Ona has found happiness in her bonding. Some aren't so lucky."

"I would never hurt her," Di'Nay vowed.

"Then it is I who am thankful," Rai admitted.

Elana opened her mouth to tell her mother of her plans to leave Aggar, but the words stuck in her throat. Not yet. Not without her father and brother present. She closed her mouth again. Di'Nay noticed the uncharacteristic hesitation, but her eyes shone understanding.

Rai untied her apron. "Continue your snack. I'll prepare your room and bath. You'll want to wash up by dusk for dinner."

Elana nodded. "Of course. Thank you, mother."

Rai leaned down and kissed her daughter's brow before hurrying off to the upper level of the house.

Elana let out a soft breath and leaned on Di'Nay's shoulder as she chewed on her mother's savory bread crust. "I told you they would understand."

"Don't pretend you weren't nervous," Di'Nay muttered.

Elana kissed her jaw. "I'm just glad you can relax now."

"I still have to pass muster with your father."

"If you have my mother's approval, you already have my father's."

"We'll seen."

"Then if you refuse to stop worrying, focus on our bath instead of my father."

A slow, pleased grin spread across Di'Nay's face. "That's a much more pleasant thought."

"Soon, Love. Soon."

Elana chuckled at the mixed feelings swirling in her lover's amarin. There was something endearing about such a strong warrior of a woman so afraid of confessing her love to her mate's father. Elana wondered what she would have done if she'd fallen in love with a woman of Aggar who wasn't a Shadow. A woman whose parents would demand a bride price. Elana was silently grateful that, as a Shadow, she was considered her own. Di'Nay wouldn't be willing to buy her.

"Is this something you do on Yemaya?"

"I wouldn't be this nervous at home. But seeking approval from a lover's parents knows no gender."

"But a mother on Yemaya would be more happy to welcome you into her family than the people here?"

Di'Nay snorted. "Perhaps, but only because there would be no surprise at my gender. You'd be surprised how many mothers are nervous of seeing their daughters partner with Amazons. We're restless. We're guaranteed to leave home, some the planet. Most women on Yemaya aren't Amazons. It isn't a life many mothers would wish for their daughters."

"Then it's good you fell in love with another adventurous spirit."

Di'Nay kissed her, the faint flavor of berries from the jam lingering on her lips. "I love you."

"I love you."

The sound of Rai descending the stairs signaled the baths were ready. Elana grinned and grabbed Di'Nay's hand. The Amazon laughed aloud as Elana led her up the stairs.

Elana ran her hand over the water, creating ripples across the glassy surface. Di'Nay tenderly brushed her fingers through the wet mass of her hair and laid a kiss against her neck. Elana pulled Di'Nay's arm tighter around her waist, relishing the silken feel of their skin pressed together, the quiet and heat of the bathing room. She closed her eyes, still existing in the tender, lightheaded bliss that followed their lovemaking.

"What are you thinking?" Di'Nay's voice was barely a whisper, her lips brushing Elana's ear. "You seem far away."

Elana opened her eyes. "I'm right here. With you."

"But your mind is at the Keep?"

Elana reached back, touching Di'Nay's neck, leaving trails like rain on a windowpane across the Amazon's skin. "Part of me is always at the Keep. With the Mistress. With whoever poisoned her. But I'm here with you now. Only you."

Di'Nay took her hand and kissed her knuckles down to her wrist, then held Elana's palm to her cheek. "I know."

A clatter of dishes echoed from the main floor. Elana sighed heavily. "Dinner will be done soon."

Di'Nay grunted. "Do we have to go?"

Elana moved to sit up but Di'Nay held her tighter. Elana laughed. "From so anxious to please my parents to wanting to skip dinner to stay in the bath with me?"

Di'Nay nuzzled the back of her neck, holding her tight like a doll. "Can you blame me?"

"Not at all. But we have a lifetime to live together and one night to have dinner with my family."

Di'Nay sighed and released her. Elana rose, the water cascading off her slender body and dripping from her hair. Di'Nay watched her appreciatively, her eyes sparkling mischief. Elana climbed out of the tub and wrapped a towel around her torso. "No ideas."

"I can have all the ideas I want."

Elana turned her attention to drying her hair. She heard the slosh of water as Di'Nay rose from the tub as well and began drying off. Elana could feel anxiety rising in her amarin again. "It will be fine, Di'Nay."

"Someday I'll find a way to keep you from reading my mind."

"I'm not reading your mind. And if I was, would you really want to keep me out?"

"I used to be a private woman, Elana."

"Everyone changes."

They dressed quickly and Elana braided her hair back with rapid, practiced fingers. She didn't like the feeling of putting dusty clothes back on over clean skin, but the bath was still exactly what she needed.

When she was finally ready for the meal, she turned to the door.

"Elana."

Elana glanced over her shoulder. Di'Nay was pale with fear. Elana smiled softly and took her hands. She led her lover to the door as she looked into her eyes, passing all her love and confidence between their amarin with her Sight. The lifestone in her wrist throbbed in time with Di'Nay's heartbeat. "I love you. They'll love you."

"What do I say to him?" Di'Nay's voice trembled with fear.

"Let me talk. You'll be fine."

"How can I tell them I'm taking you away?"

"I'll tell them. I promise."

"I love you."

"Then trust me."

Elana guided her out of the room and down the stairs. She could hear her mother setting out dinner while her father and brother discussed their day. Her father had always had a booming, excited voice, especially after his first mead of the night. Di'Nay hesitated at the stairs and glanced at their joined hands. Elana released her, acquiescing to her silent request.

They entered the dining room and Elana's family fell silent. Elana instantly sensed that Rai had told everyone about her relationship, but before she could pass the information silently to her Shadowmate, her father, Symmum, leapt from his chair and pulled Di'Nay into a tight embrace. The Amazon stiffened like a board in the burly blacksmith's grip, her eyes instantly shooting to Elana's in a plea for help.

"Congratulations!"

Di'Nay stumbled over her words. Elana touched her father's shoulder. "If you want a response, you might want to let her breathe."

Sy released her and clapped her on the back. "I'm glad my Ona has chosen someone with a taste for swords."

"You – you approve?"

Sy laughed good-naturedly, his barrel chest trembling with the raucous sound. "My daughter has always been a good judge of character. The Mother brought you together. You are bonded by lifestones. Ona seems happy."

"Isn't it breaking with tradition?"

"Rai and I were both supposed to be Shadows. We abandoned our training to be together. Alonz is orphaned but we keep him as our own. None of us are traditional, Di'Nay," Rai assured her. "Others may not agree. It certainly isn't a common arrangement on Aggar. But our daughter's happiness is important to us. And you make her very happy."

Sy clapped one hand on Elana's shoulder and the other on Alonz's. "Both my children engaged. A hearty meal on the table. My own shop. A beautiful wife. How did I ever get so lucky?"

"Sy, let them eat. Dinner will get cold," Rai implored with an adoring smile.

They sat at the dinner table as Rai carved a roasted fowl. The earthy scents of spiced, root vegetables and warm bread mingled with the tangy and sweet scents of homebrewed mead and sweet rolls cooling on the counter.

"Such a feast," Elana commended.

"Seemed fitting. There's been so much joy today," Rai agreed.

"So where are you two headed? I'm sure you didn't travel to Black Falls just for a visit," Sy observed as he loaded his plate. "Or are you traveling on secret business?"

Elana exchanged looks with her mother. She hadn't told her father about the Mistress, and the tension and pain in her amarin signaled she wasn't ready. Elana returned her attention to her father and shook her head. "Our movements aren't a secret. Only our reason. We're traveling to the southern desert."

"South?" Alonz interjected. "Then why did you come here?"

"I can guess," Sy announced. "Your mission is one of speed?"

"And discretion, the further south we travel," Di'Nay admitted.

"I have a caravan you can use. It's carrying a shipment of blown glass bottles from our forge. If you can drop them off with my merchants in Ayda, I'll let you take my cart and horses as well as food for the journey. The same provisions we would have provided professional transport. It'll save me money hiring porters and you'll be able to travel twice as fast with a solid, visual cover for heading to the desert. My people are already expecting the shipment, so you won't even have to lie about your destination."

Di'Nay and Elana exchanged glances. Elana felt a weight ease in her stomach. This was exactly what she'd been hoping for.

"I know Aydan markets well. It would be a good place to look for what we need," Di'Nay announced.

"Excellent!" Sy clapped his massive hands. "Is there anything else we can do for you or the Keep?"

Elana's stomach twisted and her tongue felt swollen in her mouth. She knew what she had to say. What she should tell them. It wouldn't be fair for them to learn about her leaving Aggar in a letter. Still, there was something so warm about the moment. Something she hadn't realized she'd been missing back in the Keep. She had never considered herself without family. She had been close to her teachers and a few of her fellow students. But it was never like this. Now that she had it, she was hesitant to shatter the illusion.

"Nothing else we need, no." Elana looked down at her food, keeping her eyes from everyone, including Di'Nay, despite feeling the Amazon's gaze on her.

"Di'Nay, how has my sword handled? I trust it's served you well."

"Very well, Tad. It saved mine and Elana's life countless times. I'm afraid, however, that it was destroyed."

"Destroyed? That steel was finely forged!"

Elana continued to eat, not looking up as Di'Nay spoke. She could tell how hard it was for her lover to find the words to explain what happened to Sy's sword, but no trace of her struggle reached her voice.

"No doubt, but it was a Terran accident. A chemical compound that disintegrated metal and cloth. I lost all my effects that day."

"Mother keep us," Sy breathed.

"They have that kind of power?" Rai questioned.

Elana looked up as her parents' shock and fear washed over her. "The Terrans are very powerful," Elana remarked. "More than they let on. We all know that."

"It wasn't a weapon," Di'Nay rushed to assure them. "It was a shipping error. Chemicals mixed that weren't supposed to."

"That doesn't mean the Terrans won't find new uses for the discovery," Sy growled, acid in his voice. "If they wanted to take our world, they could."

"They don't want to." Di'Nay's voice was confident. "Aggar is strategic for other planetary conflicts. You don't have any minerals or rare natural resources. You're not violent. You're not a threat in their intergalactic conflicts. They don't want to rule you. They just want you out of the way."

"So when they're done with us they'll let us burn," Alonz groused. They brought the wars with them. If their enemies attack, we won't be able to defend ourselves."

A strained silence fell over the table, no one meeting another's eyes. Finally, Di'Nay spoke. "The sisters won't let that happen."

"Why would the Amazons care about our planet?" Rai questioned.

"Because one of Aggar's daughters is becoming Amazon." The words slipped out of Elana's mouth before she could stop them. She didn't need to look up to feel their reactions.

"Elana?"

Elana finally looked up, her sharp features tight with decision. "After this mission, Di'Nay and I are leaving Aggar. I'm going to the Amazon homeworld to continue being her Shadowmate. If I become a Sister, our planets will be bound." Elana's family watched her in shock, none of them able to comprehend leaving the planet. "Please say something."

Rai shook her head. "I'm sorry, Ona. I never thought... of course you would follow Di'Nay. It's your duty."

"Wouldn't a Blue Sight scare the Amazons? What if they think we're a threat?"

Elana flinched and looked away. Alonz's unintentional insult stung, speaking aloud all her internalized shame at her Sight.

"Elana will be a treasure on my world," Di'Nay instantly announced, her voice sharp, not welcoming any rebuttal. "Very few women are allowed to immigrate to Yemaya. Those we accept are protected. We won't let Aggar fall after Elana joins our family. She'll be free. She'll be keeping you safe. And she'll be happy."

Sy drew his hands together, resting his chin on his thumbs as he thought. His normal exuberance had diminished as he tried to come to terms with what Elana and Di'Nay were telling him.

"All I've ever wanted is for Ona to be happy." Rai's voice was raw in her honesty and pain.

"Di'Nay found her way here. We may be able to return again in the future," Elana tried to assure her.

Di'Nay hesitated before responding. "Perhaps, yes."

No one was fooled by Di'Nay's forced confidence.

"Well then." Sy's voice rose over the overwhelming tension in the room. "We have more reason to feast than ever. We're bidding Ona congratulations on her partnership and her journey. She was always an adventurous soul. Who are we to condemn that drive?" Sy lifted his mug of mead. "Let us drink to their good health and fortune!"

Everyone raised a glass. "Good health and fortune!"

The stiff drink and the sharp clatter of mugs hitting the table seemed to shatter some of the tension. By the end of the meal, they were laughing and reminiscing. Elana's cheeks turned dark with a blush as Rai insisted on sharing embarrassing stories of her childhood with Di'Nay, but she was silently pleased at how easily her Amazon seemed to fit in with her family.

"Do you like them?" Elana questioned. She leaned on Di'Nay's shoulder as they returned to their room for the night.

"You know I do."

"Do you think we really could return someday?"

Di'Nay closed their door behind them and let out a tense breath. "I'm not sure. Transport isn't easy at such great distances and our Council isn't prone to sending Sisters abroad who aren't Amazons. We have to be very protective of our secrets."

"It should be impossible for me to go to Yemaya, but I'm going," Elana reminded her.

Di'Nay smiled and wrapped an arm around her waist, kissing her passionately, but gently. "You're right. If you wish to return in the future, it will happen."

They quickly undressed for bed, sliding beneath the fine, woven quilts Rai had made when Elana was a child. Elana wondered briefly if her mother would give her one of the quilts to take with her when she left.

"Will you be able to sleep tonight?" Di'Nay questioned. Her intention was clear. She thought Elana was in mourning.

"Yes, I can sleep." Elana answered honestly. "I'm ready."

Di'Nay kissed her once more. "I'm glad."

"I am, too."

CHAPTER FOUR

Diana eased back in the carriage seat as she led the cart horses down a particularly narrow trail. The motion was natural, taking her back in time to the years she'd spent as a trader. She was still unfamiliar with the northern forests, but she knew how to handle a cart and Sy's horses were obedient. It had been hard to part with Kaing and Leggings, but she trusted Rai and Sy to care for them until their cart was returned. It was good to be in her element again.

The forests were already thinning and soon would open to the plains north of the desert. The scents of pine and sap were becoming less fragrant, mingling with the sweet and earthy scents of the wildflowers that dotted the underbrush and would soon burst in riotous clusters when they reached grassier plains.

That was the beginning of the land Diana had traveled for so long. Where she could rely less on maps and more on intuition and known trade routes. The path wouldn't become any less treacherous – in fact, they would have to be more wary of bandits and highwaymen – but the dangers would be more in line with her skill set. She could fight off thieves. She couldn't always predict the pitfalls mother nature had littered through the forests and mountains.

She had spent so much time with Elana traversing land that was foreign to her. It would be good to be familiar with her surroundings again.

Elana glanced at the sky. "We're making good time."

"Your father's horses are strong, and his name seems to carry a lot of weight. Between his papers and my contacts, we could stop at any trader's way-stop without question."

"I don't want to stop." Elana's words were hard, almost desperate. She caught her tongue and soothed her voice. "Unless it's to care for the horses, of course."

Diana felt a momentary warmth of pleasure that always accompanied Elana's outbursts – evidence that she trusted Diana enough to be honest with her emotions – but that warmth quickly disappeared at Elana's pain. "Of course, Soroi."

Diana wiped a bead of sweat from her brow. It was getting warmer the further south they traveled. She was surprised how accustomed she'd become to the colder northern climates.

"Do you want some water?" Elana questioned.

"Please."

Elana turned into the cart and dug out a waterskin. Diana took a grateful drink. Elana sighed. "It's nice, being able to travel so quickly without the strain of riding. Being able to eat and rest while continuing on, only camping when the horses have need."

Elana smiled briefly. "I like that." She touched Diana's shoulder. "Do you need to rest?"

Diana shook her head. "Guiding a team again... it's invigorating. I don't need to stop yet."

"You want to see the plains."

"Very much."

Elana slummed, resting her elbows on the back of the bench seat. Diana felt the familiar buzz of Elana's blue eyes flitting across her, reading her amarin. She was searching for something. "Will you miss anything of Aggar? Is there anything you wish to see or experience again before we leave?"

Diana considered. "There are parts of Aggar I find intensely beautiful. Some of her wilds rival the wildernesses of home. But I've spent most of my time here hiding who I am. It's hard for me to see women sold as slaves. Women used as property or goods to be sold. No matter what beautiful things I find here, I will always long for home."

Elana continued to watch her in silence. Diana didn't know if her answer had been what the young woman expected or wanted, but it was the truth. After a long moment of silence, Diana touched Elana's hand and added, "If I could explore Aggar as myself without fear of reprisal, if it could always be like this, I think my experience would be different."

Elana squeezed her hand and shook her head. "You don't have

to qualify your answer. I understand what it's like to be an outcast on Aggar."

"Because of your eyes," Diana confirmed.

"Yes."

Diana wasn't surprised Elana felt like she didn't quite belong to Aggar. Most women of Aggar were voluptuous beauties. Subservient, or at least submissive upon command. They were raised as less than the men and all their desires, hopes, and interests were built around their belief that they should be guided by others. Elana couldn't be more different than the average Aggar woman. Willowy, strong, powerful, and inquisitive. She didn't suffer idiocy or unwanted commands. She might be a Shadow. She might take pride in providing for and dedicating herself to her Shadowmate, but she had quickly corrected Diana when the Amazon had thought the dedication was anything but her own choice.

Still, Diana could sense a growing nostalgia in Elana the closer they came to leaving. Even after her training and a lifetime dreaming of adventure, Diana had been terrified to leave Yemaya for the first time. Her longing for home was a constant, deep ache in her heart. She hoped Elana wouldn't find the same void in her soul when she left Aggar. More than anything, she wanted Elana to feel like Yemaya was her home.

"I wasn't made to be tied to a single place." Elana's voice cut through Diana's thoughts, as if she'd spoken her fears aloud. "You know that, Di'Nay."

"Sometimes we don't know how deeply we've rooted ourselves to the familiar until it's time to tear them up."

"My only home is with you. Where we stand is irrelevant."

Diana smiled softly. "You often know just what I need to hear."

"I always know what you need to hear. Sometimes I don't say it."

Diana turned to find Elana grinning. She couldn't help but smile at her dry joke. "I'm sure that's true."

The horses huffed at each other and the trees trembled as a flock of a half dozen birds streaked across the path. The sudden movement was jarring and unexpected. The horses paused, but they didn't buck. Diana felt a familiar tension along her back. Something wasn't right. She hadn't seen a flock that large streak out of the underbrush before.

Elana touched her hand, her fingers curled and her grip tight. "Di'Nay."

"I sense it, too."

With a single swift motion Di'Nay drew her sword, Elana grabbed her crossbow and seven bandits dropped from the trees.

The thieves didn't speak, they instantly charged. Diana bounded forward, putting herself between the thieves and the horses. The highwaymen paused in shock, unable to make sense of a woman with the presence and strength of a warrior. The moment was long enough for Elana to notch an arrow and send her first bolt between the eyes of the man at the center of the band.

Diana lashed out, stabbing the nearest attacker in the stomach and twisting as another grabbed her from behind. The whir of another crossbow bolt and the gurgling scream of a thief signaled another death.

Diana thrust her sword at the man who'd grabbed her, but he parried her blow, more focused than his comrades. They exchanged blows in a flurry while Elana continued defending the horses and cart. Two of the men ran away, trampling the forest brush as they went. The horses whinnied and one lashed out, nearly upending the cart as it kicked a bandit attempting to hobble him. Diana tried to ignore the sound of the thief's bones shattering.

Diana grunted as her opponent's sword slashed her arm. It was just a nick – shallow – but she was already starting to bleed. She tightened her grip. If she bled too much, it would make her hands wet, destabilizing her grip.

She lashed out again and dropped to her knees to avoid his counter. She swiveled in the dirt, rolling around him and stabbing him in the back. She wiped her bloody arm on her shirt as her assailant fell to the ground. She looked around at the carnage. Five men dead on the road. Two gone. Diana let out a deep breath she hadn't realized she'd been holding. She could hear Elana breathing heavily as well as she slowly lowered her crossbow.

It had been so sudden, the shot of violence. She hadn't even heard them speak. The silence and blood unsettled her in a way that a fight never had.

"Are you all right?" Diana called to Elana as her eyes still flitted across the forest, looking for more signs of danger.

"You're bleeding."

Diana turned to her lover and held out her arm. “It looks worse than it is.”

Elana's eyes widened, a vision flitting through her Sight a breath before an arrow whizzed through the air and buried into her shoulder.

Elana screamed in agony and fell back. She ground her teeth, pushing back her pain, and before Diana could find her attacker, the Blue Sight grabbed her crossbow with her good arm and shot into the woods, sending one of the bandits who'd fled crashing from the treetops to the ground.

“Elana!” Diana cried as she bounded toward the cart, her panic palpable enough to make the already-nervous horses shudder and shift.

Diana scooped Elana into her arms. Elana grabbed her shoulder in a vice-like grip, her hands shaking and her words shooting past clenched teeth. “Pull it out.”

“Elana!”

She rustled, showing Diana her back. The arrow had passed clean through the muscles of her shoulder, barely missing her bones. “It's clean. The arrowhead passed through. We need to bind it before it becomes infected.”

Diana let out a heavy breath of relief at seeing the arrowhead. If the stone had caught inside her body, she would need surgery. With such a clean shot, she would heal if careful attention was paid to infection.

Diana clenched her jaw and nodded. She circled around the cart and found the medkit. She grabbed the reigns to their cart and Elana bit down on the leather as Diana leaned her back against the riding bench. Her piercing blue eyes burned through Diana as her good hand grabbed Diana's shirt in a tight fist.

Diana cut Elana's sleeve away from the injury. “Ready?”

Elana nodded. She didn't flinch as Diana broke the end off the arrow and pulled the shaft free from the wound. As the arrow clattered to the ground, tears streamed past Elana's cheeks and her skin rippled between mahogany and oak browns with her pain.

Diana applied a thick layer of antibacterial salve to both ends of the wound. Her fingers numbed and Elana let out a gasp of relief as the cream eased some of her pain. With all her tenderness and care, Diana wrapped the wound in fresh gauze.

“Elana?”

Elana removed the strap from her mouth, the leather scarred with the marks of her teeth. Her breath came in fluttering gasps, but she was regaining control. She nodded. “Thank you.”

“We'll ride a bit ahead, get away from the stink of these bodies, and make camp.”

Elana shook her head sharply. “I'll be fine. We can ride on.”

“Elana --”

“No. We can't let this get in the way!”

“Elana--”

Angry tears streamed down her cheeks. “This is nothing!”

“Elana!” Diana's voice was sharper than she intended, silencing the frantic Blue Sight. “I won't lose you for speed. You need rest. We need to cool your injury. The horses need to be calmed. We should stop.”

Diana could tell she wanted to argue more, but instead Elana covered her eyes with her hand. Her fingers were still tight, curled like claws as she hid her tears and her Sight, shielding Diana from her emotions. The motion sent a shock of pain through Diana's chest. She'd seen Elana cover her eyes before -- closing them, hiding them behind her hair, or looking pointedly away. It was an impulse born of fear and forced control.

“Elana, you don't have to hide from me.”

“Just go.”

The words spit past her teeth almost like a hiss, instantly flaring Diana's temper. The heat died almost as fast as it rose as she focused on Elana's injury. She was speaking out of pain.

Diana thought she'd seen the peak of Elana's anger, but this feral woman, consumed with physical and emotional pain, was another new glimpse at the woman she loved. The thought flashed through her mind that she hadn't yet seen what Elana was capable of.

Diana strode away from the cart and put all her energy into clearing the trail. She dragged the bandits' bodies into the brush, focusing on the strain of her muscles as she lifted their dead weight instead of looking at their blank faces or internalizing the rough weave of their worn clothes. Diana had never liked taking a life, but she refused to feel guilty about defending herself and her loved ones.

By the time she returned to the cart, the horses had calmed enough to stand still again and Elana was sitting up, her eyes locked on the ground. Diana could still feel her anger, so instead of tempting her frustration she just grabbed the horses' reigns and urged them forward in silence.

Diana led the cart off the path into the forest. The trees were sparse and thin, making it difficult for more attackers to hide. The canopy was thick enough to provide shade, but the land was softer, grassier. They were finally out of the old growths and mountains of the north.

The plot of land was even, a narrow stream cutting through the undergrowth. The horses immediately made their way to the water as Diana untethered them, running her hands gently over their backs, now damp with sweat from their panic and day of travel.

Diana then set about unloading the tent and sleeping mats. Elana didn't move. She hadn't spoken since the attack. The silence wasn't doing much to ease Diana's frustration. She tried to keep her emotions in check around Elana. Her Blue Sight made her sensitive to the heat of Diana's anger, but Elana's silence and emotional distance was starting to feel personal.

Since the beginning of their relationship Elana had demanded open communication. It hadn't been easy for Diana to break down her emotional walls and allow herself to connect with a new lover. It hadn't been easy to bond. But she'd done it. Now Elana's quiet and seething, her refusal to be as open as Diana had been, felt like a passive aggressive attack.

Diana struggled with the tent and bit the inside of her lip. She wasn't being fair. Elana had as much right to her emotions and pain as anyone else. But Diana had never done well with feeling helpless.

"I'm not what you thought I was, am I?"

Elana's voice was dark as it drifted through the clearing. Diana tensed. "I never thought I knew everything about you."

"Does that make you angry?"

Elana was still turned away, unmoved from the carriage bench, her eyes still fixed on the ground. "You make me angry. You also make me blissfully happy. You make me hopeful. And scared. You make me feel many things because I love you. This doesn't change anything."

"But you're mad at me."

"I'm scared for you."

"I don't want to stop traveling."

"We need to. You need to rest."

"I don't want to be injured."

Diana hesitated. There was so much she wasn't saying. "I don't know what to say," she admitted.

Elana shook her head and finally climbed down from the cart, holding her arm close to her chest. "You don't have to say anything."

Diana watched as she wandered to the horses and tore the other sleeve from her shirt to fashion a sling. For the first time Diana considered that Elana might not understand why she was angry either. She seemed so controlled all the time. So well-trained and observant. She often forgot that Elana's wisdom had been born from a lifetime of controlling and repressing her emotions.

Diana shook her head and continued setting up the tent and preparing the bedmats. Elana didn't return until Diana had a fire going. She seemed more calm. Diana handed her a slice of her mother's bread.

"Thank you," Elana whispered.

"What else do you want to eat?"

"Do we have any cheese?"

Diana smiled, happy she was willing to eat, and pulled out a serving of honey-brown goat cheese. They ate by the fire in silence, but Diana could tell their energy had changed. After Elana finished eating, she leaned against Diana's shoulder. Diana gently ran her fingers through her hair. Her natural scents mixed with the ash of the fire and the cool minty scent of the salve at her shoulder. Knowing Elana still wanted to touch her, to rest against her shoulder, relieved some of Diana's fear. No matter what happened, as long as this beautiful woman was still in her arms, everything would be all right.

Diana tilted her face toward the sun and closed her eyes. She smiled. They were finally out of the forest. The grasslands had turned to sedgebrush. They were less than a day out of the desert. This was the Aggar Diana knew. The heat. The scents of dust and brush. She could already feel her cheeks tanning darker from the sun.

Elana sighed and shifted her thick braid. Her brow was lined with beads of sweat. She had traded out her riding dress for breeches and one of Diana's vests, but she was still over-heated. She used a cloth to dry her neck, carefully moping beneath the strap of her arm sling.

"Will it be this hot in the desert?" she questioned.

Diana laughed. "Hotter, Soroi. You'll grow accustomed to it soon."

Elana shook her head. "Is it this hot on Yemaya?"

Diana leaned forward on her knees, holding the carthorse reigns. She sighed softly as memories of home flooded her thoughts. She could smell the complex mingling of herbs from her mother Estelle's garden, feel the wiry yet somehow silken tall lavender grass against her bare legs. She could hear the music ringing from the hills during the Feast of Helen or the winter festivals. She felt so close to returning home. She'd been gone for so long.

"Not so hot, no. And if it's too hot for you still we'll live in the mountains."

Elana smiled softly and readjusted her sling. "Do you think they'll like me there?"

Diana glanced at her in surprise. "Elana, you know they will. You're already a sister."

"Are there any amazons with blue eyes?"

Diana leaned back, reading the true intent of her words. "There's no Sight on Yemaya, but there are Sisters with blue eyes. No one will see you as different."

Elana's voice lowered. "But they'll feel it."

Her walls were instantly back up, hiding whatever emotions she was feeling. Diana shifted uncomfortably, but Elana forced a smile, instantly trying to ease the tension. "Are you hungry?"

"Not really. How are our supplies?"

Elana leaned over the carriage bench into the bed of the cart and sifted through the supplies with her good arm. "We'll have to stop for more soon. We camped for longer than father expected us to."

"It was two days."

"Still too long."

Diana tensed, but she let the comment slide. She didn't want to fight anymore. "Before we reach the desert there's a village called Dagan. It's small, but it's a popular stop for merchants to gather supplies. There's a grocer there who owes me a favor. Saved his market from a raid the second year I was here. We'll be able to get what we need without drawing much attention."

Elana nodded. "Sounds good. Maybe he'll have a lead about the plant."

"Possibly."

Diana held the reigns in one hand and leaned into the cart, reaching for her bag. She grabbed a vest.

"What are you doing?" Elana questioned.

"None of my old contacts know me as a woman."

Elana pouted. "Tad Di'Nay again?"

Diana smiled. "Only for a time, Darling."

"Do you want me to be a man as well?"

Diana shook her head. "I wouldn't have you use so may of your Shadow abilities with an injured arm. I think it's high time Tad Di'Nay took a wife."

Elana smiled gently and leaned in to kiss Diana, the embrace so tender, so sudden, Diana nearly dropped the reigns. "Thank you."

"Of course, Soroi."

"I should wear a skirt."

"My wife can wear pants," Diana countered, the words rolling easily over her tongue like honey. She savored the word. Wife. Elana. Her heart skipped a beat with joy.

"No respectable woman of Aggar would travel like this. I'd shame your name."

"We won't be on Aggar much longer. There's a good chance I'll never pass through Dagan again. I could care less what happens to my name now. You'd roast in a skirt."

"I care what happens to your name."

Diana chuckled. "Do whatever you wish, Elana Min Di."

Elana laughed at the sound of the name she would have taken, were Diana a man of Aggar taking her as a wife. "Perhaps instead I should call you Di'Nay Tad Ela."

"How scandalous."

"Well, if you really don't care about what happens to your name, we might as well aim for legendary scandal."

"I love the way you think."

"Will I change my name on Yemaya?"

Diana's brow furrowed in shock and surprise. "Because of

me?"

"As your mate, yes."

"No. The Sisters don't believe in ownership. Even as mates we are both our own people."

"So what will my Yemaya name be? Here you are Di'Nay, but at home you're Diana. Will it be the same for me?"

"Your name is whatever you choose. Most will call you Elana or Elana n'Aggar until you choose your house."

"So I will one day be Elana n'Shae?"

"If that's what you wish."

Elana leaned back. "I like that."

Diana's cheeks warmed at the thought. She already fit so well among the Sisters. To Diana's surprise, she could no longer imagine being home without Elana by her side. "I like that, too."

"Tad Di'Nay!" The call rang through the busy store, rising above the the cacophony of dozens of customers both in the shop and outside in the market.

Diana strode to the back of the shop and clasped arms with Tad Camal. The short, wiry old shopkeep had created an empire, buying up half the market in the years Diana had been on Aggar. Still, despite his success, he was always a welcoming host and a generous boss.

"Tad Camal. It's been too long." Diana's voice was deeper, her shoulders more squared as she easily sank back into her male persona.

"What brings you through Dagan? Heading into the desert?"

"You'd never forgive me if I secured supplies from another."

"You're right about that. What can I do for you?"

"A basic travel kit for two should suffice. We're just bolstering what we already have."

Tad Camal lifted his brows. "Two? Traveling with a companion now? That's not your way."

Diana glanced at the other end of the store where Elana inspected an array of dried meats. Elana felt Diana's gaze and immediately walked to Diana's side. Despite her teasing, Elana had eventually opted for a skirt. She took her duties as a Shadow too seriously to let heat get in the way of her disguise.

Camal looked her over. "A new mala'?"

"Wife," Diana corrected, her voice adamant and unforgiving.

She wouldn't let anyone believe Elana her slave. “Elana Min Di.”

“Wife?” Camal clapped her on the shoulder. “Congratulations, friend. I never thought I'd see the day!”

Diana glanced back with a soft smile. She briefly noticed Elana had used her abilities to darken her eyes to a stormy gray. “She's a special woman.”

“What happened to your arm, Min?”

Elana didn't hesitate. “I tripped in the woods, Tad. Hit my arm. I'll be fine.”

Camal turned to Diana. “Let me know if I can provide any medical supplies.”

“New bandages and antibacterial salve would be greatly appreciated.”

Camal waved his hands. “Of course. I'll have my boys load your cart. No payment. But this makes us square for the rats.”

Diana shook his hands. “More than fair, my friend.”

“Is there anything else I can do for you?”

Diana drew the sketch from the seers from her belt pouch and unfolded it. “We're looking for this plant. I've heard it called both Nama and Sandstars. Do you know it?”

Camal took the paper slowly, his brow furrowed. All of his verbose joy disappeared in an instant. A cold chill grew in Elana's stomach. There was something wrong. “Tad?”

Camal handed her back the drawing. “Would you like to come inspect the ration kits?”

Diana's brows rose at the obvious redirect. “Yes, of course.”

Camal moved toward the back of the shop. Diana and Elana followed. Camal tensed and turned. “Perhaps Min Elana would like to see if anything else in the shop catches her eye? I'd be happy to throw in whatever she likes as a wedding gift.”

Diana opened her mouth to protest, but Elana touched her arm. “What a kind offer, Camal, thank you.”

Elana strode back into the center of the market. Camal visibly relaxed. “This way.”

Camal led Diana to a private room in the back of the market, the walls lined with crates of merchandise and stacks of sales receipts.

“Camal, what's going on?” Diana demanded.

He handed Diana back the paper, his voice hushed and sharp. “You can't show this to anyone else.”

"What? Why?"

"There are people in Dagan. In every merchant city surrounding the desert. They've put a bounty on everyone looking for Nama flowers."

"What? Why? Is it illegal?"

"No. I have no idea why they care or who they're looking for, but these are powerful people. I've seen members of the guild and crime lords working together. The man who came to my shop was... more than intimidating."

"Over flowers?"

Camal raised a hand. "Please, Di'Nay. I won't tell anyone about you. We have too much history, and these men obviously have dark intentions."

"Do you know what brings them together?"

"I have no idea. They aren't presenting as an organization."

"What was the man like who visited you?"

"Terran. All the men who have passed through Dagan have been Terrans."

Diana clenched her jaw. "Do you think this is some kind of Terran plot?"

Camal raised his hands in silent surrender. "I wouldn't dare to accuse your people. I just know who have come through my city and threatened my shopkeepers."

Diana let out a tense breath. She clasped arms with Camal. "Thank you for watching out for me, friend."

Camal squeezed her arm. "Be careful who you associate with. I can't promise you won't be watched now."

"Are you afraid for yourself?"

Camal shook his head. "I'm a very powerful man. I don't think they'd attack me directly."

"Is there anyone you trust? Anyone who might be able to help me? It's important I find the plant."

"Where are you headed in the desert?"

"Ayda. We're delivering a shipment."

Camal thought for a moment. "I have a supplier in Ayda. An alchemist. Worked with him for years. If you're looking for a rare plant, he'd be the one to talk to. He seems trustworthy, but I would still be careful with him."

"What's his name?"

"Darius. He has a botanical shop near the eastern wall of

Ayda."

"Thank you."

"Travel safely, Di'Nay. You and your lovely wife."

"Stay safe yourself. If you find yourself in need, send word to the guild hall in Restin. The head of security owes me a favor. He'll be able to protect you for a time."

"Trying to indebt me to you again?" Camal teased.

"Not at all. Just trying to keep you alive."

Camal shrugged. "I'm harder to kill than you'd think."

"I'm sure of it."

Camal led her back into the market, his usual joy back. "Good enough kits, yes?"

"More than I could have asked for."

Camal beckoned to a team of apprentices, who rushed to his side. "We'll have everything to your cart in moments."

"My thanks, Tad." Diana glanced around. Elana was no where to be seen. "Have any of you seen my wife?"

"I believe she returned to your cart, Tad," one of the boys offered.

"Thank you."

Diana sped out of the market. Elana was sitting with the cart in front of the shop, fanning herself with a painted fan.

"A gift from Camal's shop?"

"A blessing in this heat," Elana agreed. "Your conversation went well."

Diana arched an eyebrow. Elana's words weren't a question, but a statement. A slow grin came to her lips as Elana met her eyes. Of course she had found a way to listen in. She wasn't called Shadow for nothing. "Yes. Our supplies should be out in just a bit."

"Wonderful."

They didn't have to wait long before their cart was nearly overflowing. Diana oversaw the loading and tipped each of the young carriers before returning to the carriage seat. Elana leaned back, fanning herself, her eyes closed. Diana paused as she took the reigns. It was such a simple position. Elana looked tired and overheated. She was injured. She was playing a role that didn't quite fit her. But to Diana this simple, natural moment was beautiful.

Elana opened her eyes. "What?"

"I'm just... I'm so thankful I found you."

Elana's smile glowed brighter than the sun. “Charmer.”

Diana shook her head. “Not charm. Just joy.”

“Let's go, Di'Nay. I want you to myself again.

Diana held tighter to the reigns and guided the horses out of the bustling marketplace, along the narrow rows of tall, slender buildings with colorful canopies and roofs. Despite the heat, she couldn't wait to reach the isolation of the desert.

CHAPTER FIVE

Elana walked out into the desert, the sand shifting under her feet. She glanced down in frustration. She was used to stone and hard packed dirt. Even ice seemed easier to walk on. For the first time in her life she didn't feel confident in her ability to cover her footsteps, to disappear. What was a Shadow in full sunlight? There was nowhere to hide.

Elana paused and stared out at the waves of sand and mountainous dunes in the distance. Grains of sand rose with the light breeze and skimmed across Elana's bare arms and caught under the lining of the vest she'd borrowed from Di'Nay. She ran her fingers over her arm, the constant, sharp ache in her shoulder flaring with her touch. There was something oddly focusing about the pain. If she had to be crippled, at least there was one benefit from her injury.

Elana closed her eyes and drew a deep, calming breath. There weren't as many living things here as there were at home, but it wasn't dead. There were animals, plants, water, and soil. Somewhere there was the cure for her Mistress. And somewhere there was a band of men. Terrans. Men who had placed a bounty on the blossoms that would heal her family.

Di'Nay wasn't convinced the men were behind the assassination attempt, but Elana knew better. There was only one reason the exact ingredient they needed would be guarded. Di'Nay had lived on Aggar for a few tenmoons, but she didn't seem to grasp how important the Keep was to the world. How many enemies had tried to invade in the past. Most trusted the Keep and Council, but there were still those who were scared of the Seers and those with the Sight. People who resented their power.

Elana wondered if any of their kind might be in Ayda. Perhaps if she could just find them, use her Sight to learn who they were working for...

"Elana?" Di'Nay's voice was clouded with sleep as she called out of the oasis.

Elana turned. The tiny spit of green surrounding a shallow watering hole was an ideal place to rest for the night. The brush was just thick enough to hide sleeping mats.

She moved back into the oasis. Di'Nay's Amarin filled with relief and she laid back down, laying her arm over her eyes. "I know it's hard to sleep in the day, but you'll appreciate it when we can travel in cooler weather."

Elana sat beside her. "I know. It's my mind that won't rest."

Di'Nay looked up at her and rested her hand on Elana's thigh. "We're almost to Ayda. Should be there by dawn tomorrow. We'll find the Nama. Once we have it, we can race back to the Keep."

"What if the Terrans that threatened Camal have made it to Ayda as well?"

"Then we'll search the desert until we find the blossoms in the wild."

"We don't have time for that or the supplies. The horses aren't strong enough for wandering in the desert. And that only matters if Camal's contact is willing to lie for us as well."

Di'Nay sat up again, concern in her eyes. "Soroi. We don't even know that anything will be off in Ayda. We're a long way out of Dagan. We shouldn't worry about our next step until we encounter problems."

Elana sighed and buried her face in her knees. Di'Nay made sense, but Elana's mind was spinning. She knew something would go wrong. She could feel it in the air, in the amarin of the world around her.

Like walking on the sand of the desert, she felt like she'd lost all her training, all her skill. She had always been in control. What was undoing her now? She needed to stop it. An unstable Blue Sight was a weapon. A disaster. And the first person hurt would be Di'Nay.

"Elana?" Di'Nay sounded helpless. Elana clenched her jaw. She knew how she was making Di'Nay feel. She didn't want to hurt her or shut her out. Di'Nay didn't understand what a Blue Sight was capable of when she was undone.

"I'm fine."

"You're not."

"You don't understand."

"I understand that you're pulling away from me."

"I'm not."

Di'Nay growled and pulled away, her anger flaring. "You can't tell me nothing is changing, Elana. I can feel it. I'm right here. I'm not blind or stupid."

Elana's own frustration exploded beneath her skin. A thousand emotions, fears, and urges tangled together, feelings she didn't even fully understand. The only emotions she was sure of, the only thing that kept her together, was her love for Di'Nay.

Without thinking, she sprang, straddling Di'Nay's legs and kissing her deeply. If she couldn't make sense of her mind, she could retreat to her love.

Di'Nay fell back, catching herself with her hands in shock. "Elana?"

"I'm not pulling away from you. You're the only thing that makes sense," Elana whispered, holding Di'Nay close with her good arm.

Di'Nay's breath came in quick gasps, her Amarin dancing. As her heart raced, Elana's sped to match, their blood running in time together through their bond.

"Your shoulder," Di'Nay questioned, already kissing Elana's good arm.

Elana caressed her cheeks as Di'Nay kissed the palm of her hand. "I'll be fine."

Elana caught Di'Nay's chin and tipped her face up for another kiss. She melted into Di'Nay's strength, closing her eyes as she let everything else go. Di'Nay's grip was careful but desperate. She held Elana close with one arm as the other undid the laces of her vest.

Elana sighed at the silken feel of Di'Nay's hands on her skin, her touch somehow warding off the heat of the desert sun. Elana wrapped her arm around Di'Nay's neck as her lover left a wet, jagged trail of kisses down her neck, over her chest, and across the softness of her breasts.

"Please," Elana whispered in Di'Nay's ear, her intention clear.

Her fingers entwined in Di'Nay's hair as the Amazon's hands traveled lower, undoing the ties of her breeches and sliding down her body. Elana held her tighter, sharp gasps and sighs of pleasure flooding past her lips. Her body instantly responded, her hips rolling in time with with Di'Nay's caress.

Her head swam as waves of pleasure overtook her pain, her fear. For a moment there was nothing but Di'Nay. Nothing but love and their bond. Di'Nay rested her head on Elana's shoulder as their bond passed a taste of Elana's pleasure into her Shadowmate. Her muscles trembled, tensing and relaxing under Elana's body, exciting Elana more.

They moved and felt as one, entwining body and soul as Di'Nay's touch wound them higher and higher, finally crashing into a climax that made Elana lose all sense of herself, drowning her in their bond. This was what she needed. This was what was real. Only Di'Nay.

Elana ran her hand over her brow, her breath coming in deep, steady gasps. Her skin was covered with sweat from the heat of the desert and her passion. Di'Nay had collapsed beside her, just as exhausted and disheveled. Elana smiled as her sense of Di'Nay's individual amarin returned, their shared energy separating once more into two separate beings. Elana wasn't the only one feeling better.

Di'Nay wrapped an arm around her, pressing their bodies together as she kissed her gently. She laid her head on Elana's healthy shoulder, her hand tracing gentle spirals across Elana's bare stomach. "Thank you."

"I needed it just as much as you did," Elana assured her.

Di'Nay shook her head. "That doesn't mean it wasn't a gift, Soroi n'ti mee."

Elana kissed her again, but the embrace turned to a wince. The pain in her shoulder was steadily coming back as the emotions and adrenaline of their lovemaking faded.

Di'Nay leaned up on her arm, her eyes shining concern. "Your shoulder?"

Elana forced a smile and touched her bandaged arm. "I got a little overzealous."

Di'Nay turned and crept to the cart, drawing out the medkit. Elana watched her move, the sun shining off her damp, bare skin. She seemed to glimmer like a swath of silk. Elana marveled at her shape, her strength. Di'Nay often waxed poetic about Elana, insisting she was blessed to find a woman like the Blue Sight, but Elana couldn't believe a woman like Di'Nay would fall in love with her.

"We should re-bandage you. Clean out any sand that got into the wound."

Elana sat up and tried not to wince as Di'Nay removed the ragged bindings and cleaned her injury. She drew deep, focused breaths to ignore the pain until Di'Nay smeared a thick layer of the numbing salve over both wounds. The pain was a stark reminder of what she'd been trying to ignore. By the time Di'Nay was unwinding new bandages, Elana felt her dark mood returning.

"Almost done," Di'Nay promised. "It doesn't look too bad. I tried to be gentle."

Elana grinned. "I could have stopped you. I didn't want you gentle."

Di'Nay let out a slow sound of pleasure. "Maybe when you're better."

"We'll see if I last that long."

Di'Nay laughed and nipped at her neck. "I can be creative until then."

Both women glanced up as the horses made restless sounds near the watering hole. They were rested and well. They wanted to travel again.

"I stole your rest time, didn't I?" Elana muttered.

"That was so much better than sleep," Di'Nay insisted as she wrapped her hands in Elana's hair and kissed her. "But yes, we should leave soon if we still want to reach Ayda by dawn."

Elana sighed gently. "We should get dressed."

Di'Nay grunted in disappointment. "Do we have to?"

"It might be hard for you to hide your gender walking around Ayda naked."

"Perhaps a little."

Elana smiled. "When we reach Yemaya, we'll never have to get dressed again."

"Promises promises," Di'Nay whispered as she kissed her once more and stood to retrieve their scattered clothes.

Elana held her injured arm close as they approached the Ayda city gates. She had been to large towns before, but never a city with so much grandeur. Thick, sandstone walls rose high, the turrets bearing crimson and golden flags inscribed with the language of the desert people. Stained glass windows caught the light, reflecting it like gemstones set into the highest towers so the height of the city glittered. Red silk banners and canopies rippled like oceans of color that rivaled the dawn skyline.

Hundreds of people already streamed in and out of the front gates, the sounds of carts, horses, camels, and people haggling rose in a chorus the Blue Sight found nearly deafening. Their amarins were a chaotic web of emotion, desperation, and joy.

Elana touched her good hand to her brow and blinked, warding off a headache. She had been taught how to navigate a city, but it was clear her education hadn't truly prepared her for the reality of being a Blue Sight in a sea of people.

“Are you all right?” Di'Nay inquired, her voice already pitched deep in her disguise as a man.

Elana nodded. “There's just a lot of people. A lot of amarin. I'll acclimate.”

“Let me know if you need anything.”

Elana touched Di'Nay's hand in gratitude as Di'Nay led the horses away from the main gates to the smaller gate designated for imported goods.

“Papers.”

Di'Nay pulled out Sy's paperwork and presented it to the city guard. The man skimmed them, his dark eyes sharp as he looked for signs of a forgery. Unlike the guards and mercenaries Elana had met in the past, Ayda's city guards wore light leather armor, the material perforated for comfort on hot days.

The guard's ebony hair was cropped short and his skin tone seemed to stay consistently darker than the people Elana had grown up with. Elana's cheeks wouldn't deepen to such a shade unless she was angry or aroused. She wondered if the Desert Peoples' reputation as a passionate, emotional race came from their sun-darkened skin. The guard's amarin seemed to indicate a much more logical mind than Elana had been taught to expect from a desertman.

“Looks good.” The guard handed Di'Nay back the paperwork. “Do you need directions?”

Di'Nay smiled. “I can find my way, thank you.”

The guard nodded and waved them in, his attention already on the next merchant in line.

They passed through the gates into the city proper. Elana looked around in awe, instantly consumed by the bustling marketplace. Despite the early hour, most of the city was already awake and active, trading in shops and at carts, hawking their wares, and making early-morning purchases. Di'Nay had been right. If any city had the plant they were looking for, it would be Ayda.

"The city is separated into districts. Camal said his contact is an alchemist who works along the eastern wall. That means he's in the mystical and medical district."

"Can you take me there? I can investigate when you can drop off Sy's vases."

"You want to separate? With your injury?" Diana's voice was thick with concern.

"I don't intend to engage anyone. I want to do a little research before we approach him. Camal said his name was Darius?"

"Research as a Shadow?"

"Of course."

Di'Nay hesitated. "Are you still worried about Camal's Terrans?"

"I may be your mate, but I'm also your protector. If there's a chance of danger to you or the Keep, it's my duty to address it."

"And we can't do that together?"

Elana cast her a knowing glance and Di'Nay snorted. "Point taken. I never was particularly stealthy."

"And if Terrans are stirring up trouble here as well, you don't want to be seen skulking around the shadows. I work quickly. I'll have what we need by the time you're done. We're bonded. You'll be able to find me when it's time."

"All right. But if we can't find each other by noon, we'll meet right here at the gate."

"Sounds fair."

Di'Nay carefully threaded the streets and crowds of the city, making her way to the eastern wall. A wave of herbal and earthy scents washed over Elana as they passed into the medical and mystical section of the city.

"It seems odd to keep bandages and salves next to scrying crystals and star charts," Elana remarked. "The beliefs are more separate in the Ramains."

"The Desert People have a more complex view of the world.

Science, religion, and magic are almost the same here."

Di'Nay glanced at the sky and muttered under her breath as she sought out the building numbers along the wall. She paused along the side of the road and pointed out a small shop ahead wedged into the corner of the city walls. A massive greenhouse was built where the north and eastern walls met, rising higher than the shop.

"That should be Darius's shop there."

Elana slid out of the cart. "Stay safe, Di'Nay."

Di'Nay smiled. "You're worried about me? I'm just making a delivery."

"I always worry about you when I'm not there to protect you."

"Not many see me as in need of protection."

Elana smiled. "Your muscles and heritage don't matter to me."

"That's strangely comforting."

"Meet me back here."

Di'Nay nodded and led the cart away again. Elana glanced around and melded with the crowd. She made imperceptible adjustments to her posture and manner of walking. She used her Sight to twist her Amarin enough to turn her eyes brown and layer glamours to make herself look older, darker, and to persuade anyone who looked at her to instantly ignore her. She blended in. She was forgettable.

She moved slowly toward Darius's shop, listening to hagglers and merchants. She didn't hear anything alarming or interesting, but she sensed a mild, unspoken tension in the air she hadn't sensed in the other districts. She frowned as she ducked into the alleyway between Darius's store and a crystal shop.

A series of windows lined the walls of Darius's store, displaying an array of plants and gardening tools. Elana blended into the shadows as she studied them, her Sight catching the whispering amarin of the flora over the cascade of amarin in the rest of the city. The plants were obviously well-cared for, their voices strong. Darius was obviously a dedicated gardener.

As she rounded around the back of the building near the greenhouse, she caught onto new amarin. Human. She ducked around a shed as a man she assumed to be Darius stepped out of the greenhouse and made his way back toward his shop. He was an older man with a short, snow-white beard and a light limp in his step. He wore an apron around his waist with delicate pruning sheers peeking out of one pocket. There was fresh soil under his fingernails.

Almost immediately a blond man followed him, his shoulders squared and tense.

"Nama isn't poisonous. It's an herb. Has the medicinal school uncovered new properties?" Darius questioned.

"We can speak inside."

Elana's breath caught in her throat. Darius's companion was obviously Terran. If Camal's tormentors were targeting Darius and he recognized the plant, it was likely he had some. She waited until they re-entered the shop and jogged into the greenhouse.

The building was massive, housing more than a dozen long rows of planters and a riot of various plants. A maze of pipes – a hand-crafted watering system – wove overhead and misted the plants at various intervals. Elana felt her shoulders relax and a warmth fill her chest. The scents were so like the gardens of the Keep, a wild mixture of floral and herbal. Many of the plants had to have been imported.

A wheelbarrow full of dark soil sat beside a planter where Darius must have been working when the Terran arrived. If he was only half-way through with the project, it was likely he would be back soon. Darius didn't seem the type to leave something undone.

Elana strode down the paths of planters, her eyes flitting back and forth looking for the flower from the sketch. She saw a few likely candidates, but on closer inspection she found the wrong number or petals or the wrong shade of purple.

As she reached the final row, she heard a shuffling outside as someone left Darius's store. Elana immediately dropped to the floor, curling into a tight crawl as Darius stepped back inside. At least the Terran didn't hurt him.

Elana ignored the pain in her arm as she crawled forward. She watched Darius's shoes under the brackets of the planters. As he crouched down to return to work with the soil, his amarin clear of any suspicion, she moved forward, rushing on silent feet out the door before he could spot her.

She moved with purpose. If there was no nama in the greenhouse, it had to be in the store. The back door of the shop had been left unlocked. She glanced over her shoulder, confirming Darius was occupied with his work, and slipped inside.

The back room of the store was filled with potted plants, hand tools, and soil samples. The wooden benches were cluttered, but organized. Every plant was labeled. Her heart stilled in her chest as she spotted a small pot holding a scraggly, woody bush with purple flowers. A tag sticking out of the soil was labeled "Sandstar."

Elana gasped. She hadn't expected it to be so easy. No searching the desert. No fighting with the Terrans.

She grabbed a set of shears off the work table and clipped a dozen stems. She then left a bag of gold on the counter and tucked the flowers into her vest, concealing them from view. The stems were wiry and sharp against her skin, but her joy at finding the ingredient wiped away any discomfort.

She moved back to the door, but she hesitated. She heard a shuffle of feet in the front of the store and caught the feeling of three distinct amarin. She pressed against the wall and focused. Her breath caught in her throat. Terrans.

"How long will he be?"

"You saw the plot. It won't take long to plant a couple bushes."

"Why did we even let him go?"

"We're not supposed to make him suspicious. He won't believe we're from the university if we threaten him."

"He wouldn't be suspicious if he was dead."

"Don't be overzealous. We have more important marks. We don't need soldiers breathing down our backs."

"We should just destroy the nama and go. He can't sell it if it's ashes."

Without thinking, Elana grabbed the sheers she'd left on the counter. Her hands trembled as her blood boiled, warming her skin to a deep brown. These were the Terrans who had threatened Camal. The Terrans who were trying to stop her from finding the plant she needed. They had to be connected to the assassins. They might even know who was threatening the Mistress.

Elana wanted to challenge them. She wanted to threaten them until they told her what she wanted to know. She wanted to punish them for what they'd done to her grandmother. For what they were trying to do to the Keep. She wanted to know why.

She tried to think herself out of it. She had an injured arm. As far as she knew, they still didn't know her face. It would be suicidal to challenge them, even with her Sight, and Darius might be hurt in the brawl. No matter what she told herself, however, she only held tighter to the sharp sheers, grinding her teeth, imagining the men pinned beneath her blade.

If you die here, she'll never get the antidote.

The thought sliced through her anger, calming her heart. What she wanted didn't matter. She needed to get home.

It took all her willpower, but she put the sheers aside. The moment she released them, leaving them on the workbench, she was able to gather her wits again. It was time to leave.

Elana shuffled out the back door, racing back to the alley way and the safety of the shadows. She could feel Di'Nay near as she moved into the light of the main street. She spotted Di'Nay driving down the street, the cart now empty. Di'Nay smiled and nodded to Elana, but the smile faded as she noticed Elana's expression.

Elana bounded into the cart.

"Elana?" Di'Nay questioned.

"We have to get out of the city."

"What?"

"Just go!" Without another question, Di'Nay turned and drove the cart as quickly as she could through the ever-growing crowd back to the main gates of the city.

CHAPTER SIX

I can deliver the nama."

Elana shook her head. "I have to see this through. Go back to our room and rest."

"Are you sure?"

Diana pulled into the courtyard of the Keep. Elana kissed her cheek and leapt out of the cart, answering her lover without words. She hit the ground running and sped into the building to deliver the nama to the healers. Diana brought the horses to a slower stop and collapsed back against the bench.

They'd been traveling at a break-neck speed since leaving Ayda, sleeping in the back of the cart in turns. The entire way back Diana had been feigning health, insisting that Elana take as few turns leading the cart with her injured shoulder as possible. Diana was weak with exhaustion and her stomach roared. She shivered, her body confused by the sudden weather changes between the north and south. Now that they were back, she didn't have a reason to continue clinging to false strength.

A band of adepts ran to her, two immediately moving to the horses.

"Well take care of them. Get some sleep." Their leader, Telias, the current Eldest Prepared of the Keep, helped Diana to the ground.

"Is the Mistress well?"

Telias's face was pale as her lips pressed into a tight line. "She still lives."

Diana understood her unspoken warning, but the fact that she was alive, that they hadn't been too late, lifted a massive weight from her shoulders.

"Is our room prepared?"

"I sent someone to build a fire when we spotted you on the horizon. There should be food and drink in your room as well."

Diana clapped Telias on the shoulder with a weary sigh and stumbled toward the Keep. "My thanks."

"Di'Nay."

Diana turned. "You'll want to be with Elana. The Mistress has... faded since you were away. I think the sight of her might upset her."

Diana nodded. "I promise."

She barely reached her room before her head started spinning. She kicked off her boots and cloak then collapsed into bed. The fire warmed her chilled skin and took what was left of her strength. She felt a momentary surge of guilt at climbing into bed as Elana worked with the healers, but the feeling faded as the lifestone set into her wrist started to warm, signaling Elana's approach.

Before Diana could fall asleep, Elana slipped back into the room, her face resting in her good hand. Diana noticed fresh bandages around Elana's shoulder.

"Are you all right?"

Elana shook her head in a quick, tremulous motion. "She's skin and bones, Di'Nay. I can't believe she's still alive. They don't even know if the antidote will work anymore."

Diana reached out and Elana climbed into bed with her. She curled into a ball, hiding her face behind her hands. Diana gently removed her boots and untied her cloak, letting the uncomfortable attire fall to the floor. Elana slipped into her arms, pressing tight against her, making an effort to connect with Diana despite hiding her eyes. Diana notice a couple tears slide down her hands, glittering in the firelight.

Diana ran her fingers through her hair and laid soft kisses along her brow and hands. "We did the best we could. You did the best you could. Her fate is with the Mother."

"I don't want her to die." The admission was weak, barely audible.

"Soroi. Soroi n'ti Mee," Diana whispered gentle words of love against her skin. "Sleep. Rest in my arms. What will be will be. We found the plant. She's still lives. Don't be afraid. Just be with me." Diana was able to gently ease Elana's hands from her eyes. She met her entrancing, blue irises and fed every loving emotion she could muster into their locked gaze. "Sleep, my love. I'm here."

Elana melted into her arms, finally giving away her pain like she had in the desert before reaching Ayda. Within moments she slept, but Diana could still feel her muscles jumping and her heart pounding in her sleep. Diana held her tighter, hoping her touch could bring her peace, and drifted into her own dreams.

Diana eased quietly into the seat beside the Mistress's bed. Elana didn't look at her, but she reached out and took Diana's hand. In the week they'd been back, Elana's shoulder had healed enough for her to have limited mobility and the healers gave her regular treatments to reduce the pain. She wasn't allowed to shoot or even ride, but she could hold Diana's hand and she could help treat the Mistress.

The antidote had only taken a day to brew, but Elana's grandmother hadn't wakened. Diana swore she could see color returning to the elderly woman's face, but Elana continued to despair. Diana worried what would happen if the Mistress passed before she woke. Elana would never forgive herself.

"How's she doing today?" Diana questioned.

"The same, but at least she's still breathing. How are you?"

"I'm fine, Soroi. Leggings and Kaing were returned this morning, along with word that the cart reached Black Falls safely. Your father said his vases have already sold."

Elana smiled softly. "I'm glad. He was always proud of his glasswork. Is there any word from Ayda? Darius is all right?"

"I wrote Camal and he hasn't heard of any problems, but he admits it's been a while since he's spoken with him."

Elana sighed. "I suppose that's all I can ask for."

"You didn't do anything wrong, Elana. It would have been more dangerous for him if you had confronted him directly. The Terrans might not even know you took the plants from his shop."

"I suppose."

"It's the truth, Elana."

"I know. I just don't like it."

"You wish you had done something wrong?"

"I wish I had killed them."

Diana sat back in shock at the venom in Elana's voice and the intensity of her words. The rage that had been steadily building since the attack had gone quiet. Deadly. Without a mission, without something she could do to help her Mistress, Elana was turning inward. Obsessing.

Diana searched for the right words to say. She didn't want to invalidate her lover's rage, but at the same time, she found herself increasingly lost trying to understand or predict Elana's moods and wishes.

All I can do is take her at her word.

"You don't know what's really going on. You would have regretted killing them without any answers."

"I'll get answers. I already have the seers searching for the men I heard in the shop. I implanted their amarin into the hive mind. It won't take long."

Diana nodded toward the Mistress, lying in her bed. "Would she want you seeking vengeance? What if she wakes?"

"That's irrelevant. Whoever poisoned her threatened the Keep. The Council. They need to be dealt with or they'll attack again. We need to know how they infiltrated us."

"The seers will do that, sae?"

"The seers can identify the threat. It's up to the Shadows to act."

Diana sat back, her fingers brushing across the skin of Elana's hand. "Were you trained to assassinate? As a Shadow?"

Elana glanced at her, her blue eyes burning framed by her raven curls. "Would it change the way you think of me if I was?"

"No. But perhaps what I understand of the Keep."

Elana turned back to her grandmother. "I wasn't trained to kill anyone. Just to defend myself and my bondmate."

Diana relaxed a fraction. "That's good to know."

"But the skills lend to it. Secrecy. Moving unseen. I'm a good Shadow, Diana. If I know who did this, I can stop them before they strike again. I can take care of this without it coming to public blows."

"You'd be all right with that? Killing someone in the shadows?"

Elana's voice was sharp and sure. "I will defend my Keep."

Diana was about to rebut when the Mistress shifted. Both women gasped and stood. Elana grabbed the Mistress's hand in a tight grip and a moment later, the Mistress's fingers tensed and wrapped around Elana's.

"Mistress." The word tore past Elana's lips like the cry of a scared child.

The Mistress's eyes fluttered open and she drew a deep breath past pale lips. "Your amarin is screaming," she groused.

Tears spilled down Elana's cheeks, a wet laugh filling the room. "I'm sorry."

The Mistress smiled and slowly closed her eyes. "You were always loud. I wouldn't ask you to change."

Diana rushed to the doors and called out for the healers. They ran to the Mistress's side, checking her vitals as the Mistress weakly complained about the attention. Elana never released her hand but for a moment Diana saw the smile return to her eyes. She breathed a sigh of relief. No matter what happened now, Elana would know they had succeeded. She had healed her Mistress and given her the best chance to survive that they could.

Diana sat on the ground, the icy stones freezing her skin even through her pants. She hugged her arms closer to her chest, trying to retain warmth. She grit her teeth and silently chided herself. She should be inside by the fire. She should find other ways to spend her time – do something useful. But she couldn't stand another minute within the Keep.

Diana had become much more open since meeting Elana, but there was still something unnerving about being around seers and shadows trained to read body language. She felt exposed, all her thoughts and secrets laid bare before the members of the Keep. She needed privacy.

"Almost not worth it," she grumbled to herself as she hugged her arms closer to her chest. She needed to find somewhere to be alone with a fireplace. Or perhaps a hot bath.

The gardens had succumbed to Aggar's winter, the flowers and trees that weren't evergreen had worn away to twigs and naked stems. Everything was sleeping, waiting for the sun to return. Diana wondered what it would be like to be able to fall in on herself, to hide away until conditions were better.

She silently chided herself for being so selfish and childish. She was a grown woman. She shouldn't be hiding in a sleeping garden from her young mate, grumbling about feeling useless in a community and system that wasn't her own. She had spent her entire life training to be sensitive to other cultures, to reign in her personal prejudices and concerns and be a good diplomat. Why was she having so many problems now?

Perhaps it was just that she'd never been in love with a woman from another culture before. Everything felt more personal. More intense. More frightening. Elana was changing. Anything with Elana had a way of undoing Diana.

As the Mistress healed, the Council moved forward with how they wanted to respond to the attack. Diana had only lived among the traders and rulers of Aggar, never the leaders of the Keep. Their processes and abilities were still foreign to her, and they were moving too quickly for Diana to keep up. She could voice her opinions, but at the end of the day this wasn't her world or her people. Her opinion didn't matter. It shouldn't matter. But she couldn't help but want to stand by Elana's side as she made these big decisions.

"The council of dey Sorormin would ground me if they could see me," she whispered.

"They would be making a horrible decision."

Diana spun around as Elana stepped out of the shadows of a cluster of evergreens. Diana hadn't even felt her approach in her lifestone.

Elana smiled smugly at Diana's shock. "I told you, I'm a very good Shadow."

"I never doubted it, Soroi." Diana stood, her legs numb from the cold and lack of movement. "How did your meeting with the seers go?"

"They found the Terrans I sensed. They believe the organization that threatened the merchants originated in a nearby Terran stronghold. They have ties with the Maltar. The Council thinks the attack was in response to our mission."

"I know the one. But an assassination attempt?" Diana's brow furrowed. "That's too personal for the Terrans."

"You put too much faith in them, Di'Nay."

"I don't put any faith in them. I just know the way they operate. They don't care enough about Aggar to sanction an attack on a major power center. Attacking the Council of Ten would be like a declaration of war."

"We've known for a long time that Terran eyes have started to focus on Aggar more closely. They've been here long enough to have a personal stake in our world. The Council has never actively meddled in their schemes before. They've had a taste of our power and it scares them. They may decide it's easier to take control of the planet."

Diana grit her teeth. "That doesn't sound right."

Elana's eyes flashed her hatred of the Terrans. "You haven't seen what we have, Di'Nay."

Diana lifted her hands in surrender. "I didn't mean to question your Sight or the power of the Council. I just know the Empire."

Elana crossed her arms over her chest. "You might be right. Perhaps it was a solitary band. You know as well as I do the corruption Aggar-bound Terran soldiers can inflict."

"It's more likely than an official action."

"I don't care about their politics. I care about what they did to my home. And I'll find them."

"They're sending you out again? Another assignment?"

"No."

"You're going alone?"

"Not if you go with me."

"Elana... There's a legion stationed at that stronghold. One of the largest on the planet."

"I'm a Shadow. I can slip past an army."

"Let me reach out to my Terran contacts. The Empire won't like a force destabilizing their relationship with a base planet. They'll help us."

"No. I don't trust any Terran."

Diana's hands balled into fists. How could she make Elana understand? "You don't want to make them angry. They're powerful."

Elana's lips curled away from her teeth. "So am I." She turned away. "They should be scared of me." Diana raced after her. "I'm going. I want you with me. But I'm still going even if you stay."

Diana's heart gave a painful jolt. She had no other choice. "I'll help you prepare for the journey."

PART TWO

BETRAYAL

CHAPTER ONE

Elana crouched low in the foliage, creeping forward on her hands and knees. She was hyper-aware of her surroundings. Her crossbow strapped to her back was a comforting weight as the pine needles prickled under her hands and her Sight filled the clearing, scanning for movement and life.

The trees whispered to her, reporting back the locations of scouts and spies. The Terran stronghold sat nestled in the base of the mountains, sprawling across the land like a stony cancer. Thick cement walls surrounded a series of bunkhouses, offices, practice courts, and four landing strips. Soldiers moved in uniform formations as they ran drills in the courtyards. The relentless buzz of their electronic devices were hard on Elana's Sight, the chaos of the artificial devices stirring up a powerful headache.

Their forces were impressive and unsettling. Elana knew the Terrans had heavily infiltrated Aggar, but she had never seen so many in one place before. Her lips curled with anger. Someone in the stronghold knew about the attack on her Mistress. Their walls and numbers couldn't keep Elana out.

"There are two transport ships on the landing strip. That means the hangers are full. Potentially six transport vehicles. They must be swapping forces. There will be twice as many soldiers as usual." Di'Nay's voice was soft and sharp. It didn't take Elana's Sight to know what she was really saying.

"It doesn't matter."

"Elana."

"We've been through this, Di'Nay."

Di'Nay sighed and clenched her jaw. "Do you have to go alone?"

"You're not trained to move like I can. You'll be noticed."

"I can pass as a legitimate visitor. I have supervisors that can stand up for me if I'm questioned. It's safer for me than for you."

"Not when it comes to getting information. They'll never tell you about an attack on the Keep. You're of dey Sorormin. Your people wouldn't condone assassination plots. This task requires stealth."

Di'Nay hesitated. "If they capture you, they'll put you in prison. People of Aggar aren't allowed on the bases unsupervised."

"I won't be captured."

"If you're not back by dawn, I'm going in after you. If they catch you, tell them you were looking for Tad Di'Nay. I'll be able to claim you as a cultural adviser."

"Fine."

Di'Nay took her arm, catching her eyes with a worried glance. "I don't like this, Soroi. Something feels off."

Elana kissed her. "They can't get away with attacking the Keep. Don't ask me to trust the people who would poison my family and steal my world."

"There are rules and regulations. There's a way to do this. A way I have access to."

"I'm not playing their games. I don't care how they operate. I'll be back soon. I promise."

Elana continued forward before Di'Nay could protest again. With her lover staying behind, Elana gave her whole self over to her Sight and her skills as a Shadow. She merged with the shade of the forest, her amarin interweaving with the life forces of the trees and grass, shielding her from view. She moved on silent feet. The rustle of her clothing and arrows blended with the sound of the gentle wind dancing through the forest canopy. Unless she was intentionally being sought out, she would be able to move unnoticed.

She used her Sight to search for any weaknesses or openings in the stronghold walls. She was able to sense a small shipping access opening near the mountainside. It had to be used for maintenance crews during times of high capacity. She timed her movements with the shifting of the guards along the wall. She grinned to herself. The Terrans had never been particularly observant. They were too dependent on their technology to find threats for them.

She easily slipped through the access door and ran for the shadow of the bunkhouses. The sharp tread of boots filled the air as a larger-than-normal troop practiced their formations. Elana silently thanked the Goddess for the distracting sounds. With less natural cover to draw from, her sounds would be more apparent.

She crept toward the first bunkhouse and peered into the windows. The house was filled with Terran soldiers unpacking their gear. She could sense they were new to Aggar, most of them novices. There was no way any of them had arranged an assassination. They probably hadn't even made landfall when the attack occurred.

She moved to the next bunkhouse. This one was empty, its soldiers among those marching on the field. She didn't hesitate before slipping inside, her eyes scanning the room. There were rows of simple bunks, each bed made the exact same way with the same deep green blankets. Rows of hooks holding canvas bags lined the far wall.

Elana looked through a half dozen bags, the satchels seeming to hold the soldier's only personal effects. She found letters from home, trinkets, and paltry bags of gold coins. It didn't seem the soldiers were paid much. Not nearly enough to hire assassins. And judging by the cleanliness and order of the soldier's routines, they weren't like the bands of soldiers from other bases that roamed Aggar townships and abused the people. Elana doubted these soldiers often even left the base.

Elana grunted in frustration. It was clear any attack from this base must have been ordered by someone with more authority. Elana had a moment of doubt. Perhaps she should have listened to Di'Nay.

Elana shook her head. This wasn't the time to doubt. She slipped back out the front door, leaving no trace of her presence.

She flitted between buildings, glancing in windows and pausing to listen in on conversations. She steadily made her way to the central office buildings. She shot every negative thought out of her mind. She understood there was a slim chance she'd find anything. But she had to keep going. She had relied on the Mother's grace most of her life. She couldn't stop now.

The central office building was an ugly, square cement structure dotted with small glass windows. There was more activity here. Soldiers and administrators bustled about their usual duties, shuffling paperwork and grouping together for meetings. Elana eyed the building warily. It was so unlike the structures of Aggar. There was an air of fear and despair surrounding the entire camp, but it seemed to come to a head in this building of business and politics. Elana couldn't imagine Di'Nay in this world. She knew her lover was a diplomat, often dabbling in politics and peacekeeping, but she couldn't imagine an energy more opposite her loving amazon.

Elana timed her approach, shifting through the shadows and cloaking herself with her Sight. She slipped through a back door and peered into the Terran minds to find her way around the building. It didn't take her long to reach a door that led into a cellar full of records; the Terran archive. If the Terrans had sent out a team to attack the Keep – and bothered to keep any records on the venture – they would be here.

The cellar was a library of boxes and files. The shelves were made of thin metal as opposed to the wood and occasionally stone shelves of Aggar libraries. Elana ran her hand over the manufactured structure with distaste. The Terrans had no respect for beauty or living things.

No one stood guard over the files. The Terrans were arrogant, thinking they were safe in the center of their base. Elana clenched her jaw. They clearly had no idea what Shadows were capable of.

She moved through the files quickly, scanning the labels and flicking her long, slender fingers through stacks of paper. She grunted softly to herself. She wished her Sight would allow finding paperwork to be as quick as reading people.

She hesitated as she found a case labeled "The Council of Ten." Her blood ran hot. She hated seeing the name of her beloved council written in Common. She pulled the box from the shelf and sifted through the files, curious what the Terrans knew about the Keep.

She found a collection of stories from the local people of Aggar and blueprints of the areas they'd allowed the Terrans to visit. There were rumors and mysteries. There were local legends and a few truths. She found a series of reports from within the Keep from more than a tenmoon before that seemed strangely accurate. Elana wondered if one of the recruits had been spying for the Terrans. Elana wanted to think the student changed their mind and grew loyal to the Keep, but chances were they had just gone home. It wasn't uncommon for Shadow students to drop out of the program as youths.

Another series of files detailed the comings and goings of various known Council members and identified Shadows. Elana saw her own name in a few of the reports. It made sense that they would keep an eye on her as one of the only Shadows they had confirmed to be working outside of the Keep.

Her hands trembled with a seething rage. She wondered how many spies were regularly posted in the forests surrounding the Keep. How many traitors had slithered into her home. She would have to remind the Council to keep the perimeter defenses up to date.

Elana's skin tingled as her eyes scanned past a mention of the Mistress. She quickly backtracked. Her lips pressed into a tight line. There was a report that the Mistress had taken ill and the rumored suspicion of foul play. There was nothing about an attack and no note about the poison. It seemed all they had was hearsay, information they could have gotten from one of the traders who serviced the Keep.

It was clear whoever was maintaining such a detailed file on the Keep wasn't involved in the attack. It didn't rule out the possibility of secret actions, but it was clear the base archive wasn't going to be of any use to her.

Elana replaced the files and the box on the metal shelf. She considered her next steps. The most likely scenarios now were that the attack had been a private operation that wouldn't be kept with the other files or it had been a band of soldiers working without the permission of their superiors.

Whoever it was either worked with someone of Aggar or they had been on the planet long enough to have a strong understanding of rare Aggar plants. The more she thought of the understanding it would take to both brew the poison and sneak it into the Keep, the more Elana was convinced it couldn't be any of the short-term soldiers who constantly filtered through the base. It had to be someone who worked in administration. Someone who had been here for years.

Elana squared her shoulders and stood. She was tired of thinking and plotting. It was time to be direct.

Elana slipped out of the archive and, instead of returning to Di'Nay, she made her way to the base commander's office. Elana was a representative of the Keep. The former Eldest Prepared. The Terrans had to respect her. And if they didn't, Di'Nay would storm the base at dawn and save her. She needed answers more than she needed to move unseen.

Elana burst through the commander's doors and three Terrans leapt to their feet, drawing swords.

“I'm Elana, bondmate to Diana n'Athena and representative of the Council of Ten. I demand to speak to the commander of this base.”

Two of the Terrans instantly advanced and she dodged the attack. The third, an older woman in a worn soldier's uniform, stood. “Stop.”

Her voice was clear, crisp and sharp. It cut through the chaos of the fight, demanding everyone's attention. The Terrans instantly snapped to attention, their swords at their sides. Elana turned to the woman, her face still feral from the fight, but she fought to remain calm.

The woman walked around the desk. Her stride reminded Elana of Di'Nay when approaching her Terran superiors, but Elana doubted the woman was an Amazon. Her eyes reflected her amarin – determined and controlled.

“I'm commander Alexandra Turner. What are you doing on my base?”

Despite the fire, Elana found her confidence and hesitance to leap into violence reassuring.

Elana stepped around the Terran guards to address the commander directly. “I know your people have been watching the Council's Keep. You know our Mistress was taken ill. You might even know that she was poisoned.” A flash of shock rippled through Alexandra's amarin and Elana's stomach clenched. She genuinely didn't know. “We've cured her, but we have reason to believe her would-be assassins came from this base. We demand answers.”

Commander Turner turned to her guards. “Leave us.”

“Ma'am --”

“Now. And shut the door.”

The guards traded glances, but followed her orders. Once they were gone, Commander Turner leaned back against her desk and folded her arms across her chest. Elana relaxed slightly. She wasn't emitting any dark intentions.

"My people do trade with the Keep. We work hard to maintain a peaceful relationship with the people of Aggar. Why do you think we would try to kill your Mistress?"

Elana snorted. "Peaceful? Terran soldiers rip through our towns. They raid. They deal in illegal trades and abuse the poor."

Commander Turner tensed. "Not my soldiers."

"You're so sure?"

"Yes. My soldiers spend most of their deployment here on the base. Those that do go into Aggar towns do so to weed out the violent and exploitative Terrans abusing their power. My base has charged more Terrans – Terrans from other bases – than any other settlement. It isn't us."

Elana's breath caught in her throat. Commander Turner's conviction shone like the sun. Despite her heritage, Elana sensed a truly noble soul. The realization was like a shower of cold water. This was her only lead. The only path that made sense.

"If it wasn't you, who then?"

Commander Turner shook her head. "I don't know. Are you sure the attackers were Terran?"

"I know Terrans were involved, yes. "

Commander Turner circled back around her desk and picked up her communicator. "This is Commander Turner. I'm calling an emergency council. I want every leader of a deployment team in my office in one hour."

A burst of static was followed by a man's voice. "Yes, Commander."

Commander Turner flicked off the communicator. "I've worked too hard to be the scapegoat for dirty soldiers. If your Keep is under attack -- if my base is being blamed – I'll do everything in my power to help you find those responsible."

Elana leaned back in her chair as the Terran soldiers debated. Her eyes were sharp, scanning every face and amarin, attempting to catch someone in a lie. The leaders of the stronghold had been discussing Elana's tale for three hours, picking apart everything she and Di'Nay had seen on their trip through the desert.

Di'Nay leaned forward, her elbows resting on the table as she joined in the discussion. Elana had sent for her the moment Commander Turner had gone to organize her meeting. While Di'Nay had never met the commander before, they seemed to get along quickly. Their similarities were more apparent when they talked. Their conversations moved quickly, bouncing between topics and ideas faster than Elana could follow. Elana wasn't stupid, nor was she a stranger to politics and intrigue, but she wasn't a Terran. The more they spoke, the more she realized she was clueless about the way the humans interacted with each other when they were unconcerned with the presence of someone from Aggar. Elana was surprised to find herself a bit jealous of the Terran commander.

"O'Donnell is commander near Dagan and Samuelson is north of Ayda. Both contingents have had their problems, but I don't see them working together," a lieutenant with a blonde beard streaked with silver grunted. "Some kind of sports rivalry. They take it very seriously."

"You think sports could keep soldiers from working a paying job? Whoever masterminded this has a lot of money, or at least a lot of power."

"We couldn't even get them to work together when the Sand Plague blew through both camps. Men died while they squabbled over who would carry the antidote."

Di'Nay snorted in disgust.

"We're assuming whoever is involved is staying close to their base or that they even belong to a base in the first place. Soldiers defect every day. Someone poisoned the Mistress of Council's Keep and their trail led at least to Ayda. This could be a private job or someone could be traveling," Commander Turner announced.

"If that's the case, what can we do? Finding the trail of an unknown defector from any base between the Keep and Ayda would be next to impossible," another lieutenant, a man with bushy red eyebrows, stated.

"What do you think, Elana?" Di'Nay was attempting to include Elana in the conversation but Elana only clenched her jaw.

She couldn't sense a shred of guilt or insight in anyone at the table. Her feelings danced between anger at having her plan stalled and frustration that they were still on the base. These Terrans had nothing. For all their resources, they were just as clueless as everyone else. The longer they worked together, the more the Terrans would focus on the Keep. Elana couldn't stop thinking of the files and reports she'd found tracking the movements in and out of her home.

"I think there isn't much we can do for each other."

Commander Turner rested her chin on her hand, obviously either not catching Elana's frustration or ignoring it. "Why not?"

"With all due respect, we've survived this long by keeping the Terrans at arm's length. We have our own resources. If you had nothing to do with the attack, we should move on. The less we have to do with each other, the better," Elana grunted.

Di'Nay tensed, surprised and shocked by her bondmate's uncharacteristic bluntness. "Might we have a moment, Commander?"

Commander Turner watched Elana suspiciously, but she slowly nodded. "Of course."

Di'Nay stood and Elana followed. She didn't want to be in the meeting anymore anyway.

Di'Nay led her from the council room to Commander Turner's office across the hall. She shut the door.

"Is something wrong?"

"We don't need them," Elana sighed. "They don't have any leads. They don't hold power in the right districts."

"They're powerful. They have an immense intelligence agency. They're peacekeepers. They're the perfect allies," Di'Nay argued.

"I'm well aware of their spying," Elana grunted. "I don't need them to focus more closely on the Keep."

Di'Nay hesitated. "Elana, they aren't going to use this as an excuse to infiltrate the Keep. They want to help. Commander Turner has fought for a good reputation among the locals. Her work is on the line here, too."

"No Terran can maintain good standing with Aggar. They're invaders. Off-worlders. They shouldn't even be here in the first place."

Di'Nay cocked her head to the side. "I'm not from here either. Am I so dangerous?"

Di'Nay's words caught Elana off guard. "You're not Terran."

"Commander Turner is doing good work. She showed me her records and exploits. You want her on Aggar."

"So I'm supposed to just let her walk into the Keep? They tried to kill my grandmother!"

Di'Nay drew a deep breath and understanding filtered into her amarin. She took Elana's hand. She chose her words carefully, trying to sound comforting. "I understand why you'd be angry. I understand how you feel about the Terrans and I know you feel violated that someone would come into your home and try to kill someone you love. But rejecting someone who wasn't involved, someone who is trying to help, won't undo what happened and it won't help us find the people responsible. Commander Turner and her lieutenants aren't the enemy. They fight the same enemy you do."

Elana pulled away from her. "You don't understand, Di'Nay. You're not from here. Your people weren't invaded. You came here to help us, but we wouldn't need any help if the Terrans had left us alone in the first place. I don't care what her intentions are. The Mistress wasn't poisoned by a stranger. The seers would have sensed an assassin's intent if one had simply slithered into the Keep in the night. This had to have been someone we trusted. Someone who seemed good. I can't trust seemingly good intentions and I can't trust amarin."

"Give her time."

"I'll give her three days. Unless she can do something useful, I don't want her help."

Elana stormed out of the room and Di'Nay didn't try to stop her.

CHAPTER TWO

Diana sat in a chair beside the bed, watching Elana as she tossed in her sleep. She had tried to wake her more than once, but like every other time she'd had psychic nightmares, she couldn't be disturbed.

They had only been on the base a single night before the nightmares began again. Diana would hold the smaller woman tight in their sleep and Elana's dreams would bleed into her own, waking her within moments from their intensity and ferocity. Diana wasn't sure if she was seeing the same things Elana dreamt or if her Sight, wild without Elana's conscious mind to control it, was lashing out at her.

Tears sparkled on Elana's cheeks and she gasped for breath. Soon she would wake with a start but without a sound. She would hold her head for a moment and catch her breath. Sometimes she would tell Diana what she had seen, but most of the time she would pretend nothing unusual had happened. Diana had never told her that her nightmares affected her as well.

Diana leaned back against the wall. Elana was always pale and a bit unfocused after her nightmares. They drained her energy instead of restoring her, and with her stress so high Diana worried what too many nights with such vivid dreams would do to her Love.

It was clear the Blue Sight's fears and prejudices were growing. She was turning into a different woman. The calm, careful Shadow who had gently pursued Diana's heart and trust was replaced with a brash, restless avenger. She couldn't predict what Elana would do next. She knew she wasn't saying the right things. Diana feared they'd soon clash so hard, so violently, that they wouldn't be able to pull themselves back together again.

Diana shuddered at the thought. It had only been a short time, but already she couldn't imagine a life without Elana. Just the thought made her sick. She had to find a way to help her lover – to be more sensitive or perhaps more helpful. Elana had been right. Diana didn't know what it was like to live in an occupied world. She grew frustrated with the stupidity or carelessness of various Terrans, but she didn't have a reason to hate them. To fear them. Elana was fully aware of their power and presence.

Perhaps Elana was right. Maybe they should leave. At the very least, Diana knew she couldn't keep taking Elana's hatred of off-world invaders to heart, no matter how much the words stung.

Elana sat bolt upright, sweat running down her cheeks and her heart pounding so hard Diana could feel it through her lifestone.

"Di'Nay?" Elana's call was weak and desperate. Diana was instantly at her side.

"What is it, Love?"

Elana grabbed her, burying her face against Diana's chest. Tears stained Diana's shirt and Elana trembled in her arms. Elana didn't talk about her dream, and Diana didn't ask. Whatever she'd seen, Diana wasn't going to make her relive it.

Diana moved to adjust to a more comfortable position and Elana held her tighter. "Don't leave me."

Diana settled and ran one hand through Elana's hair. "I wasn't going anywhere. I won't leave you. I promise."

She held Elana as she wept and tried her best to comfort her. After nearly an hour, the Blue Sight's tears dried and her heart started to calm. "I'm sorry," Elana whispered.

Diana kissed her brow. "Never be sorry for needing me."

"I don't like it here, Diana. I don't want to be on a Terran base anymore."

"Then we'll leave."

Elana looked up, her cheeks dark olive from crying. "But you want to stay."

"I want you happy and safe. No chance at help is worth a nightmare like that. Where do you want to go?"

Elana wrapped her arms around Diana's neck and kissed her, the embrace slow and gentle. "Thank you."

"They're not my people, Elana. You are my people. My mate.

My partner. My sun. My moon. My life. If you say it, I believe it. If you wish it, it's yours."

"You stayed awake thinking?"

"Yes."

Elana glanced down as her fingers mindlessly curled and twisted at the strings of Diana's night shirt. "Do you really trust this commander? Do you really think she'll be of any help?"

Once more, you surprise me. "I think she's our best chance right now, yes. And she seems honorable."

"Then I'll try to be more understanding."

"I thought you wanted to leave the base?"

"I do." Elana looked back up, meeting eyes with Diana. Even in the darkness her magical, icy blue irises seemed to glow. Elana's confusion, fear, and a lifetime of oppression was laid bare to Diana in a single glance. "But I *need* answers. And I trust you more than I fear them."

Diana kissed her again, letting Elana feel the awe she inspired in her Amazon lover. "Do you want to sleep, Ona?" Diana whispered against her ear. "I'll hold you, even if you have another nightmare."

Elana shook her head. "I don't want sleep. I want comfort. I want to feel you. Please."

Elana's kiss was as gentle and warm as the silk of her skin in Diana's hands. She felt her blood rise and her heart quicken, but the fire of her passion was low and steady. She touched Elana with all the gentleness of her love.

"How could I ever leave you?" Diana's lips formed the words against the curl of Elana's throat, more a sigh than vocalization.

Elana relaxed into her caress, their bodies melding into a single being. "You couldn't. As I could never leave you."

And they both knew it was true.

The sunlight seemed sharp, the light bright enough to make Diana squint as she glanced across the base at the marching soldiers. The air was crisp. She had come to associate the feeling with snow coming. She grunted softly at the thought. She was so sick of snow.

Commander Turner rushed out of her office building and rubbed her hands together to warm them. Diana smiled softly. The motion reminded her of a family friend – Sera -- a woman close enough she might as well have been blood. Much about the commander reminded Diana of Sera. She was sharp. Focused. Intelligent. In-control. But Diana could also see a gentleness in her. A side she was too afraid to show while commander of such a prominent Terran base. Women held positions of power in the Empire, but not many. Any sign of weakness from the commander would be fodder for the dozens of people that had to be waiting to replace her.

If someone of prominence among the Terrans was involved with the assassination attempt on the Mistress, Commander Turner would lose her job. She had to know it was a possibility. The fact that she was still willing – and eager – to offer her help spoke volumes about her character.

"Any updates?" Diana questioned.

Commander Turner shook her head. "Not a trace. But I have my best investigators on it. I did find the shopkeepers you wanted me to look in on. Tad Camal and Tad Darius. Both are alive and seem to be well. Tad Darius doesn't even seem to realize anything has happened."

Diana let out a breath of relief. "Elana will be happy to hear that."

Commander Turner hugged her arms over her chest. "She seems pretty tightly wound."

Diana bit back a laugh. "She doesn't like Terrans. Can't really blame her."

"I suppose not." Commander Turner shifted uncomfortably. "I'll never get used to this cold."

"Neither will I. I've never stayed long in a place like this. I prefer deserts."

Commander Turner looked her over slowly, her eyes inquisitive. "I never expected to see a Shadow bonded with an Amazon."

"It's a long story," Diana admitted.

"You're mates, yes?"

Diana glanced at the Commander from the corner of her eye. "Yes. Does that make you uncomfortable?"

Commander Turner shook her head. She seemed unphased by the answer, but Diana could see a familiar light in her eyes. "You're not used to working with Amazons?"

"No. Between school, my first off-base missions, and then my time here, I haven't met many people."

"What do you think of them?"

"I think there's more to your people than you let on."

"Have you ever wanted to find out more?"

Commander Turner shrugged. "I'm not a lover of women. It didn't seem my place to investigate the Amazons."

"You love men?" Diana was genuinely surprised. "I admit, you could pass for a Sister."

Commander Turner smirked. "I've been attracted to a few men, yes, but generally I don't find romance or attraction a big part of my life. I don't have many drives outside of my work. It keeps me focused."

"There are Sisters like that. Those who are happily unattached or prefer not to engage in intimacy with anyone. That doesn't make it impossible to join our ranks."

Commander Turner cocked an eyebrow, good-natured amusement sparkling in her eyes. "Are you trying to recruit me, Diana?"

Diana laughed aloud. "I try to bring every good woman into the fold of Yemaya. I don't see why any would ally themselves with the Terrans."

"There are challenges, but there's also good work to be done. Look at what I've built here. Most of my soldiers are new, fresh out of the academy. I give them a purpose. I teach them about honor and respect. We keep the people of Aggar safe. I don't like what our presence on this world has done to the people of Aggar, but like it or not, the planet is necessarily strategic to keep the galaxy at peace. If war broke out, there would be a lot more for the people here to worry about."

Diana nodded slowly. "That's the bit I don't think Elana understands. She doesn't see or know what threats lay outside of the Terrans and the Empire."

"Mother willing, she never will."

Diana glanced at her in surprise. "A Terran invoking Aggar gods?"

Commander Turner shrugged again. "I like the idea of a female goddess."

"Are you certain you have no interest in becoming an Amazon?"

Commander Turner laughed. "Right now I just want to find out what happened at the Keep. Is there anything else Camal told you about the men who approached him? Something you might have forgotten before?"

Diana wracked her brain for anything helpful. "Nothing, I'm sorry."

Commander Turner shook her head. "Don't be. You've already given us more than we usually have. We'll just have to keep looking."

"Thank you."

Commander Turner nodded and strode back to her office building. Diana returned her attention to the soldiers. Normally the sight of so many warriors would put her on edge. She didn't like fighting and soldiers were rarely interested in using diplomatic approaches. But knowing why they were training – that they were under Commander Turner's thumb – gave her hope. At least they were trying to make the world better.

"Di'Nay?"

Diana turned as Elana approached. Her cloak billowed behind her as she moved. Dark circles ringed her eyes – evidence of her restless night. She was looking pale. Diana pressed her lips tight together. Lately she seemed to see Elana exhausted, sick, or hurt more than happy and healthy.

"Is everything all right?"

Elana nodded, but she still took Diana's hand and stood close beside her. "Did Commander Turner have anything to say?"

Diana shook her head. "No leads. She did tell me Camal and Darius are alive and well."

Elana smiled. "I'm glad."

"Whoever is doing this seems to have gone into hiding. If Camal and Darius are well, then they may also be trying to stay nonviolent."

"Nonviolent? They tried to kill my Mistress!"

"Yes. Still, they could have silenced everyone we came into contact with. They haven't even harassed them. It seems staying invisible is more important to them."

"Perhaps."

"You don't think so?"

"I don't doubt it. I just... something feels off. Different. There's more to this story, but I don't know what it is."

"I'm sure you're right."

A communicator buzzed at Diana's hip.

"Diana?" Commander Turner's voice echoed from the speaker.

Elana cocked an eyebrow at her lover. "You two have communicators?"

Diana winked. "Jealous?"

Elana snaked an arm around her waist. "After last night? No."

Diana kissed her cheek and pressed the button on the device. "Here. What's going on?"

"Partel asked to move up the morning meeting. You wanted to sit in?"

"Yes. Thanks. I'll be there soon." Diana switched off the communicator.

"You're going to their meetings?"

"I figure if we're going to be staying here for a while, we might as well learn as much as we can."

"Do you want me to go with you?"

"Only if you want to."

Elana took Diana's hand. "Let's go."

They walked together toward the meeting room. Commander Turner leaned over the table, studying a thin stack of paperwork. A travel-worn, middle-aged soldier leaned back in his chair and ran a hand through his salt-and-pepper hair. "It's strange. I don't know what to make of it."

Diana could see the confusion and frustration in Commander Turner's eyes. "What is it?"

Commander Turner glanced up and shook her head. "Nothing about the assassination attempt."

"But something about the Keep?"

Elana's statement surprised everyone in the room. Diana looked at her in shock. She could feel Elana's heartbeat quickening through their lifestone connection. "Excuse me?" Commander Turner questioned.

"I can feel it in you. There's something wrong with the Keep."

Commander Turner exhaled deeply. "Not the Keep directly. Seers are going missing."

"What?" Elana and Diana gasped together.

"How is that possible?" Diana questioned. She turned to Elana. "Wouldn't the other seers know something was wrong?"

"They're not being taken from the Keep. These are potential students, coming to prove their worth to the Keep."

"Are they hurt?" Diana asked in concern.

"We don't know. For all the evidence we have, they could have left voluntarily. It isn't rare for potential students to run away."

"How many?" Elana's voice was sharp.

"A dozen or so."

Elana tensed. "We haven't gotten word of a dozen recruits, and nothing about students disappearing."

Commander Turner's brow furrowed thick over her eyes. "How many have you been told to expect?"

Elana grit her teeth. "Can I use your satellite? I need to reach home."

Commander Turner walked around the table. "Of course. Come with me."

Diana slowly hiked into the forest. She could see Elana in the distance, sitting beneath a pine tree with her knees tucked against her chest. Her long, blue skirt splayed across the floor, covering everything but the tips of her boots. She closed her eyes, pressing her face against the curve of her thighs.

"Elana? Soroi?"

Elana looked up, her eyes ablaze. "Commander Turner was right. The seers searched for recruits. Fifteen have been taken. They've disappeared. The seers can't even find them."

Diana sat next to her love. "That's awful. Do they have any idea what has happened to them?"

"Nothing. Di'Nay, what if someone saw what the Maltar did to his seer? What if they're twisting these children? Using them and destroying them? You saw the horrors the Maltar did with one seer, but fifteen?"

Diana hugged her arms across her chest, as much to ward off her sudden fear as to block out the cold. "First the assassination attempt, and now this. It's too much for the Keep to investigate at once. What can we do?"

"I think it's the same people."

Diana lifted an eyebrow. "The same? Why? The crimes don't seem related."

"Someone is targeting the Keep. Killing our Mistress and kidnapping our seers both create chaos. They cause fear. Who would send us their child if they're going to disappear before they can reach our gates? We can't even feel safe behind our walls anymore."

"But the children aren't being killed. If they were, the seers would be able to find their bodies, yes?"

"This isn't about killing anyone," Elana grunted. "It's about tearing us apart. The people are already afraid of us. They trust us because we're still useful to them. If the tides change – if we stop being a safe place – the people could turn on us."

Diana studied her mate, trying to understand. She could see the fear and erratic anger in her eyes. She wasn't thinking logically. She wanted to tell her everything would be okay. She wanted help her see that the cascade of pain and chaos raining down on her home could be a horrible coincidence without being a conspiracy. She just couldn't find the words.

"I'm not stupid." Elana's voice was acidic. "I know it's more likely that these are coincidences. I know there are plenty of people who would want the Mistress dead and want to use seers. I don't know why I'm so sure it's the same people, but I am. I thought you trusted me?"

Diana blinked in shock. She thought she had seen the worst of Elana's anger. The almost casual ferocity in her voice was like a punch in Diana's stomach. Everything about her seemed to shift for a second – her scent, the sound of her voice, even the taste of the air around her. Diana rested her hand on Elana's shoulder. "I didn't mean to imply you were stupid or that I don't trust you. I just want to be sure we don't act rashly."

Elana's shoulders sagged. "I'm sorry."

Diana shook her head. "Don't be."

Elana looked out into the forest, her eyes searching for something Diana couldn't see or understand. "The Ramains and the Keep have been conversing. The Ramain royalty has asked for the Council's aide. Commander Turner knows where to look for information. We aren't doing anything just waiting here for her people to tell us something new. The Mistress wants us to travel to Markessa to offer our help to the King and Queen of the Ramains."

"She wants us to abandon the assassination investigation?"

"She said this is more important. That she'll send others out to continue our work. She likes that we can approach the Ramains royalty as representatives of both the Keep and the Terrans."

"I'm not a Terran," Diana argued.

"I know. So does she. But you work for them. People of Aggar know what Amazons are, but not many of your kind have openly traveled among us. To the people of the Ramains, you are a Terran."

Diana clenched her jaw. Elana was right, of course. She still didn't like the thought of presenting herself to Aggar world leaders and being confused as a part of the Empire. "I suppose."

"I can't argue with her, as much as I want to. I don't want to abandon the work we've done and I don't trust anyone else to pursue this case as closely as we can. But these are children. Seers. We can't let them get hurt."

"Perhaps you'll be right and the two cases will be connected."

Elana drew a sharp, deep breath. "Perhaps."

Elana fell silent. Diana couldn't tell what she was thinking, but she knew it wasn't pleasant. "Do you want to get some sleep? It might make us both feel better."

"I won't be able to. Not well, anyway."

"What would help?"

"Moving forward. I don't want to wait anymore."

Diana glanced at the sky. It was about midday. "I'll prepare the horses."

Elana looked at her in shocked surprise. A smile curled her lips. "Really?"

"I told you last night, Soroi. If you wish it, it's yours."

Elana wrapped her arms around Diana's neck and kissed her. Diana lingered in her embrace, relishing the silken touch of her lips and the solid weight of her arms across the top of her shoulders. She breathed Elana's scent deep into her lungs and ran her hands gently over the lines of her waist and hips. Dear Goddess, she would do anything for this woman.

"Come," Diana whispered, feeling her own breath warm Elana's lips. "We have a long way to go before we make camp."

CHAPTER THREE

Leggings moved at a steady pace beneath Elana, her hoof beats sharp on the cobbled stone road. Elana fought the urge to nudge her faster. She wanted to gallop. She wanted to push herself as far and fast as she could go to Markessa. It always seemed there were urgent matters to attend to – information to find – but so much traveling in between. She almost wished the Terran transport ships were more common on Aggar.

"It will be all right, Love," Di'Nay's response was soft and encouraging.

Elana knew Di'Nay could sense her frustration. They were too close to the capitol to gallop. They weren't hiding their presence – if they could force whoever was attacking the children to attack them as well, it would save them a lot of research – but they didn't want to catch the attention of the local authorities until they could reach the castle where the Ramains royalty held court. They needed to move casually. They needed to blend in.

"I know." Elana fought to keep her voice even.

The air seemed to crackle with tension and power. Elana felt... disconnected. Off. Something was steadily warping her Sight and she couldn't tell if it was her own frustrations or a corruption in the amarins around her. Whatever it was, it was leaving her unfocused and anxious.

She gripped Leggings' reigns tighter. She would fight through it. She could fight through anything. Lives depended on it.

Di'Nay scanned the sky, her eyes narrowed. Elana studied her. "You feel it, too?"

"Hmm?"

"You can feel something is wrong."

Di'Nay shifted uncomfortably. "I'm not sure what I feel. But the air seems still. Quiet."

"It makes you feel sick?"

"A little. Does that mean something?"

Elana drew a deep breath. "It could. But we're so connected, you could just be feeling a hint of what I am."

Di'Nay laughed. "Sorry I can't be of more help. I'm not known for my psychic abilities."

Elana smiled. "At least you're strong."

Di'Nay reached out and squeezed her hand. "Glad to be good for something."

The strangled cry of a horse split the air, sending a shock of panic through Elana's senses. She gasped and fell back, paralyzed for a moment by the animal's pain. The sensation was more intense than it should have been, as if amplified by something else. Something uncontrolled. Young.

"Elana?

"We have to help!"

Elana charged forward, following the waves of agony leaving a glowing trail in Elana's Sight. She rounded a sharp corner into a grove of fruit trees to see a carriage toppled on its side, a dying horse flailing on the ground. Two soldiers already laid in pools of their own blood, one trampled in the horse's death throes. A half-dozen men dressed in black with black cloths covering their faces circled the carriage.

A third soldier's throat was slit as Elana whipped her crossbow from her back and notched an arrow.

"Bandits?" Di'Nay called as the sharp swipe of her sword leaving its sheath echoed in the air.

"No."

Elana let a bolt fly, felling one of the attackers. Four others raced toward them as the fifth survivor climbed on the toppled carriage and threw open the door.

"No!" Elana shouted and shot the attacker at the carriage, ignoring the men rushing toward her. Her bolt narrowly missed, embedding in the wood.

Di'Nay leapt down from her horse and ran to meet the four. Her sword flew, knocking aside the attack of the first man and swinging back around to stab him in the stomach.

Elana shot at the man at the carriage a second time and once again missed.

"Elana!" Di'Nay called as she fought off the other three men at once.

Elana grunted in frustration and forced her attention back to Di'Nay. She carefully aimed and took down one of the three as Di'Nay beheaded another. Their clothing seemed to be made for speed and stealth, not defense. Their techniques were crude. They weren't trained. Di'Nay quickly dispatched the third as well.

A child screamed in the carriage as the remaining attacker pulled him out of the carriage. He was no more than three tenmoons, his eyes wide in terror. He wasn't able to fight back. He probably didn't even speak yet. Seers rarely did until they were with their own kind.

Elana shot again, her bolt catching the man in the foot, pinning him to the ground. The man cried out in pain, but he didn't drop the child seer. He tried to run, but he stumbled on his injured foot. Within moments Di'Nay was upon him, pulling the child out of his arms and pushing him to the ground.

Elana leapt off her horse and strode to the man. He fought to get up and Elana shot another bolt into his arm, sending him crashing to the dirt once more.

Di'Nay held the child tight, whispering soothing sounds in his ear. Elana glanced at him nervously. His power was still growing, but it was wild and heightened in his panic. If he turned his attention on Diana, it could easily knock her out. Elana engulfed him in her Sight like a heavy quilt and fed him all the soothing energy from the trees and flora in the grove. He started to calm.

Elana stepped on the attacker's chest. He fought against her, but with his wounds he was too weak. She bent down and removed the headcloth. He winced and tried to cover his face. Elana tensed. He was of Aggar.

"Who are you?" she demanded.

He struggled against her again. "Blue-eyed demon!"

Elana sent a third bolt into his unscathed arm. He screamed and Di'Nay held the young seer tighter.

"Who are you?" Elana repeated.

"Can't you read my mind?"

He continued to cover his face. A sharp laugh escaped her lips. "I don't need to see your eyes to read your amarin."

"Go back to the Fates' Cellar!"

Elana fell to her knees and peeled his hands away from his face so she could look into his eyes. “Why are you kidnapping children?”

“Demons!” he spat. “Possessing our children!”

Elana scowled. It wasn't the first time she'd heard the theory. It wasn't as common in cities as it was in the smaller towns across the Ramains. Elana couldn't believe someone who espoused such ignorant hatred could recruit a following skilled enough to hide from the Council.

Elana leveled her crossbow at his head.

“Elana?” Di'Nay sounded nervous, but Elana couldn't show any sign of weakness now.

“Who sent you?”

The man looked at her crossbow bolt and his lips curled into a snarl. “You're scared?”

Elana barely heard his taunt as she felt something in his amarin. A whisper he was almost hoping she'd sense. He knew what had happened to the Mistress.

The man froze in horror as Elana met his eyes, ripping into his mind with her Sight. He hadn't been involved with the assassination attempt of the Mistress, but he knew what had happened. She saw snippets of his memories. His mind was too simple to keep her out. She saw groups of men, mostly of Aggar, meeting in cellars and in forested groves at midnight. She saw unnecessary ritual and men in black robes wearing metal amulets.

She saw seer children curled in on themselves, unable to cry out as they were pulled from carriages and inn beds. The man wasn't high enough in the organization to know what happened to the children that disappeared.

Elana broke contact with him by turning to Di'Nay. He whimpered and collapsed, falling unconscious from the intensity of her power. A trickle of blood ran from his nose down his lips.

Di'Nay was pale as she watched her lover's ferocity. Elana felt a punch of guilt and tried to soften her face. “I was right.”

“About what?”

“He knows about the Mistress. He's part of an organization that's targeting the Keep.”

“He got involved with Terrans?”

Elana clenched her jaw and shook her head. Her stomach turned. “I only saw people of Aggar.”

"What? How?"

"I'm not sure. But I know there's a major sector of the group in the capitol. I can't sense the other seer children."

Elana eased the child out of Di'Nay's arms and cradled him close to her chest. The child made a weak sound of distress, but his seer abilities latched to Elana's powers more firmly than his tiny hands clutched at the collar of her tunic. She kissed his silken brow and used her Sight to soothe him to sleep.

Di'Nay watched them, her eyes soft. "Poor thing."

"He'll be better when he's with his fellows. Born Seers need each other to understand the world."

"That must be hard for their families. Do many call on the Keep when a seer is born?"

Elana tensed, a cold shock flashing through her stomach. She kept forgetting how little Di'Nay really knew about her world. "Some. Not all seers have such strong abilities at birth. Some don't grow into their abilities until they're coming into adolescence or even adulthood. Some can even live outside of the vault." Elana patted the seer child's back. "But they're often like him. Their families are supposed to call on us. But many don't know their child is a seer. They assume the child is broken. It's not uncommon for them to be abandoned or worse."

Di'Nay blanched. "They're so young."

Elana rubbed the child's back, his dreams peaceful, possibly for the first time in his life. "They're seers. To most on Aggar, they're born dangerous."

Di'Nay clenched her jaw. "I'm glad they have the Keep to protect them."

Elana glanced away. "If the Keep stands."

Di'Nay touched her shoulder. "We'll defend it. The Mistress is still alive. The defenses are intact. And if any who would threaten the keep are as poorly trained as the ones attacking seers, your novices could fight them off. They're weak."

"Perhaps physically. But they're hiding seers from us. They have some kind of power that interferes with the powers of the Keep. That's nothing to take lightly."

"We've dealt with people who can hide from the Keep before," Di'Nay reminded her.

Elana tensed. "I don't want to think of someone like the Maltar with a dozen seer children."

Di'Nay sucked in a sharp breath in agreement. She patted the young Seer's back, instantly pulling away when he made a tiny sound of distress at contact that wasn't Sighted. "What do we do about him?"

"I'll contact the Keep. They'll send Shadows to bring him to safety," Elana assured her. "There are inns in Markessa that are friendly with the Keep. Some that are hidden. We'll be safe there." Elana scanned the clearing, with the carriage overturned and the dead kidnappers littering the ground. "Any authorities will assume it's a robbery gone wrong. It would be better for everyone but the Keep to think the child and his caregivers are dead. Less of a trail."

Di'Nay nodded and started back toward the horses. "Then the sooner we get to the capitol the better."

Elana closed the door tight behind her, instantly shutting out the noise of the busy inn and the city surrounding it. The Dancing Lark was no stranger to housing Shadows and Blue Sights. The top floor of rooms had been enchanted and glamoured to make them unnoticeable to those who didn't already know they were there.

Elana was most appreciative of the wards that kept out sound. The overwhelmed seer child was taking so much of her energy and Sight that she could barely deal with the massive crowds wandering the Ramains capitol. Thankfully, Di'Nay knew the city and was able to lead both horses through the bustle. Elana just had to direct her to the inn.

Di'Nay dropped their bags beside the washbasin as Elana sat on the edge of the bed. The sound of bottles clinking against each other, barely padded with cloth diapers, echoed through the small room. They were lucky the landlady had small children and supplies to spare.

The seer child was still cuddled against her chest. Every time she tried to move him or even settle him in a different position, he would start to cry. The squall was weak, mournful, older than his handful of years. It broke Elana's heart.

Elana could see very little in his fractured mind – images of his kidnapper. A memory of his caretaker. She couldn't see anything of his parents or home. Elana wasn't surprised. If his family was wealthy enough to hire a carriage and porter, they probably wouldn't want it known they had a seer in the family. He would have been hidden away. Probably didn't even live with his parents.

His amarin was all fear and darkness. He would heal among his own kind, but it would take time. Still, trauma wasn't uncommon among the seers that came to the Keep. He would fold into the hive of his people and find himself finally connected to the world. To the endless ebb and flow of nonlinear time.

Elana never envied the seers their intense connection to the world. She valued her independence and individuality. But she knew the intense joy the seers sang through the halls when they found a new member of their ranks. She could hear them reverberate through the stones of the Keep and knew the kind of happiness that was in the child's future. She ran her fingers though his silken hair and smiled.

"That's quite a sight." Elana glanced up at Di'Nay, the Amazon leaning back against the wall with a gentle grin.

"What would you do if I bore a seer child?" Elana questioned.

"Would that be possible off Aggar?"

Elana rocked the child slowly. "I have no idea."

"We would love her, sae?"

"Even if she could never speak to us? Even if she couldn't understand her world?"

"You underestimate the love and care of the crones n'Shae. They would be able to help her. Or give her comfort."

Elana cocked her head to one side, appraising her confident bondmate. "You're so sure?"

"I would have to be, Love. I would do anything for our child."

Elana glanced away, savoring the care in her words. The certainty. Di'Nay might not understand the realities of a child with the Sight, but she was loving. And Elana knew she would rise to whatever challenges came their way.

If you survive long enough to have children.

The thought was sudden and sharp, breaking through her happiness like an arrow in her heart.

The seer child whimpered at the change in her amarin and Di'Nay's brow knit with concern.

"Did I say something wrong?"

Elana shook her head. "No. What you said was beautiful." She raised her chin, her eyes teasing. "Perhaps I just wondered what I'd do if I bore an Amazon."

Di'Nay laughed aloud in true glee, the sound a snort of

surprise. "I'm afraid, Soroi n'ti mee, that a n'Athena child would be far more trouble than any seer."

"And a n'Shae child?"

Di'Nay's cheeks were flushed with excitement and joy at the conversation. Elana could feel her emotions, strong enough to flow through the lifestone at her wrist that bonded them together. The seer child soothed once more as Elana's love swelled at the sight of her lover's hope.

Di'Nay pushed away from the wall and sat beside Elana. "Speaking generally, of course."

"Of course."

"A n'Shae child will want to experiment. My cousin was dear friends with a future n'Shae. The girl was always mixing things. Playing at making medicines. She burned her eyebrows off trying to make a tonic for a head cold. Lucky she didn't poison anyone."

"I once paralyzed my teacher trying to use my Sight to cheer her. I was only six tenmoons."

"N'Shae," Di'Nay accused as she nipped at Elana's cheekbone.

"Child," Elana gasped, indicating the seer in her arms.

"He's sleeping," Di'Nay protested.

"He's listening," Elana corrected.

Di'Nay wrapped Elana and the child in her arms, Elana's lifestone humming with pleasure and peace.

"What kind of child would bring us peace? N'Huitaca?"

"Fire dancers."

"N'Hina?"

"Plowing accidents."

"N'Minona?"

Di'Nay scrunched her nose in annoyance. "Bossy."

Elana laughed. "So judgmental."

"Is there any kind of child that doesn't bring risk and pain?"

"I suppose not."

"Do you really have any preferences for what our child becomes?"

Elana shook her head. "I just want my children to be good. To be kind. And to be happy."

"No doubt of that with you as their mother."

"And you."

Di'Nay's blush was light and pleased. "I'd like to think so. Though I fear my influence may increase the likelihood of troublemaking."

Elana smirked. "You really underestimate my capacity for trouble."

"I would never underestimate you."

"Then our children are doomed."

Di'Nay held her tighter. "I can't wait to meet them."

The seer child let out a contented sigh and Elana kissed the top of his head, his sweet new baby smell waking impulses and instincts she'd rarely allowed herself to dream about. Before she met Di'Nay, before she knew she could go to Yemaya... It had never seemed possible. It would mean giving up her life as a Shadow. It meant fundamentally changing everything she had fought to become, everything she had trained for. It would mean leaving the Keep. Trusting it to people who had already allowed the Mistress to be poisoned once before. Would it be abandonment?

The uncertainty filled her once more with doubt, but for a moment she closed her eyes and allowed herself to sink into Di'Nay's arms, the weight of the child who needed her resting heavy on her chest. She smiled as she dreamed. As she hoped. She wasn't gifted with the ability to see the future, but for one night at least, there was no harm in imagining.

Di'Nay ran her fingers through Elana's wild mass of Ebony hair and gently caressed the child's cheek with a single finger. For the first time, the touch didn't disrupt him. It was a moment of pure sweetness. So pure Elana could taste it, could feel it even with her eyes closed.

In a moment she felt transported. She was in the home, all wood and tile, nestled in the forest in autumn the way Di'Nay described. She felt the heat of a fire on her face. Could smell dinner mingling with the bitter, earthy scents of the herbs in her medicines and concoctions. Was she teaching a child to heal? Was it the smell of homemade paints for an artistic child? Or a strange, favorite dish of an adventurous child?

She could hear children laughing. She could sense the amarin buried in objects around the house – treasures from adventuring with her love across the Amazon homeworld. They would never stay still for long. Not even as mothers. There was nothing dark. Nothing sad. Nothing bitter or lonely. There was only family. Only home.

Elana couldn't open her eyes for fear the vision would shatter.

She couldn't breathe, afraid that if she did, if anything disturbed this moment, it would disappear forever.

"Someday, Soroi n'ti mee. Someday this will be our life. If you want it."

"I want it." Elana was surprised at the way her voice shook and her eyes filled with tears. *I just don't know if I'm allowed to have it.*

The Keep was shrouded in darkness, the hallways unnervingly silent as Elana stood in the middle of the great lecture hall. She stood at the center of the circular room, the rows of benches surrounding her like ripples in a pond. Parchment and books were scattered across the stone seats as if left in haste. The lecture hall was never left cluttered.

The room was so familiar, she'd been there hundreds of times, but now it was off. Haunted. It took her a moment to realize why.

Even when everyone was asleep the Keep was never silent. The vibrations of the Seers, communing with the world even in their dreams was a steady heartbeat. The gentle waves of rolling amarin from the largest concentration of Blue Sights on Aggar was like the dull thud of blood pumping behind her ears.

But now everything was quiet. Desolate. Elana trembled. She could feel the trees and the earth outside and around the Keep. She wasn't entirely cut off from the world. But there was nothing else. Nothing inside the building. Was the Keep abandoned? Was everyone dead?

She ran through the room, her feet skipping steps as she climbed between the rows of seats and raced out the tall, wooden double doors. She sped through the building, searching the bunks and libraries. The bedrooms were abandoned, most of the student's belongings gone, but a few bits of clothing, notebooks, and quills were scattered about. What could make the Shadows abandon the Keep so fast? There were no signs of struggle or war. Something else must have happened.

Elana clenched her jaw. No matter what happened, the Mistress wouldn't abandon the Keep. But if even the Seers were gone...

Elana shook her head. She couldn't imagine it. She just needed to find her family.

Elana sped away from the students' quarters into the heart of the Keep. Her sense of dread grew with every step. The hallways seemed to stretch out too long. As Elana reached the Mistress's favorite study, her vision began to blur and swim. Elana couldn't sense the Mistress's presence, but she had to be there. The Keep was her home.

Yet as Elana finally reached the Mistress's door, she hesitated. There was still no trace of the Mistress's amarin. No sound of anyone else in the Keep.

The hollow clank of wood hitting the ground echoed through the hall. Elana spun around as a dozen wooden mugs rolled toward her feet, appearing out of nowhere. Trickles of crimson wine spilled across the stones like blood. An acrid, sulfurous scent filled the hallway and burned Elana's nose.

"Mistress?" Her voice was hushed in terror. She could suddenly feel the Mistress's hand in her's, as thin and fragile as paper as she healed from being poisoned. She remembered the pallor of the Mistress's skin and the way her Amarin dwindled in and out of existence as she struggled to survive.

"So many cups."

The world around her felt incorporeal. The air was growing thinner.

Elana spun around, reaching out for the Mistress's door, but the knob had disappeared. Elana pushed against it, trying to force it open, but it wouldn't budge. She pounded and cried out, praying to the Mother that someone, anyone, would answer. But no one heard her screams. The Mistress was silent. There was nothing left.

Elana's eyes flew open, but she sensed the weight of the seer child on her chest fast enough to keep herself from leaping up and waking him and Di'Nay. She drew a deep, calming breath and cradled the child, patting his chest to keep him from sensing her fear. It was just a dream.

Elana was exhausted despite having slept. The child was like a parasite, suckling at her psychic energy as if it were the only thing keeping him alive. She wouldn't be able to care for him for long without getting sick. Elana had never been sent to retrieve a seer and she rarely worked with one so young and wild.

"Elana?" Di'Nay's voice was heavy with sleep, her grip around Elana's waist weak. Elana smiled. Di'Nay was so soft and warm when she was only half awake. Almost childlike.

"Just a nightmare, Love. Go back to sleep. I'll be fine."

Di'Nay didn't have the strength or awareness to argue, she only held tighter around Elana's waist and surrendered to her dreams.

As Elana felt her drift away, her loneliness and fear from the nightmare returned. She'd been worried something was coming. She'd felt it as surely as any intuitive vision. But she couldn't see or interpret the future. But perhaps there was something about her connection with a seer – a child born outside of linear time – that had enhanced her abilities.

Was the Keep safe? Was the Mistress? She imagined her home abandoned, the people she loved scattered or dead.

She ran her hands gently over the child's back, lost in thought. She couldn't let herself panic. Not with a child so dependent on her stability. A Shadow would be coming from the Keep in the morning. If something had happened in the last couple days, the Shadow would know or wouldn't even arrive. It was counter-intuitive to be scared now. It would upset the child.

But still.

Elana pressed as tightly into Di'Nay's arms as she could without upsetting the child and tried to fall asleep again. She drew on the bond in her lifestone for comfort. She let the rhythm of Di'Nay's heart vibrating through the stone embedded in her wrist draw her focus from her fear to her love for her bondmate. She concentrated on Di'Nay's amarin. Her gentle dreams. And she let herself fall into the peace her Amazon gave her.

Elana stood at the small window, staring down at the crowds gathering for the day in Markessa's marketplace. She leaned against the windowsill, trying not to fall asleep.

"Is it wise to stand at the window? Will that effect the illusion?" Di'Nay questioned.

"Yes. But It's more important that I see our contact coming."

Di'Nay pulled on her boots. "You think they may be attacked?"

"No, nothing like that. Just my own insecurities."

Di'Nay looked her over. "Does it have anything to do with your nightmares?"

"A bit."

"Do you want to talk about it?"

Elana shook her head. "Not with the child here. I have to keep my emotions even."

"But you'll be all right?"

"I'll be fine," she confirmed.

Di'Nay stood. "Good. I'll get us something to eat and fresh formula for the child. Do you have any preferences for the meal?"

Elana shook her head, her eyes still locked on the people below. "Anything."

"A test," Di'Nay teased. "I know your favorite foods well enough to bring a passable meal."

Elana smiled. "You'll be fine."

Di'Nay held her from behind and curled around Elana to kiss her. "I'll be right back."

"Thank you."

Di'Nay disappeared into the inn hallway. She shut and locked the door behind her.

Elana returned her attention to outside the inn. "Please, Mother," she whispered aloud. "Let them come."

Elana let out an audible gasp of relief as an unmarked black carriage turned down a nearby street. The seer child trembled and clenched at her shirt as he sensed her sure of emotion. Elana held him tighter and he quickly quieted.

She raced from her room and down through the inn. She spotted Di'Nay near the bar, a basket of food in her hands, and strode up behind her. "They're here."

Di'Nay glanced out the front door as the carriage pulled up to the inn. "Wonderful." She turned back to the bartender. "I'll be back."

The bartender nodded, no interest in interfering with Council work. He regarded Elana and the seer child with a wary gaze, but his prejudice didn't phase Elana. She had other things to worry about.

"Come," Elana beckoned Di'Nay and they made their way to the courtyard.

A young man Elana had seen in passing but never trained hopped down from the carriage and instantly strode to Elana's side. Elana regarded him carefully. He didn't have the Sight. Why would he be sent to care for a seer?

"Well met," the Shadow greeted her. "Elana, yes?"

"You are?"

"Frisk," he offered without any further explanation. "The

Mistress sent me."

"Is the Mistress well?" Elana wondered if Frisk could hear the strain in her voice. If he did, he didn't acknowledge it.

"She's recovering slowly, but she's doing better every day."

"And the rest of the Keep is well?"

Frisk cast her a sideways glance. "Is there a reason it wouldn't be?"

Elana shook her head. "No. I was just inquiring."

"Everything is as it was when you left."

Frisk carefully eased the child out of Elana's arms. The young seer instantly started to howl, flailing wildly at the air. Elana's heart ached for him. She fed him as much of her Sight as she could without holding him, but he was too scared and confused to be comforted.

"You have to be careful," Elana insisted, but Frisk only nodded and smiled. "It will be fine."

He opened the carriage door. The windows inside had been boarded and the seats removed. An elderly seer sat cross-legged in the darkness. Elana let out a soft breath of relief. She thought she had sensed another seer, but her powers were exhausted.

The young seer quieted the moment the elder pulled him into her arms. Elana smiled as their amarins wove together, harmonizing joyously in the ether. Seers were meant to be together. They didn't lose energy helping each other, they only grew stronger. They were pieces of a whole. And now the child would catch his first glimpse of the world as he was meant to experience it.

Elana felt her shoulders sag with relief. He would be safe. He was happy. It was all worth it.

Di'Nay stepped up behind her as the Shadow closed the seers into the dark carriage. "Will they be all right?"

"Yes. The sensory deprivation helps them connect with each other. He's happy. He's where he's supposed to be. Soon he'll be part of the song of the seers and connected with his people."

"And they'll be safe?"

"Two seers together guided by a shadow shouldn't have trouble reaching the Keep."

"Good."

The carriage pulled away into the bustle of the city.

Di'Nay's voice was soft as she considered aloud. "It must have been very brave for the elder seer to leave the safety of the Keep."

Elana leaned back against Di'Nay and closed her eyes. "It was. And incredibly rare. But of everyone on Aggar, the seers care for their own. They can't physically fight. But they can bring him comfort."

"Are you all right?" Di'Nay questioned. "You're exhausted. You should sleep."

Elana shook her head. "We have a lot more to do. There are still fifteen missing children and apparently more being targeted every day. I'll be all right."

Di'Nay started to argue, but she stopped herself. She squeezed Elana's shoulder. "What do we do now?"

Elana smiled softly as Di'Nay fought her urge to coddle her. "We need to present ourselves to the court of the Ramains. They called to the Keep for a reason. They may have information that will help us."

"That makes sense. Have the Ramains lords taken interest in the seers before?"

"We have an understanding. They don't interfere with the Keep and we don't hold power in court. But the people of Aggar respect and fear our power. And missing seer children... Whoever is kidnapping them may as well be stockpiling weapons in the eyes of the Ramains. The nobility will take notice."

Di'Nay couldn't find the words to respond but Elana could feel her anger and frustration at Aggar's prejudice against her most powerful people. "Well. The least we can do is eat before we head to the castle."

Elana tried to argue but her words were cut short by a fierce rumbling in her stomach. Di'Nay smirked. "I already ordered a meal before the carriage arrived."

Her smug joy at caring for Elana was contagious. Elana smiled up at her. "Did you get me any sun melon?"

"No."

"I wanted sun melon."

Di'Nay furrowed her brow in mock frustration. "You said you didn't care what I brought!"

"I thought you knew me."

Di'Nay shook her head and sighed. "Such trouble. We'll eat in our room and plot how we should approach the Ramains."

"I don't know if eating alone together is conducive to getting work done quickly."

Di'Nay smirked. "I *am* capable of focusing on a mission even when I'm alone with you."

Elana only squeezed her hand and guided Di'Nay back into the inn. "I'll send word to the royal steward that we've arrived."

"You're insufferable."

Elana let out a tired laugh. "True."

The Ramains castle rose high into the sky, its dozens of turrets and towers adorned with crimson banners and pennants, each flag bearing the mark of a different duke or baron that sat on the Ramains council. There was no banner for the Keep.

The castle was built entirely of marble from the northern Ramains mountains. The veining in the stones glowed faintly opaline in the noon sunlight. It reminded Elana of amarin and lifestones, a living representation of the auras she could see with her Sight. She wondered if it was intentional. If a Blue Sight had been involved in building the palace. She doubted it. The Ramains, while not publicly anti-Blue Sight – no country would dare insult the Keep like that – wouldn't intentionally let a Blue Sight take part in building one of the most prominent buildings in the country.

Still, Elana liked to think that someone with the Sight, someone in hiding, had a hand in the castle's construction. That there was one magnificent structure in the Ramains that recognized her people and their place on Aggar.

"It's beautiful." Di'Nay's voice was full of awe as they stood together in the courtyard before the palace.

"You've never seen it?"

"Only once. When I first arrived. I didn't spend a lot of time in the Ramains."

"Are there any buildings like this on Yemaya?"

Di'Nay smiled. "Many. Each house headquarters could rival this castle. You should see where the Shaes train."

"What's it like?"

Di'Nay closed her eyes and her amarin grew warm with thoughts of home. Elana could see bits of her memories; golden skies fiery with sunset, massive, looming trees that reminded Elana of where she'd grown up, and great, emerald hills dotted with windows, woven curtain doors, and stone chimneys.

"The Shaes don't prefer buildings made of stone. They make massive tree houses and homes in the hills. Vast, twisting, natural structures that twine around nature instead of demolishing it. As a n'Athena, I've never traveled their depths, but I've spent summers sitting at their fires. I've been healed in their sanctuaries and studied basic aide among their masters. I can imagine you there so easily. Surrounded by rich, vibrant life. Embraced for your skills."

Elana's eyes fluttered closed at the power of Di'Nay's memories. She could hear the gentle scrape of a mortar and pestle. She could smell herbs and spices she couldn't identify, she could taste them in the back of her mouth. She felt a gentle breeze on her skin and the warmth of a fire on her face.

Elana's entire body trembled at the strength of Di'Nay's thoughts. She wanted to reach out with her Sight. To see this place with her own eyes and her own abilities. She couldn't imagine a life so connected with nature and living things. Not even the Keep could compare.

"Elana."

Di'Nay touched her shoulder and Elana gasped, coming out of her vision. "I'm sorry."

Di'Nay shook her head. "Did you see something?"

"You know what I saw."

Di'Nay smiled. "I should have dressed as a man so I could kiss you."

Elana squeezed her hand. "Later, Love."

They strode through the front doors of the castle. The grand hall stretched out before them. The floors were polished to a gleam, reflecting the peaks and hollows of the vaulted ceiling above. The air smelled of wildflowers, the scarlet blossoms decorating every corner in crystal vases.

Dozens of people waiting to be seen by the Ramains Council of Lords milled around the room with various castle servants. Elana's eyes scanned the crowd. She caught sight of an elderly man in a scarlet tunic and a silver beard standing near the doors to the throne room. His amarin carried an air of self-importance and watchfulness.

Elana touched Di'Nay's shoulder. "There. The steward."

"I'll follow your lead."

Elana led her bondmate through the crowd.

"Excuse me?"

The steward glanced at Elana with thinly-veiled contempt. “There are many people who wish to address the council. You'll have to wait your turn.”

“My name is Elana. I'm a Shadow the Council's Keep and this is my bondmate, Di'Nay. We were invited.”

The steward's expression instantly changed. “Oh! Yes! Of course. Forgive me. I was told you were coming. A moment please.”

The steward ducked into the council room before returning shortly. “The King requests that you meet with him outside of the council chamber. If you'll follow me?”

“I was led to believe that we were going to be speaking with the entire Council of Lords,” Elana remarked.

“I'm afraid his Majesty was very insistent on privacy.”

Di'Nay and Elana exchanged glances, but Elana didn't sense any ill intent in the steward. She nodded to Di'Nay and they followed him out of the waiting area deeper into the castle.

Elana had never been outside of the main hall and the Council of Lords. She made a point to memorize their path as the steward quickly led them away from public areas and stopped before a simple wooden door.

The steward indicated the door. “Please wait inside.”

“Where is this?” Di'Nay questioned.

“A study.”

“The King's?”

The steward shifted uncomfortably. “Please, just wait inside.”

Di'Nay took a step forward, ready to press for more information, but Elana took her hand. There was something going unsaid. She studied the Steward. “We'll wait. Thank you.”

The steward seemed relieved to be free of the conversation and sped away.

“Elana?”

Elana didn't respond, she only opened the door.

“Elana of the Council Keep? Diana n'Athena of Yemaya?”

A man's voice called to them as they entered and Elana tensed. She hadn't sensed anyone in the room. She still couldn't sense anyone.

“Would you close the door?”

Di'Nay closed the door as Elana took a single step closer to the man at the desk. He was tall and slender, a well-groomed ebony beard and the jeweled rings on his fingers marked him a noble, but Elana had never seen him on the Council.

"Who are you? How do you know us?" Di'Nay demanded.

The man stood from his velvet chair in front of his polished cedar desk. He stepped closer and smoothed his quilted maroon doublet.

"I'm sorry for misleading you. His Majesty thought it would be better if I met you myself but due to the sensitive nature of this conversation, a little subterfuge was in order. My name is Tristan and I'm a Royal Marshal for the Ramains court."

"Marshal?" Di'Nay questioned.

"I wouldn't expect you to have heard of us, Amazon. We aren't a public organization. The Empire sees us as primitives. It keeps us practically invisible. But perhaps *you* know who we are, Blue Sight?"

Elana studied him harder. When she focused, she could sense a glimmer of his amarin. He seemed sincere, but his ability to keep her Sight at bay was disconcerting. "My name is Elana, not Blue Sight."

"I apologize. I didn't mean to offend you."

"Who are you really?" Elana's voice was sharp.

"I already told you. My name is Tristan. I'm a Royal Marshal for the King of the Ramains. Truth be told, I assumed the Keep would know of our existence by now. How interesting."

Elana raised her chin in defiance. The Keep had long suspected the Ramains had more resources than they let on, but they had never caused any trouble, so the Keep had never pried. "Tristan? No surname?"

His eyes narrowed. "No." He studied her closely and a knowing smirk spread across his face. "You can't sense if I'm telling the truth, can you?"

Elana clenched her jaw. She didn't like someone so blatantly calling out her Sight. Di'Nay took a step forward, moving between Tristan and Elana.

"What's going on here?" Di'Nay demanded.

Tristan raised his hands in silent surrender. "I didn't mean to threaten. Please allow me to explain."

Tristan pulled a chain bearing a small, brass amulet out from under his doublet and laid it on the table. The moment he lost contact with the necklace his amarin flooded Elana's senses. She took a step back at the rush. She couldn't believe she had such trouble sensing him before. For someone who claimed to be so secretive, his amarin was unusually open and honest, allowing her deep into his intentions and emotions with barely a glance.

"Elana?" Di'Nay took a step toward her, her face etched with worry.

Elana shook her head. "I'm fine. He's telling the truth."

"The Royal Marshals are a private band of warriors and spies. We're the first and last line of defense for our King. We don't usually announce our presence."

"Then why meet with us?" Elana questioned. "You know I'll report your existence to the Council."

"Because there's something more important than our anonymity at risk right now. The Keep understands the importance of privacy. I trust that after helping you save your seers, you'll find it in your hearts to keep our organization a secret."

Elana's eyes narrowed. "Are you a threat to the Keep?"

Tristan didn't even flinch at Elana's gaze. "We're not a direct threat to anyone. We defend our country and our King. Most of our dealings are with the Terrans or our own people. The Keep has never been a real danger to the Ramains, so we're not a real danger to you."

"But you gather information on us?"

"We gather information on everyone. It isn't personal."

"But why would you want to help us?" Di'Nay questioned. "You're taking a lot of risks revealing yourself. I don't see the benefit to you."

Tristan gestured to two seats before his desk. "Would you like to sit?"

Di'Nay shot him a wary look and he sighed. He leaned back against his desk and crossed his arms over his chest. "You know as well as I do that this situation could quickly become dangerous for the Ramains. You saw the damage the Maltar almost did with a single broken seer. But there's more going on than you understand and I need to know you're invested in working together before I say anything else."

Elana looked him over once more. The Keep had never announced the source of the Maltar's power, but she didn't think it would be hard for an intelligence organization to find the truth on their own. Many members of the Maltar's court would have fled south, all knowing about the seer trapped under the Maltar's control. Still... "Do you have contacts in the Keep?"

Tristan fell silent, his eyes intense and his lips pressed into a tight line. His charming demeanor suddenly shifted into a quiet, piercing intelligence. The change was so sudden and complete it took Elana off guard. When he finally spoke, his voice was soft, his words precise.

"The Marshals had nothing to do with the attack on the Mistress of the Keep. We found the assassination attempt as disconcerting as you did."

For the first time in years Elana found herself truly at a loss for words. He shouldn't have known about the Mistress. His claims about the nature of his organization and his abilities would make him the most obvious suspect Elana had met in the poisoning of the Mistress. He'd all but admitted to having a source in the Keep and he'd been able to confuse Elana's sight. But his amarin remained as open and honest as ever. Elana had never met someone whose actions and amarin conflicted so dramatically.

To her surprise, she found herself believing he truly wanted to help.

She moved purposefully to the seat Tristan had offered. "I'll hear you out."

Di'Nay followed suit more slowly, but Elana could feel how much her bondmate trusted her judgment. Tristan beamed as he sat in his chair once more. "Thank you."

Elana folded her hands over her knees. "What do you have to share?"

Tristan pushed the brass amulet he'd left on his desk closer to Elana. The moment his finger touched the circular pendant, Elana lost her ability to read his amarin. It returned as he sat back. The sensation made her nauseous. But more unsettling was how familiar the little pendant etched with the image of an eye was.

"What is that?" she demanded.

"So you do have a response to it."

Elana glanced at Di'Nay. "I've seen it before. In a vision."

"Really?" Tristan leaned further forward, resting his elbows on his desk. "What did you see?"

Elana shook her head. "Tell me what it is first."

Tristan didn't hesitate. "This is an amulet worn by members of the Order of Blinding. A relatively new secret organization that has started interacting with various elements of the Ramains underground."

"Order of Blinding?" Di'Nay questioned.

"Anti-Blue Sight and Seer. They're not uncommon. But they're usually small. Relatively harmless."

"There's nothing harmless about a mob willing to kill Blue Sight children," Elana snapped.

Tristan nodded in agreement. "But not on a national level."

"Everything that happens in small towns affects the nation at large," Elana countered. "You claim to specialize in gathering intelligence and you don't believe the small-town prejudices against Blue Sights and Seers is becoming epidemic?"

"My focus is on preventing things that could destroy the Ramains. War. Major political upheaval. The mistreatment of people with the Sight is unfortunate and unacceptable, but it isn't catastrophic."

"We'll have to agree to disagree," Elana countered. She pointed toward the amulet but couldn't bring herself to touch it. "That necklace isn't just a symbol. There's power in it."

"We have some evidence the pendent shield the wearers from scrying and seers. They're cloaking devices, if you will. And judging by your expression and reaction, I would say our theories are founded. How does it affect your Sight?"

Elana shook her head, ignoring his questions. "They're using these to kidnap seers from us?"

"As far as we can tell. We haven't been able to find the children, but if members of this organization can shield themselves with amulets, I imagine they can veil their hideouts. Kidnapping is already a crime, but the fact that the victims are all seers? They're planning something. Something potentially very dangerous. We never thought they were a serious threat. Just a few radicals meeting at midnight to drink and complain about the government. Obviously they found new leadership."

"Do you think they're behind the attack on the Keep?" Elana demanded. "Did they poison our Mistress?"

"I don't know for sure. But with these amulets, they would have a distinct upper hand in remaining hidden in a fortress full of seers and Blue Sights."

The thought made Elana's blood run hot in her veins and her

cheeks flush dark. She glanced away from Tristan and Di'Nay, unable to keep her rage buried.

"Who leads them now? Rebel Terrans?" Elana seethed.

Elana felt the response coming before the words escaped Tristan's lips. A whisper of future sight that left her sick. "There are Terrans in the organization, yes. But the ringleaders and dissenters are of Aggar."

CHAPTER FOUR

"Please put that down."

Diana set the necklace back on the nightstand. Elana paced their room at the inn, her bare feet padding sharply against the wood floors. Diana didn't have the ability to read amarin, but even she could feel the tension and frustration in her lover. Her lifestone ached in her wrist, throbbing in time with Elana's frustration.

"I'm sorry." Diana rested her hands on the armrests of her chair to avoid the temptation to touch it again.

The pendent was circular and flat like a coin, a rough etching of an open eye scratched into the surface. The pupil of the eye was wide and tinted white, as if clouded with blindness. Diana couldn't believe such a crude object could be powerful enough to disrupt Elana's Sight, but the effects were obvious. Elana still refused to touch it.

"Is it really that dramatic?" Diana questioned. "When I touch it?"

"It turns my stomach and makes my head ache," Elana complained. "But... mostly I just don't want you to disappear from my Sight."

"It affects me, too? Even with our lifestones?"

"I feel you stronger than I felt Tristan, but you still fade away." Diana glanced at the amulet anew. It had felt light and solid when she touched it. There was no sign it was electrical or technological. She considered nanotech for a moment, but there didn't seem to be any evidence of a containing field. And if the technology to specifically target Blue Sights with nanobots was available on Aggar, Diana was sure someone would have taken advantage of it long ago. An organization with the technology to target Blue Sights wouldn't have had to resort to poisoning with local flora.

What could possibly imbue it with so much power?

If it had only been the one, Diana might have thought it was some kind of spell or curse. She didn't tend to believe in the magical, but she certainly didn't know how to describe the nature of Blue Sights and seers without using the phrase. And it was clear through the use of lifestones that the natural properties of Aggar had an unusual and intimate affect on the people of Aggar. But Tristan had revealed a box with five of them, collected off various members of the Order of Blindness across the Ramains. There had to be something more to them than a curse or spell. Something more proprietary to the Order itself.

"Could it be in the type of metal? A property that interferes with whatever gives you the ability to See more than the rest of us?"

"If there was a natural property on Aggar that could blind seers and Blue Sights we would have found it already. Or it would have been used against us already."

"Even if it was hidden from you?"

Elana hesitated. Diana saw a flash of panic cross her face as a sudden blush of olive skin.

"I feel blind, Di'Nay. I don't know what to do when I can't trust my Sight." Elana sat on the bed, her hair falling like a curtain of curls around her shoulders as she stared at the ground. "Do you think people have been using them for a long time? That we just haven't encountered one before? Were we too proud to consider their existence?"

Di'Nay considered her words carefully. "I don't think they're widely known. If a trinket as portable and powerful as a necklace that could hide you from seers was readily available, even for a high price only on the black markets, the Maltar would have made use of them. Whatever they are, I think they're made by the Order and kept fairly secret."

"You think Tristan would be that much better at uncovering secrets than a man like the Maltar?"

"I don't know anything for sure about Tristan. But the Ramains King called out to the Keep and Tristan was his representative. He seems very official for a traitor. The Ramains wouldn't want a war with the Keep. The King would choose his mouthpiece wisely. And regardless of whether what he said was true or not, the amulets certainly do as he claimed." Elana fell silent. Diana sighed. "I didn't like him. He seemed arrogant. Disconnected from the average citizen. And I know he offended you with his talk of Blue Sights. I just don't want to discount his information. It's the most solid lead we've had."

"So you do trust him?"

"I'm reserving my judgment until he's proven wrong."

Elana nodded slowly, deep in thought. "I think I might trust him, too. I just don't like what that entails."

Diana leafed through the documents Tristan had given them. Information on what his organization had discovered about the Order of Blindness. Maps of their local headquarters. Lists of suspected members. "Whoever he is, he's thorough."

"Very trusting for a man who deals in secrets," Elana agreed. "If he's not lying to us, that information isn't everything he has. He would have to have something that would silence us if we turned on him."

"That's not very comforting," Diana muttered.

"Nothing about him is."

A sharp knock on the door silenced them both. Diana stood and answered. A young woman Diana had seen serving dinner curtsied quickly.

"Forgive the intrusion, but the lady of the house wishes to know if you'd like a warm drink or something to eat? Normally we'd wait for you to come down to the common room, but we understand that often the secrecy of your endeavors might make coming down to dinner difficult."

Diana raised an eyebrow. She hadn't been shy about going to the common room for meals and the staff knew it.

"What's your name?"

The young woman shifted uncomfortably. "Jessa. Jessa Min Carlo."

"You're related to the innkeeper?"

"My mother," Jessa confirmed.

"And you often work with the Keep representatives?"

"Since I was a child."

"Then you can be frank with us. What's happening downstairs?"

Jessa blushed chocolate brown as she was caught in her

misdirection. "I beg your forgiveness. The last thing we want is for you to feel unsafe or disrespected. We just... if we are to remain a safe haven for members of the Keep, we can't publicly show a preference for those who study there. A band of men have come in for the night. They're loud and brash, but they've done nothing we could throw them out for. Not without causing trouble. I'm afraid they're getting rather boisterous about their hatred of certain members of the Keep."

"Blue Sights?" Elana called from within the room. A moment later she was at Diana's side.

Jessa nodded. "I'm so sorry, Min. We don't condone their actions..."

"No, I understand," Elana stated. "Do you recognize them? Are they a common problem around here?"

"I've never seen them in such numbers before, but I'm afraid it isn't uncommon to hear some anti-Keep sentiment once the ale starts to flow. My mother is waiting for any excuse to ban them. Unfortunately, despite their prejudice, they aren't being particularly violent or destructive."

"I'm glad of that," Elana remarked.

"Thank you for the warning," Diana replied. "We'll stay in for the night."

Jessa let out a soft breath of relief. "Thank you. I'll try to be available to you. My room is just down the hall if you need anything. Perhaps I can get you some spiced mead? It's a fresh brew tonight."

"That would be wonderful," Diana responded.

Jessa curtsied once more and rushed away to fetch the drinks.

"She's a nice girl." Diana closed the door and turned to Elana, who sat on the bed tying her boots back on. Her cloak was already bound around her shoulders. "Is something wrong?"

"She was scared. She was supposed to find out if we knew the men in the common room."

"What? Why? Who would be talking about us?"

"Have a guess."

Diana paled. "You think they're members of the Order? But how would they know where we are?"

"I don't know. But I'm going to find out."

"You're going down there? What if they're dangerous?"

"I won't be seen. And it won't take much for me to ascertain if they're from the Order if any of them are wearing amulets."

"Elana..."

Elana stood and kissed her, silencing her concern. "I'll be right back. I promise. The room is public. They can't hurt me without being seen and you'll either hear a scuffle or the staff will come to my aide. At worst, I'll be recognized. And I'm far too good a Shadow for that. Trust me. Stay here."

Diana sighed. "One day I'll make the Mistress train me as a Shadow, then you won't see me as such a liability in stealth situations."

Elana laughed. "Hopefully, soroi, you'll never have the need. I am bonded to you not just as a lover, but as your protector. Let me use my skills to keep you safe."

They kissed once more and Elana slipped out the door, pulling the hood of her cloak over her head.

Diana sat on the edge of the bed with a heavy sigh. She rubbed her face once with her hands and settled into waiting.

When had she become the one staying behind while her partner left to gather information? She had never been bad at stealth and she was excellent at bartering and talking her way out of trouble. She had never been the liability on a mission before, even if that mission caused for subtlety and moving unseen.

But every day she spent enmeshed in the business of the Keep, she started to understand how out of her element she was. She could fight her way through any obstacle. She trusted her sword. Her wits. Her diplomacy. But in a battle of Seers, lifestones, magical amulets, and Blue Sights, she was missing an entire sense. She felt crippled. Like being on a battlefield and suddenly loosing her hearing.

This is what you get for wanting to love a woman better at something than you. The thought flashed through her mind and she smiled. She had always said that aloud. Her ideal mate would be better than her at something she was passionate about. But she'd always imagined the skill would be very different from her own, like cooking or taming animals or something more artistic. It served her right she should find a woman who would fight by her side – and do it in ways Diana could never hope to replicate.

The minutes seemed to drag on forever as evening fell into night and Elana still hadn't returned. She asked about the men in the common room when Jessa arrived with her mead, and then again when the young woman came with dinner. Nothing seemed to have changed. There had been no fighting. No sign that Elana had been discovered. But Elana still hadn't returned.

"Z'iki sak, Diana!" Diana growled to the sky as she took another swig of her mead and plopped down across the bed.

She looked out the window at the twin moons in the sky. In reality, Elana couldn't have been gone more than an hour, but it felt like days. She was just about to let caution be damned and run down the stairs into the common room when Elana swept into the room, closing the door behind her.

"What took so long?" Diana's voice was more panic than accusatory, but whatever she was about to say died on her lips as Elana turned, dropping her cloak to the ground.

Tears streamed down her pale cheeks. Her sapphire-blue eyes seemed somehow duller than usual and her shoulders sagged as if she were exhausted nearly to the point of collapse.

"Elana?"

Elana dropped a small collection of parchment on the table beside the information Tristan had given them.

"They were from the order. At least three of them were wearing amulets. One of them mentioned a meeting place not far from here, so I went. I thought it they were all drunk at a bar the building wouldn't be hard to search alone. There were barely any guards. They were easy to sneak past."

"Did you find something?"

Elana indicated the paperwork. Her voice cracked as she spoke. "They did it, Di'Nay. They poisoned my Mistress. There was no official information, but I found letters they wrote to each other. Jokes. They tried to kill her and they're laughing about it."

Diana pulled Elana into her arms. Elana sank into her embrace like a child too exhausted to pretend anymore. Diana ran her fingers through her hair as Elana continued, barely holding back from sobbing. "The amulets are old. Older than the Order. People have been wearing them for generations to avoid us."

"Generations? But how?"

"I don't know if they worked before. I only found sketches. Stories in journals. But the hatred is real. The distrust. I know people fear us. I know they think we're controlling them. I know the stories and myths that surround the Keep and Blue Sights. I even understood why some kill us or hunt us. I thought it was ignorance. But I never realized... I was so naïve. I didn't understand how much they *hate* us. How much they delight in making us suffer. They things they were saying about the Mistress... About the children! I was lucky to have good parents. To be sent to the Keep as a child. I never saw this part of Aggar."

"It will be all right. I promise." Diana whispered the words against Elana's cheek. She had never wanted to take Elana home more fiercely. Home where no one would hate her. Home where she would be valued.

"Not for everyone. Not for my people." Elana sounded utterly dejected and Diana didn't know if she meant her family at the Keep, her fellow Blue Sights, or the people of Aggar as a whole.

"Did you learn anything else about the organization? About the seers?"

Elana pulled away slightly, wiping the tears from her eyes as she shook her head. "Their headquarters is small. Most of the men stationed there seem to be grunts and thugs. I'm sure there are locations with more elite members of the Order in town but I don't want to stay anymore. We have to get the amulets back to the Keep so they can be studied. We need to warn the Council so they can be on guard for threats we can't sense."

"I can have one of the amulets delivered to Cleis. There are a few Sisters on a nearby Terran shuttle. Scientists. They may be able to break down their chemical compounds, find out why they're so powerful. If they can somehow be reverse engineered, your seers may be able to use them to track threats. To find the children."

Elana's face tightened into a grimace. "I don't want anything with this kind of power anywhere near a Terran base."

Diana felt the sting in her words almost like a slap. "Not Terrans. Sisters. We wouldn't let the amulets fall into Terran hands."

"I still don't trust the situation. We can solve this on our own. Leave Aggar's affairs to Aggar."

"But you're a Sister now, too. You have every right to request their aide."

Elana shook her head. "Please. They wouldn't understand."

Once again, Diana tried not to take Elana's othering of dey Sorormin personally. She had lived her entire life on Aggar. She had only agreed to come to Yemaya very recently in the grand scheme of things. How could she expect Elana to completely understand her place with her new people yet? To trust the discretion and loyalty of her Sisters? Still, the realization of how little Elana still trusted the Amazons in her everyday life stung. It dug up her deepest fears that Elana wouldn't be happy off Aggar. She just had to have faith it would change.

"I won't send them anywhere. I promise, Soroi."

"Thank you." Elana turned away and drew a deep breath, trying to compose herself once again. Diana was quickly learning to recognize her rituals for repressing her pain and her emotions. "Did you drink my mead?"

Diana smiled. Elana's humor had returned right on time to bury the last of her pain. "You were gone a long time."

"An hour."

"You said you'd be right back. You're lucky I didn't go after you."

Elana forced a disappointing sigh. "At least you saved me dinner."

"There was lexion. Of course something would be saved for you."

"The best partners have opposite tastes in food. It will keep me from starving." Elana glanced over her shoulder with a teasing smile. "Now if only I could get you to hate sweet rolls!"

"I don't know if you're making a comment on my weight or wishing all the sweet rolls for yourself."

"Serves you right for drinking my mead."

Diana opened her arms and Elana eased herself into them, fitting tight against her. "We'll solve this. I promise."

Elana didn't say anything, but her tight grip around Diana's waist and the fear Diana could feel through their lifestone bond said more than Elana could with words. "Let's go. Let's leave now."

"You need rest."

"I know. But I want to feel like we're making progress. And I don't want to spend another night in this city."

Diana kissed her brow. "Well make camp in the hills."

"Thank you."

"Of course, Soroi. Of course."

Diana led the horses into a secluded grove nestled between two rolling hills. It had been nearly six hours since Jessa had let them out the back of the inn, helping them creep past the members of the Order in the common room. They'd traveled longer than she'd intended. Elana had been so set on continuing on, determined to leave the capitol far behind, that Diana hadn't had the heart to insist they stop until Elana started falling asleep in her saddle.

Diana dismounted and helped Elana down from her saddle. The Blue Sight was already half asleep as Diana sat her on the ground and turned to pulling the bedmats off Kaing.

It was a clear night. The stars blazing in the sky, dotting the expanse surrounding the twin moons. There was no need for tents.

Diana smiled as she laid the mats together and returned for her bondmate. Elana sitting up, leaning over her knees, already asleep. She let out a gentle sigh as Diana helped her to her feet, cradling her as she led her to bed.

"We should keep going." Elana's plea was barely audible, her eyes still closed.

"I think the world will stay in one piece while you sleep for a few hours."

"You don't know that."

"No. But I know you can't ride until you get a little rest. If Leggings was even a touch more unwieldy, you would have fallen."

"I didn't fall."

Diana chuckled. She couldn't tell if Elana was even awake anymore, her voice so distant and her steps faltering. "No, you didn't."

"There are two eitteh in the trees."

"You can sense them with your Sight?"

Elana only leaned on Diana's shoulder and fell silent.

Diana laid her on their bed mats and pulled off her boots before tucking her under the quilt Elana's mother had given them. She sat beside her for a while, enjoying the gentle sounds of Elana sleeping and the sparkling galaxies above them.

Yemaya was too far away to make out clearly in the night sky, but she could feel its call. Sense its position among the stars.

A rustle in the trees caught her attention. Two young eitteh, a silver cat with soft white wings and an orange and black mottled tabby, leapt out of the foliage and watcher her with large, curious eyes. Diana smiled but she didn't reach out to them. She didn't want to startle them. Instead of fleeing, they curled up on the ground, wrapping their wings tight around their fluffy bodies, and fell asleep.

Diana rang her fingers over Elana's hair. "They can feel you, can't they? Feel your amarin."

The eitteh purred, the sound like a rumbling landslide far away. The horses nickered softly and prepared themselves to sleep as well. It was one of the most peaceful nights Diana could remember on Aggar. It seemed wrong that it should be the same night Elana had been so upset by a group of her people turning on her. It seemed even worse that after worrying about her lover, Diana's first thought at discovering the evils of Aggar was how much more she wanted to take Elana away from this world... and how much easier it might be if Elana broke ties with the world that had spurned her.

Diana didn't know if she should feel bad for hoping the pain would help Elana move on or not. She didn't want to take Elana away from her home, but she wanted her to be safe. Supported. Loved. Elana didn't know what her life could be like. She'd lived for so long on a world that largely rejected her. I world that had proven it would kill her given half a chance.

It couldn't be wrong to want to take her Love far away from that.

Diana pulled off her boots and climbed under the covers with Elana. She held her bondmate close, wrapping her arms around her waist as she'd grown accustomed to do. With all her traveling and time alone on other planets, Diana had rarely shared a bed with a partner, even just to sleep beside each other. She had spent so much time alone. And now she couldn't imagine sleeping without Elana curled up beside her. Her mate's body, her warmth, the sound of her breath were now necessary for rest. It was a part of her, like her heartbeat and the breath in her lungs. She never thought she'd find someone who could become so crucial to her life, let alone in such a short time.

"I love you." Diana whispered the words against Elana's neck before closing her eyes and falling into a deep sleep.

Elana rustled in Diana's arms, drawing her out of her sleep. Diana opened her eyes slowly. The sun was already high in the sky. How had they slept so long?

"Diana?" Elana's voice was tense.

"Love?"

"We've slept so long."

Diana sat up slowly. The horses were wandering nearby, nibbling at the grass. The eitteh were still near, wrestling with each other in the brush. It was peaceful. Almost dreamlike.

"Do you feel all right?" Diana questioned.

Elana was pulling on her boots, her anxiety starkly out of place in the idyllic setting. "I'm fine."

"You look a lot better."

Elana tensed and Diana prepared for a sharp retort, but Elana caught herself. "Thank you. I feel better."

Diana breathed a mental sigh of relief that she wasn't upset at the delay. "Let's pack up and get back on the path to the Keep."

Elana didn't need any urging. She was already on her feet, rolling up her bedmat. She hesitated for a moment as she strapped her bedmat to Leggings. "Look, eitteh!"

Diana laughed aloud and glanced at the eitteh, who had stopped their wrestling and were cleaning each other, licking and preening each other's wings. "They've been with us all night! You told me you sensed them as I took you to bed."

Elana blushed a pale olive. "I don't remember even arriving here."

"You were very tired," Diana agreed.

"Did I talk a lot?"

"Enough."

"What else did I say?"

Diana rolled her mat, purposefully not meeting her lover's eyes. "Oh, this and that. "

"Di'Nay!"

Di'Nay chuckled. "Nothing embarrassing, Soroi. You didn't want to stop for the night. And you were very proud of yourself for staying in your saddle when you fell asleep on Leggings."

"That sounds like me."

"You were adorable."

"I'm too old to be adorable." Diana snorted and Elana's eyes narrowed into a glare, but her Sight only transferred amusement to Diana's heart. "If you're about to make a joke about my age --"

"No! No, Ona. Being gentle and soft and sweet in your exhaustion knows no age, just a particular nature."

"Using my childhood name isn't very convincing in this argument."

"It's a term of endearment!"

Elana's expression melted into a sly smile and she glanced at the sky. "If we don't want to have to make camp another night, we need to start riding now."

"It will be well after nightfall before we can reach the Keep," Diana warned.

"You made the mistake of letting me sleep to my heart's content. Now I can travel for as long as I need to."

Diana sighed gently. "Ah. My mistake. I should have woken you an hour earlier."

"Your mistake."

Diana strapped her bedmat and their quilt to Kaing's saddle. "I'm glad you slept."

"I needed it more than I could admit. Thank you."

Diana smiled at her. "Well then. We should get moving or you'll take it back."

They mounted their horses. Diana took one more fond look back at the eitteh, who were suddenly still as they watched the two women leave. She allowed herself one more memory of the night before, of the quiet, of the peace, before she turned her back on it and followed Elana back to the path toward the Keep.

Diana hunched over Kaing's reigns, shivering beneath her fur-lined cloak as the air grew more chill. No matter how much time she spent in the north, she never seemed to fully acclimate to the cold. Riding at night only seemed to make things worse. There was something about the darkness that made everything feel even colder than it was.

"When we get back to the Keep, there will be a hot meal and a warm fire," Elana assured her.

"Sounds wonderful."

Horse hooves pounded in the distance, their sounds echoing through the trees and drawing steadily closer.

Elana and Diana nudged their horses to the edge of the trail, trying to make room along the narrow trail for whoever was riding past. Elana gasped as the hooves drew closer. "Di'Nay..."

The rider came into view: A shadow from the Keep galloping with desperate intensity.

"Brother!" Elana called out.

The shadow slowed. "Elana!" It was Frisk. He was pale enough his face seemed to glow in the light of the twin moons. "You're supposed to be in Markessa!"

"We're coming home early. We have something for the Council," Elana announced. "What's going on? Were you coming to find us?"

"We need you home. Both of you. There have been more attacks. Three more poisonings and... and Counselor Karis is dead."

"Dead?" Elana gasped. "He was our strongest Blue Sight!"

"He was stabbed in the garden. We don't know who did it. There was no weapon at the scene. But the Keep has clearly been infiltrated."

Elana was stunned into silence. Diana instinctively reached out to her in an attempt to comfort her, but Elana jerked away from her touch. Diana withdrew slowly in surprise at Elana's sudden emotional withdrawal.

"What of the Mistress?"

"Unharmed. We've been watching her too closely to let anyone hurt her. We didn't realize so many others were at risk as well."

Diana turned to Frisk. "And the poisoned. Are they..."

"Alive. Elana... one of them was the Master."

Diana's heart froze. She could feel Elana's shock and horror through their bond.

Frisk looked between the two women. He raised his hands as he sensed their shock. "We had enough antidote from when we healed the Mistress, and we were able to administer it quickly. All of the poisoned are recovering well. But the attacks are coming more frequently and we can't find the assassins."

"We should be able to help with that." Elana's voice was dark, hollow. Diana glanced at her again in concern. She didn't wait for an answer before nudging Leggings forward into a gallop.

Frisk and Diana followed, fighting to keep up with her as she expertly navigated the pathways that were so familiar to her.

They reached the Keep as the moons were high in the sky. Elana leapt from her horse, grabbed the bag containing the amulet from her gear, and raced into the Keep.

Diana dismounted, looking from the horses to her bondmate.

"Go. I'll care for the horses," Frisk offered.

Diana ran after Elana. The Shadow quickly outpaced her, but Diana knew where she was going. By the time she reached the

Mistress's quarters, Elana had already emptied the amulet onto the Mistress's bed.

"They have dozens of these. Tristan had five himself. The attackers have to be using them as well."

The Mistress was obviously stronger than the last time Diana had seen her, but she still looked far more fragile than the woman she'd been before the poisoning. Her cheeks were colored bronze as Elana finished her explanation.

"This is far more serious than I thought."

"Should I deliver the amulet to the seers? Or perhaps the alchemists?"

"The seers have cloistered themselves in their vault. They're worried about their new child you found. They're afraid he'll be poisoned as well. I'm loathe to disturb them. They wouldn't understand."

"It's been a long time since the seers pulled away from the rest of the Keep," Elana considered.

"They've always felt safe before this." The Mistress's voice was heavy with sadness and fear.

Elana touched The Mistress's shoulder. "It's not your fault."

The Mistress patted Elana's hand almost dismissively. "It doesn't matter now. We just have to ensure it doesn't happen again."

The Mistress looked up to Diana with a sad smile. "How are you, Di'Nay? All this work with seers and Blue Sights must be very foreign to you."

"I admit I feel out of my element from time to time, but I can keep up. Unfortunately, it seems my sword is always helpful."

"It can be a very violent world," the Mistress agreed. "I'm glad you're both safe."

"If the seers are cloistered, I'll take the amulet to the alchemists. They might be able to discern its properties."

"Bring it straight to Lila. She specializes in metals."

Elana nodded to the Mistress and grabbed the amulet, covering her hand with the bag before picking it up. Diana watched her leave, not knowing if her mate wanted her to follow or not.

"Give her time," the Mistress advised.

"You know her better than I do."

"Perhaps not better."

"Then longer." The Mistress acknowledged Diana with a polite nod. “I've never seen her… angry before. I admit I don't know how to approach her. She seems to want me to leave her alone.”

The Mistress patted the end of her bed and Diana sat with her, anxious to hear whatever insights Elana's mentor might have.

“She isn't trying to push you away. Elana has always been a solitary creature. It's what brought her to the Shadows. It's kept her alive as a Blue Sight. Distancing herself from you isn't personal, it's survival instinct.”

“I thought we'd worked through that. We've broken down so many barriers.”

“When Elana felt sure of herself, yes?”

Diana considered everything they'd been through and nodded slowly. Until recently, Elana had always seemed so sure of herself. “I suppose.”

“You're seeing her as she was when I met her. When she was still scared and lost. She feels like her home is under attack and she can't do anything about it. And she's probably scared of hurting you when she feels so emotional.”

“She has been avoiding my eyes. And my touch.”

“She's trying to protect you. She'll find her way again. And you'll both be stronger for it.”

Diana considered the Mistress's words. She made sense, but they didn't sit well with her. All she could do was imagine Elana lost in the dark, pulling herself away from everyone that cared about her. She didn't want to leave her love in that place.

Still, she didn't pretend to know everything. And she didn't want to push Elana further away.

“Thank you. Your insight helps,” Diana admitted. “You're looking better.”

The Mistress smiled, acknowledging Diana's attempt to change the subject with grace. “I'm feeling better. Soon I'll be able to get out of this bed.”

“Take your time to be well. The Keep needs you healthy.”

“Oh, don't worry. I don't think I could rush healing even if I wanted to. I'm too old to push myself anymore.”

Diana smiled. “My aunt used to say the same when people were worried about her.”

“Your aunt was a clever woman.”

“That she was.”

“I would have liked to see your world when I was younger. I

used to be very adventurous."

"Yemaya would have embraced you."

"Just as your world will embrace Elana."

Diana studied her face. "Elana will be well-cared for. She'll be happy," Diana swore.

The Mistress glanced away, smiling softly to herself. "For one without the Sight, you see a great deal."

"I know Shadows aren't supposed to hold onto family ties, but it's obvious they aren't destroyed completely."

"If I were any younger, I would deny it. But that seems foolish now."

There was an odd sense of finality in her voice that Diana couldn't place or understand. "Mistress?"

The Mistress brushed aside her unspoken question with her hand, silently begging the same grace she'd given Diana when changing the conversation. "Your dedication to Elana is more than I could ever hope for her. I'm very happy you came here."

"Thank you. Your approval means a great deal to me."

The Mistress's eyes twinkled. "I couldn't possibly understand why."

Diana chuckled. "Of course not."

"Would you like some tea while we wait for Elana to return? I wouldn't put it past her to stay up with the alchemists while they work. Or would you like to go to sleep?"

"I'm afraid after recent events the tea makes me nervous."

"Understandable."

"But I don't mind staying up with you if you'd like the company."

The Mistress considered. "Has Elana ever shared with you the Tales of the Blue Wanderer?"

Diana shook her head. "I've never heard of them."

The Mistress pointed out a tall bookshelf across the room. "It's a small book. Silver cover. A children's book."

Elana found the palm-sized booklet sandwiched between the collection of massive tomes on the shelf. She flipped through the pages. Colorful illustrations of a young man in blue filled every other page.

"It's the oldest collection of stories about a Blue Sight ever discovered. It's very popular for Aggar children. Many of the myths, good and bad, that Elana lives with comes from these pages."

Diana thumbed through the pages again, curious what they might reveal about her bondmate. "Did Elana read it as a child?"

"She loved it, for better or for worse. Would you like to read it aloud to me? I haven't heard its stories in many tenmoons."

Diana sat at the base of the Mistress's bed and turned to the first page. "Many a moon ago, when the great whales of the sea were like islands and the cats of the north built castles in the sky, there lived a young boy with blue eyes."

The Mistress settled back against her pillows and closed her eyes, her lips occasionally moving perfectly with the words Diana read aloud.

"Blue eyes that could see into the darkest soul and the kindest heart for he had been taken by the very spirit of Aggar..."

CHAPTER FIVE

Elana stood at her window, letting the cold night air seep through her skin, piercing her like dozens of tiny needles. She hadn't started a fire. She didn't wear a cloak. She grabbed the stone window frame, letting the biting cold burn her palms. She welcomed the cold. She welcomed the pain. She welcomed anything that made her feel, bound her to the present. Anything she couldn't hurt with her despair.

The Alchemists were running sensitive tests on the amulet – tests she couldn't be present for. She'd visited the infirmary to check on the poisoned council members and the Master. They had all been her teachers as a child. The people who had taught her to read. To write. To ride a horse. To lace her boots. And they had almost died.

She hadn't been able to stay long. The council members were still unconscious and the Master was resting. But they'd all survive. At least they would if they weren't attacked a second time.

She'd passed the Mistress's room and heard Diana reading children's stories to her. The moment had been so peaceful Elana didn't want to disturb it. She wasn't feeling strong enough to reign her emotions back – to not spoil a beautiful moment.

She was a storm. She was chaos. She was dangerous. And she couldn't find the strength or the will to pull herself back together.

This was why so many in Aggar thought Blue Sights were demons from the Fates' Cellar. Why they were afraid. At her core, Elana was a wildfire. Her nature was too untamed. Too unbroken. She remembered all the times she'd hurt the Mistress as a child, when her powers were new and untested. She remembered the headaches, the nosebleeds, all the times she'd knocked the

Mistress unconscious as she tried to help her.

What would she do to Di'Nay? Someone who had never been trained? Someone who intrinsically didn't understand her abilities?

What would happen on the Amazon homeworld? Would her powers fade? Or would they be uncontrollable without her connection to Aggar?

Elana squeezed the window frame hard enough the stone left rosy creases across her palms. She didn't know how much she could take. She could never be far from Diana's side. But she couldn't be close to her, either. She couldn't be close to anyone.

There was a reason the Blue Wanderer never had a companion.

Elana released the windowsill, her hands trembling and pale. She wanted to walk outside. She wanted to spend time alone in the gardens and try to find herself once more. To stitch herself back together. But she couldn't find the energy. Instead she just climbed into bed, curling up into a ball. It's what she used to do as a child. Find a place to hide and curl up into as small a space as possible. If she could make herself small, perhaps she could make her problems small as well. Perhaps the tension of her muscles as she physically held herself together, maybe the physicality of wrapping her arms across her chest and bringing her knees to her shoulders and tucking her face against soft pillows and furs could connect her with herself.

She closed her eyes and drew deep, careful breaths. She forced herself not to think of the amulet, the poisonings, the assassins. She even shut out the Mistress and Diana. She only thought of herself. Of her own feelings. She let go of her anger as she breathed out and pulled and buried her concerns deep in her core as she breathed in.

She called on her earliest training. The guided meditations she'd taken to as a child. The children training to be shadows had fidgeted and whined about meditation but Elana had adored it. It was the only time she felt in control. The only time she was calm. Even then she'd known the dark side of her abilities. The pain she could inflict on others. She was no help to anyone uncontrolled then and she wouldn't be of any help to anyone uncontrolled now.

"Elana?"

Elana tensed at the intrusion. Di'Nay stepped carefully into the room. Elana could feel her anxiety and confusion. She thought

Elana was angry with her. She didn't understand.

"Are you awake, Soroi?"

"I'm awake." Elana fought to keep her voice even.

"I thought you'd be with the alchemists. I was waiting up for you."

"They needed space for their tests. I saw you with the Mistress. I didn't want to disrupt you."

"You could have joined us."

Elana was at a loss for words. How could she possibly explain? "I know. Thank you."

"Are you feeling ill?"

"I just like laying this way sometimes."

"Are you tired? Cold? I could start a fire."

"A fire and some sleep would do us both good." Elana didn't care about a fire or sleep, but she knew Di'Nay wouldn't feel better until she felt useful.

As she'd predicted, most of Di'Nay's fear disappeared at Elana's request. She went about building the fire in relative silence. Elana pretended to fall asleep and Di'Nay worked quietly, taking comfort in the thought of Elana resting.

Once the fire was crackling, Di'Nay stripped out of her travel clothes and climbed into bed. She smelled of lavender. She must have taken a bath at some point after reading with the Mistress. Elana was suddenly aware of her dusty clothing, the tangles in her hair, the scent of her skin.

Di'Nay didn't seem to care. As she pulled Elana closer, Elana could only feel her love and concern. She was still dreaming of home. Every night her thoughts seemed to turn more and more to Yemaya. How was Elana supposed to express her fears, especially about how her powers will manifest away from Aggar? She didn't want to rob her bondmate of her dreams.

"You're awake." Di'Nay's voice was gentle even as she accused. Elana sighed. There was no point in hiding.

"I am."

"Were you ever asleep?"

"No."

Di'Nay shifted. "Elana. We'll figure this out. We always do."

"This isn't the Maltar or an expedition to the desert or even a lost seer. This is the Keep. This is a threat to the most powerful people in Aggar."

"That's not what's bothering you."

"Di'Nay."

"I spent most of the the night talking with the Mistress."

"About the Blue Wanderer?"

"In a way."

"About the Sight?"

"Partly."

"About me, then."

"Yes, about you. About Ona."

For the first time since arriving at the Keep, Elana smiled. "I suppose my mother couldn't be the one to tell you embarrassing stories from my childhood."

"They weren't embarrassing," Di'Nay consoled. "They were enlightening."

"What did she say?"

"She told me about your first days at the Keep. About your nightmares. Your anger."

"I was a foolish child."

"You were so young. And confused. And why wouldn't you be?"

"Is that what the Mistress said? That I was confused?"

"She said you were scared. Scared of being far from home but even more afraid of hurting people with your Sight. I remember the night you knocked me unconscious when you were angry, but I didn't truly understand what your Sight was capable of."

Elana covered her face with her hand, trying not to remember the darkness of those very early days. Of discovering that she had the ability to do so much damage to the ones she loved. The ones trying to help her.

"Does it change the way you think of me?"

Di'Nay held her tighter. "Not even a little, Elana. I always knew you were Shea. You've worked so hard to control your abilities. You don't scare me. I trust you. But I think you're afraid of hurting me. You shouldn't be. I can take care of myself."

"Di'Nay. Please. Just... Let me work through this. I'll be fine. I just need a little time."

"You don't have to do this alone anymore, Soroi. You can talk to me." Di'Nay pressed her wrist against Elana's, their lifestones touching. "We're bonded. You don't have to do anything alone anymore."

"You don't know what you're saying."

"I'm not afraid of you. We can work through this together."

Elana clenched her jaw. "You really have been talking with the Mistress."

"I've been worried about you. I don't know what to do to help."

"She doesn't know everything about me. Neither do you. You need to trust that I know how to handle myself. And what's safe for me to keep private. I'm not a child anymore."

"I never thought you were."

"Then trust me."

Di'Nay let out a sharp breath. Elana could feel her confusion and sadness. The emotion turned Elana's stomach and broke her heart. She hated to feel Di'Nay so upset. She hated being the one to make her so sad. But Di'Nay didn't know what she was asking. She didn't realize Elana was sparing her from so much more heartache.

Elana held her tighter, pressing back against her until they were one. Di'Nay buried her face against the nape of Elana's neck, trying to draw comfort from her seemingly cold lover. "I just don't want to lose you."

"You're not losing me. You're everything to me. Just stay with me. Just be here. Please. I'll share with you whatever I can. But be patient with me."

Di'Nay laid a tender kiss on her neck. "Always. I'm always with you."

The Mistress's door fell open beneath Elana's pounding hands, sending her pitching forward onto the ground. The stone floor was colder than usual, almost burning her palms. Elana could smell pine in the air.

Elana pushed herself up to her feet. The Mistress's room was empty and aged, the quilts on her bed threadbare and faded. The books on her shelves – the books Elana would sit and read long into the night when she first arrived at the Keep – were all but dust. The spines were broken down, the pages scattered across the floor before the shelves.

Elana blinked and for a moment she saw Counselor Karis, his corpse draped across the bed, his blue eyes wide in horror, his hand still clutching the stab wounds littering his chest.

Before Elana could scream he was gone, the room empty once more.

A single window was open, a winter storm blowing the gauzy curtains into a tangle and creating a small pile of snow on the ground.

There were no windows in the Mistress's room.

Elana took two steps into the room and a golden eitteh appeared on the Mistress's bed. Elana fell back a step in shock. The winged cat just stared at her, its glowing green eyes wiser than any other eitteh Elana had ever encountered.

Elana tried to See it with her Sight, but she couldn't sense its amarin.

"You're not an eitteh."

The eitteh leapt off the bed and flew out the window. Elana raced after it, but it disappeared into the snow storm. The snow was so thick and the night so dark Elana couldn't see anything, not even a shadow of trees or the light of the moon.

Elana was suddenly overcome by the overwhelming urge to jump out the window. Without thinking, she threw herself into the storm, plummeting through the air. She fell longer than it would have taken to hit the ground. The snow thinned and then vanished completely.

She fell into nothingness. Her stomach turned and her breath caught in her lungs as she fell even faster. She saw a flash of gold and feathers and then she was surrounded by a blinding flash of white light.

Elana woke with a start. A wave of new amarin spread through the Keep.

Di'Nay rose with her. "Elana? Is something wrong?"

"I don't know."

Elana leapt out of bed and moved barefoot through the Keep. A dozen students were clustered around a nearby window, whispering anxiously to each other. "What's going on?" Elana questioned.

A young student clutched at Elana's tunic, her hands trembling with fear.

Di'Nay angled toward the window. "Alexandra?"

Elana reached the window, an arm around the scared child. Commander Turner and a contingent of soldiers stood in the courtyard. Telias waited at the door, but Elana couldn't sense any anger or violence in Commander Turner.

"We need to help Telias." Di'Nay turned and ran down the hall.

"Everything will be fine," Elana promised the children. "Stay here."

They nodded, their amarins full of hope and trust.

Elana raced after Di'Nay.

"We're looking for Diana n'Athena or Elana. We've worked with them before." Commander Turner was trying to stay calm.

"We don't allow Terrans into the Keep uninvited," Telias argued.

"It's all right, Telias. She's telling the truth," Elana assured the Eldest Prepared. She narrowed her brown eyes, her sharp cheekbones framed by her blonde hair. For such an excellent Shadow, Telias was brilliant at expressing her emotions with only a look.

"Did you invite them?"

Elana scowled right back. "I don't know why she's here. But she helped Di'Nay and I in our search for the seer children."

"What do you need, Alexandra? Is everything all right?" Di'Nay called as she ran to her friend.

Commander Turner was filled with righteous anger, her amarin a veritable bonfire. "We've heard about the attacks on the Council. Word is spreading that my unit is behind them."

"We know you're not. It's a group of criminals from Markessa. Mostly people of Aggar," Di'Nay informed her.

"Thugs from Aggar? Who were able to attack Council members?" Commander Turner's fury wavered with her disbelief. "Do they have that kind of power?"

"It's more complicated than that," Di'Nay remarked slowly, unsure of how much to share.

"But they're a real threat?"

"Yes." Elana's voice was sharp.

Commander Turner met Telias's eyes. "We want to help protect the Keep. I won't have the reputation of my unit tarnished by a band of petty criminals. You don't have to let us into your home. We can camp on the grounds. Or around the border of your territory. Or we can leave if you insist. But until your problem is solved, we're at your disposal."

Telias and Elana exchanged looks. "Is she really trustworthy?" Telias questioned. "I admit, the thought of more protection – at least until we can find the nature of the amulet you brought us – is tempting."

Elana looked Commander Turner over. Her natural instincts didn't want to trust her, but she'd proven herself willing to help more than once. And Di'Nay trusted her.

"I think she is. I would hate it if we allowed another attack because of our pride."

Telias considered for a moment before sighing. "You can camp on the grounds for now. The Council of Ten will have to decide how long you can stay. We have many sick Council members inside and I don't want their peace disrupted. What will you need from us?"

"We don't need anything. We won't disturb anyone," Commander Turner promised. "Just let us know how we can help."

"We'll talk and formulate a plan," Telias promised.

Commander Turner nodded and turned to her unit. "We'll camp here. Start setting up tents back toward the bridge so we don't crowd the courtyard."

"Ma'am." The response echoed from every shoulder and they moved to do as they were told.

Elana's stomach clenched at the sight of so many Terrans in the courtyard of the Keep. They'd spent so long trying to keep their secrets from the Terrans, to protect themselves from their invaders. What would the Mistress say? Were they making the right choice?

She could feel the same questions in Telias, but Di'Nay was so steady. So sure.

"They'll be able to help us," Di'Nay promised, correctly interpreting Elana's and Telias's looks of discomfort. "Alexandra isn't corrupt. She's done a lot of good on Aggar."

"They're still invaders," Telias grunted.

Di'Nay sighed in frustration. "That's not Alexandra's fault. She didn't start the war in space. She didn't decide to colonize Aggar as a base. But she *is* working to keep corrupt Terran soldiers from taking advantage of people. No one person can remove the Terrans from your world. But that doesn't mean we shouldn't accept help from the ones trying to make things better."

"We'll work with her," Elana assured her. "It's just... it's strange to see a troupe of Terrans on our land. It will take some getting used to."

Di'Nay crossed her arms over her chest, but she didn't say anything. Elana could feel her frustration at their reticence, but

Elana refused to feel guilty for her hesitance. Di'Nay didn't understand. She couldn't possibly understand. Di'Nay's feelings were nothing compared to how torn Telias felt about potentially letting a dangerous threat into the Keep after there had already been poisonings and deaths.

"We should meet with the Mistress and the Council about where to go from here," Elana recommended. "Everyone should make a decision together."

Telias nodded. "I'll call a meeting with everyone who isn't sick. We can meet in the Mistress's room."

"I'll let her know. She wouldn't want the Council arriving unannounced," Elana volunteered. "Di'Nay, will you speak with Commander Turner? Find out more about what she knows and how she can help us?

"Of course. Call for me when the Council meets?" Di'Nay requested.

Telias looked at Elana anxiously, but Elana nodded. "Of course. You can present what Commander Turner says."

"Sounds good," Di'Nay agreed. A bit of her anger at Telias and Elana's hesitance to trust Commander Turner abated.

She jogged out to the Terran unit. Telias touched Elana's elbow. Despite her strength, Telias was still young. Younger than most Eldest Prepareds. "I don't know what to do here, Elana. If you hadn't bonded with Di'Nay, you'd be Eldest Prepared. Am I making the right decision?"

Elana thought on her answer for a moment. She clenched her jaw. Everything felt so confusing. "I don't think anyone knows what we're supposed to do. We can only present the information to the Council and decide together."

Telias nodded slowly. "I suppose you're right."

"It's the benefit of having a council. We don't have to make any decisions for the Keep alone."

Telias smiled softly. "Sometimes I don't think I was ready for this responsibility."

"You were ready, Telias," Elana assured her. "You couldn't have known what would happen to the Mistress. The Council. You're a strong Shadow. And you care about the Keep. No one would be ready for what you're going through."

"You would."

Elana clenched her jaw. "I'm having a hard time with it, too

Telias. I just have to be better at hiding it."

Telias didn't push her for more information. She only looked out on the Terrans, her amarin full of tense understanding. "You're lucky to have found a good bondmate. She may be ignorant to some of our challenges, but her heart's in the right place."

"It is. And sometimes I think she may be right. Perhaps my prejudice does blind me."

"Now doesn't seem the time to take the chance that these Terrans aren't like the others."

"Di'Nay works with the Terrans. So does her companion, Cleis. They sent her here for help. They can't all be bad."

"Perhaps."

"If Commander Turner had been of Aggar, I wouldn't doubt her."

"But she's not. She's from a race who invaded us."

Elana crossed her arms over her chest. "Nothing's simple, certainly."

"The Mistress will want to hear about this from you. I'll gather the rest of the Council."

Elana nodded. "I'll see you soon."

Elana stood at the window in the lecture hall, staring out as the Terrans built their fires for the night. True to Commander Turner's word, they had brought all their own supplies. They'd asked nothing of the Keep. They'd even moved half their tents to allow for the trainees to practice riding.

A half-dozen adepts had already set off for the desert in search of more nama in case of future poisonings. The seers were still cloistered, refusing to let anyone in to see them. The amulets still remained a mystery. The alchemists had no idea what kind of metal they were made out of or what gave them their special properties. But their tests were conclusive that it hid the wearer from all Blue Sights and seers.

They had burned the body of Counselor Karis, finally laying him to rest. Elana still couldn't believe he was dead, and to be stabbed on Keep land! Knowing about the amulets, Elana wasn't surprised he was the one taken by surprise. He would have been counting on his Sight to warn him of danger. He wouldn't expect an attacker who could hide from him.

There was no telling what might happen next. But even the

Keep's most seasoned professors and Blue Sights were terrified. Their emotions rested dark and heavy over the keep, the weight of their sadness achingly familiar from her nightmares after Di'Nay's return before the poisoning. Perhaps those dreams had been premonitions after all. Or perhaps she'd felt the presence of the assassin without realizing it. Either way, it didn't bode well for her current nightmares.

The Council had voted to accept the Terrans' help. No one was comfortable with the idea, but if they could even be another set of eyes to watch for assassins – even if they could provide some form of defense against physical assaults – it would be worth having them stay. There was even some talk of having Terran guards posted at the entrance to the seer vaults and the rooms of the Council members after Di'Nay gave her testimony on Commander Turner's skills and intentions.

Elana couldn't bring herself to voice an opinion. As things moved on, she only became more confused. She only felt more helpless. For all she knew – and all she could sense – she could be watched by an assassin right now. For a woman who'd spent her entire life learning to navigate the shadows, she'd never felt so exposed.

"Do you plan to sleep tonight?" Di'Nay walked up behind her. Elana felt a sudden comfort feeling her near, not even having to look at her to know she was at her back.

"I thought you'd be with Commander Turner."

"Alexandra's meeting with the Council. She doesn't need me right now."

Elana smiled softly to herself. "You're a bit smug."

"Am I?"

"You were right about Commander Turner, I think. I'm sorry to be so hard on the Terrans."

"You have every right to be. But hopefully this will prove sometimes you can work together to take care of each other."

"If the Keep survives, I don't care how it happens." Elana's voice was soft and sure. She didn't know much anymore, she didn't have confidence anymore, but she did know the Keep had to survive. That was all she could hold onto. The only thing she knew for sure. The Keep would survive, or Elana would go down with it.

"The Keep will survive. We're more powerful than a group of terrorists."

"They're strong. We don't understand them. And ignorance is a powerful weapon. We've spent so long depending on our abilities. On the seers. I... Di'Nay, I don't know what to do when I can't See. When my senses are no longer trustworthy."

Di'Nay wrapped her arms around Elana's waist. She laid a kiss on the top of her head and Elana reveled in how close she would always feel to her bondmate. How clearly she could feel her. "That's why you have me. I could never See them. They have no power over me. I'll keep you safe, Elana. Always."

Elana leaned back against her chest and ran her hands over Di'Nay's arms. "I know you will. It's not me I worry about."

"I'll fight to keep your family safe as well."

"You can't do it alone."

"That's why the others are here. And the Shadows without abilities. You're all trained for this. You just have to adapt. And you're not alone."

Elana nodded softly. "You're right."

Di'Nay rested her chin on the top of Elana's head. "I do have a bit of intuition, you know. It doesn't require the Sight."

Elana laughed softly and leaned up to kiss her lover. "I know you do."

"Come to bed. Or maybe to a bath? You couldn't have taken a long one with all the chaos of the day."

"Just enough to get clean," Elana agreed.

Di'Nay rubbed her shoulders. Elana sighed aloud as Di'Nay eased some of the tension and pain from her muscles. She hadn't even realized how much she hurt.

"You deserve to relax after all the traveling we've been doing."

Elana closed her eyes as Di'Nay's massage moved to her neck. "I know what you're doing."

"Is it working?"

"I'm not sure we should be so distracted right now."

"Whose distracted? I just want a bath."

"Di'Nay..."

Di'Nay kissed her shoulder. "You don't have to. I understand."

Elana was torn between her fear and her need for something to focus on that wasn't death. That wasn't pain. To be close to something she could feel and know wouldn't hurt her.

Elana turned, facing her bondmate. Di'Nay's passion was a fire in her eyes, her amarin as clear as if she'd spoken her desires aloud. “I want to be close to you.”

Di'Nay kissed her, one hand cradling her head, the other arm still holding her tight. “You're still scared.”

“Yes.”

“Are you sure you want this?”

Elana smiled softly. “Maybe a short bath?”

Di'Nay's grin was more than a little triumphant. “Anything you want, Soroi n’ti Mee. Always.”

Elana woke on a cold stone floor. She was sprawled face-down on the ground, her limbs crooked and broken. She struggled to move. She didn't feel anything – not even pain – but as she pushed off the ground her limbs snapped back into alignment as if they'd never been any different.

She sat on the ground, running her hands over her eyes as her vision cleared and shapes started to form in the darkness. She let out a cry of horror as she realized where she was.

The thick stone walls suffocated her. All life had been scrubbed from the surfaces without even a trickle of water to connect her with Aggar. It was a seer's tomb. A prison cell built specifically for her.

“This isn't real. It isn't real,” she muttered to herself as her knees curled to her chest and she buried her face in her hands. “I'm free. I'm not here anymore.”

“Are you sure you ever left?” The voice echoed through the cavern. Elana couldn't place it. It seemed to meld and shift between many voices, sometimes sounding like the Mistress. Other times Di'Nay. Still other times like Counselor Karis and Commander Turner. “We go all kinds of places to escape the torture.”

Elana blocked out the doubt. She knew what was real. “Di'Nay saved me. The Maltar is gone. I'm fine. I'm safe.”

“You're never safe, Elana. Not with those eyes.”

“I'll wake up. I'll wake up.”

“You're not asleep.”

Elana folded in on herself. She was instantly back in that place: cut off from the world. Helpless. Beaten. The last of her hope was slowly draining away as her Sight and her connection to amarin was robbed from her.

“You went mad in here. You know it's true. No one with the

Sight could survive this place."

"Stop it," she hissed, finally acknowledging the disembodied voice. "Go away."

"Do you even know what's real anymore?"

CHAPTER SIX

Diana was torn from her dreams as Elana violently jerked out of her arms. She sat up, instantly awake, every sense hyper-sensitive as she searched for threats. But there was no attacker. Elana tossed and turned, weeping into the pillows and grabbing at the blankets with her fists as she dreamed.

Diana touched her shoulder, caught off guard by the raw terror on Elana's face.

"Elana? Soroi? Wake up. Come back to me."

Elana started to calm as Di'Nay soothed her out of her nightmare until her eyes opened, her tears rushing in a flood down her cheeks. Her voice was desperate and trembling. "Di'Nay?" Diana pulled her into a tight embrace and Elana latched onto her like a terrified child. "I was back there. I couldn't... I wasn't..." Elana's voice disintegrated into sobs.

Diana didn't need to ask where she'd been in her dream. There was only one other time she'd seen Elana so week and broken.

"You're not there anymore. You're here. You're with me. You're safe."

"I'm not safe. I'll never be safe. Don't make me go. I don't want to go." The words tumbled from Elana's mouth without filter or thought. She was rambling. Still half asleep.

Diana hesitated at her words, her pleas striking a cord with her darkest fears. "You don't want to go where, Soroi?"

Elana cried out and her Sight flooded out of her, making Diana sick as she held tight to her grieving lover. Diana's stomach turned and her head pounded. Her vision started to waver and the lifestone in her wrist burned red hot.

Diana fought to push her words past her lips and keep her

voice calm even in her pain. "Trust me. Elana. Please. Come back. Wake up."

Elana started to calm, focusing on her breathing. The effects of her chaotic Sight faded until Diana's headache disappeared and her eyes cleared. Her skin around her embedded lifestone was still rosy red, but the pain had disappeared.

Elana fell silent and looked up slowly. She wiped the tears from her cheeks. "I'm sorry."

Diana shook her head. "No, don't apologize. Are you all right?"

"It was just a bad dream."

"You've been having those a lot lately."

Elana shrugged, but she wouldn't meet Diana's eyes. "It happens from time to time."

"Is it because of the chaos here? Or are you having visions?"

Elana shifted uncomfortably. "I don't know. But this one wasn't a vision. Just... a bad memory."

"I know."

Elana rubbed her shoulders, her grip tense as she tried to hide a shudder. "What about you? I lost my hold on my Sight for a moment there."

Diana smiled. "I'm still conscious, aren't I?"

Elana glanced up at her, still avoiding her eyes, but at least she wasn't hiding anymore. "That's a very calculated response." Elana caught hold of her arm and ran her fingers over the crimson ring around her lifestone. "You're lucky not to be unconscious."

Diana pulled away and took her love's hands. "I'm perfectly fine. You were distressed. My lifestone reacted. There's no pain."

"I see why you're a good ambassador."

Diana chuckled. "I'm well. I promise. I can face your Sight. I can handle any part of your life as long as you're with me."

Elana fell silent for a long moment, but her grip around Diana never faltered. The sudden tension between them twisted at Diana's core, resonating with what Elana had been weeping in her nightmare. "Elana –"

"Can we go back to sleep? Please?"

Diana hesitated, unsure if she should ask the question she knew Elana was avoiding or if it would only cause more trouble.

"Will you be able to sleep?"

"I think so. Just be with me. I'm so tired, Di'Nay."

Diana ran her hand through her lover's thick hair, letting the curls – still damp from their bath – loop and twist around her fingers. How could she do anything but accept? How could she break this tender moment? "Of course, Elana. I'll stay with you as long as you want me near."

Diana knew Elana heard the silent message in her words, but she ignored it. She was just as hesitant to talk as Diana. It just didn't seem the time. Would it ever seem the time?

Elana laid back in the bed and nestled close to Diana. Curled tight together they didn't feel so far apart, but there was still something between them. Something Diana couldn't name – no, something Diana didn't want to name.

Maybe if they waited long enough it would disappear on its own.

"I love you, Soroi n'ti Mee."

"I love you, Di'Nay."

Diana closed her eyes. She could feel Elana's love like a wave of heat. At least she could still trust those words. Everything would be all right as long as their love stayed strong.

Diana jogged through the Terran camp, the brisk morning chill somewhat abated by their morning fires. The scent of roasting meat filled the courtyard as the soldiers prepared a meal. The sun had just broken over the horizon coloring the sky crimson and gold.

Alexandra stood in the distance with one of her soldiers, glancing over a map with a mug of tea in her hand. Her eyes were already clear, her face tense as she concentrated. She glanced up as she spotted Diana moving toward her and smiled.

"Send Stuart and Thompson. Have Kennison lead the scouts."

"Sounds good. Thank you, Commander."

Alexandra's soldier rushed back into the campground and Alexandra lifted her chin in greeting, silently beckoning Diana forward.

"Good morning," Alexandra greeted. "Everything still well in the Keep?"

"As far as I know. Elana is meeting with the Council again. I think I would have heard if something catastrophic happened."

"Good. I met with the Council's Keep most of the night and I still don't know how they operated."

Diana grinned. "They're certainly different than working with the Empire."

"I'm not sure that's a bad thing."

Diana snorted. "I agree. But it can be confusing. They're working with forces I've never encountered before."

"Is it genuine? I always assumed they had some trickery on their side or they were just incredibly intuitive. Maybe they created seers to protect their feeble-minded."

Diana paused. "You've never met a Blue Sight before Elana? Or a seer?"

Alexandra shook her head. "Never. I've only heard the stories. Sound like urban legends or folktales to me. Primitive people and their mythologies."

Diana looked her friend over anew, the casual condescension in her voice didn't seem intentionally offensive, but she was surprised to hear it. "They're not primitive. They just choose not to use the same technologies we do. And their powers are very real. I would never want to fight a seer."

Alexandra looked up at the towering Keep. "Fascinating."

"How did your meetings go?" Diana inquired, trying to change the subject.

Alexandra returned her attention to Diana. "Well, I think. We're running regular patrols around the Keep's perimeter and we have permanent guards posted at the hospital, the Mistress's room, the Seers vault, and the student dormitories."

"They must trust you a great deal. They don't let many into the Keep, let alone Terrans."

"We're taking their trust very seriously. I trust every soldier here with me to be at their most respectful and professional. I hand-picked them. We'll keep everyone safe until the threat is neutralized. Though I admit I don't know why there are still students on the grounds. I'd think they'd be sent home until it's safe. I saw young ones still learning to lace their boots!"

"Most of them don't have homes to return to, and the rest have disavowed their familial bonds. This is the only place they know and the only place they're safe. Even with the threat of assassins."

Alexandra shook her head. "Everything's so different here."

"It is. You can see why they have trouble understanding us as well."

"It's always hard when we set up bases on a new planet. It's hard for them to get that we're protecting them as much as anyone else. They just see us as invaders."

"Have you been involved in many colonizations?"

"A few. Enough to know how to keep my soldiers in line."

"I thought you didn't approve of colonization."

"I don't approve of the wars we're fighting either, but my disapproval doesn't make reality any different. Colonization can be a necessary evil."

Diana wondered if somewhere in the Keep Elana was smug feeling how uncomfortable Diana felt at her conversation with Alexandra. It wasn't anything she hadn't heard before from other Terrans. In fact, most conversations about the people of Aggar were much more offensive. But it was Alexandra's good intentions coupled with her words that seemed to strike Diana to her core. There was so much unintentional ignorance. No wonder Elana and the other shadows grew so tired with the Terrans.

"I know everyone is glad for your help here," Diana remarked.

Alexandra cast her a knowing glance, her serious face melting into an almost sarcastic smile. "It's an uneasy truce. I know it is. But we can help each other. My soldiers can ensure the Keep's safety and they can restore our reputation as benevolent. I can't man a base that's hated by the people around us. We don't need a rebellion. Having the Keep's favor could do a lot to ease tensions and create peace. And while I'm still not sure how genuine their abilities are, I do know the fall of the Council's Keep would be catastrophic across the planet. The people talk about the place like it's some kind of divine presence, for good or bad."

"Losing the Keep would be pure chaos, yes. In many ways."

Alexandra rolled her shoulders and raised her chin in determination. "Then we'll make sure it doesn't happen."

No matter what she thought of Alexandra's empirical views, Diana trusted her to keep her word. If the Keep had to take Terran allies, they couldn't find more powerful, committed, and well-intentioned soldiers.

"Have you found anything? Your scouts or your intelligence agents?"

Alexandra took a sip of her tea. "Nothing solid. I took what you gave me and put out feelers for more information on the amulets you discovered. No one has seen anything like them. Are you sure I can't have a sample of the one you have? I'm sure our scientists could –"

Diana shook her head, interrupting Alexandra before she could insist. "Terrans aren't allowed to handle it. I'm sorry."

Alexandra sighed. "We really should be trusting each other."

"They've already trusted you a great deal. Maybe with more time." Diana didn't believe the words even as she said them. The Keep would never give away the amulet. Elana wouldn't allow it. But now wasn't the time to antagonize anyone.

"Commander Turner!" A sentry raced forward, holding a letter in her hand. "A report from the scouts along the barrier."

The sentry handed Alexandra the message. Alexandra looked it over quickly, her brow furrowing as she read.

"Did they find anyone?" Diana questioned.

The sentry shook her head. "No. But some evidence of small campsites."

Diana raised an eyebrow. "More than one?"

Alexandra folded the letter. "Half a dozen. Just the remains of a fire and flattened branches where someone rested. Obviously recent. They couldn't have supported many people, perhaps four each, but that's more than a couple assassins. Is it common for anyone to camp around the Keep?"

"Not that I know of. I'll ask Elana. She should be done with her meeting soon."

Alexandra slipped the note into her pocket. "You can speak with the Council about the campsites, but we'll investigate anyway. I'll let you know if we find anything in particular."

"Thank you. I'll come back in the evening."

Alexandra nodded and Diana jogged back toward the Keep, silently praying to the Mother that the Shadows regularly camped around the Keep for training.

Diana ran her fingers through her short hair, flicking out the water from her bath. Her hair had gotten longer since her time with Elana. Soon it would feel completely unmanageable. She wondered if someone at the Keep would have clippers. She'd have to ask Elana when she returned from the Council. Her revelation about the discovered camps had extended the meetings. Apparently no trainees had left Keep grounds since the attacks.

Diana stepped into her bedroom and slipped off her boots. She glanced out the window. The moons were already rising high into the sky. A fire was already crackling in the fireplace. She smiled.

Elana must have asked for it to be lit for her. Even in her meetings, her mind was on Diana.

She had barely seen Elana as information continued to come in. More camps were found, some recent, others much older. No other clues were found – no amulets, abandoned gear, not even scraps of food – but they weren't made by the Terrans or the trainees. Elana and other Blue Sights had visited them, hoping to find some lingering amarin but it was if no one had ever been in the forest. More than anything, the lack of a human imprint seemed to point to the Order of Blindness.

Diana had spent her time patrolling with the Terran soldiers and working with the guards to explore the Keep. She desperately wanted to reach out to Cleis. To bring in the technology available to her through her sisters and the Empire space shuttles. But there was nothing she could do.

She crouched low beside the fire and warmed her hands. If Elana wasn't done already and she'd had a fire prepared, she didn't intend to be back for a while. Diana sighed. In such a short time, she'd gotten used to sleeping with Elana in her arms. It felt strange being away from each other.

You knew times like this would come. Stop being a child.

Diana smiled at her own chiding. There had been a time she'd been proud. Solitary. She'd spent nearly twenty years away from her home planet. Yet somehow this woman nearly half her age had made her feel like a freshly-deployed Amazon again. Strangely enough, Diana had come to feel that was a good thing.

She rose slowly and stretched her arms over her head. She undressed quickly, crawling beneath the covers before any late-night chill could seep beneath her skin. She wondered if Elana would come back at all or if she'd be cloistered all night. Perhaps Elana was less interested in the meetings and more interested in always knowing the Counselors were safe. Diana couldn't blame her, though the thought unsettled her. When this was over, would the woman she'd known before return to her? Or would this leave a permanent mark on her lover?

Diana was just beginning to slip into unconsciousness when the door opened. She spied Elana in the shadows and smiled. She knew Elana could tell she was awake, but the young woman didn't acknowledge it. She fell back against the wall for a moment, holding her chin in one hand as she thought. Before Diana could rise to ask if she was all right, she moved again, stripping out of her clothes, her body a lithe glimmer of pale skin in the dim moonlight, and climbed into bed.

"Did everything go well?" Diana muttered as Elana slid into her usual place in Diana's arms.

"As well as could be expected, I suppose."

"Did you discover anything about the camps?"

"Many are tendays old. They could even have been used more than once by the same party."

"Then there could still only be a handful of assassins?"

"We don't even know if they were used by assassins. They could be travelers who didn't want to interact with the Keep. Some of them were old enough it would even explain why we couldn't sense any lingering amarin."

"That sounds hopeful, sae?"

"It means nothing. We still don't know anything."

Diana held her tighter. "But we're still learning. And the Keep and Terrans are working well together."

"The students hate having them in their quarters."

"It's for their own protection."

"The only reason a Terran soldier may be stronger than a shadow is in the choice of weapon. Many of the students could outfight and certainly hide from any of Commander Turner's soldiers."

"But they're observant."

"Yes. And we need more eyes keeping watch for murderers. But the students don't see it that way. Many question if the assassins might not be among the soldiers. It's a matter of time before a fight breaks out."

Diana sighed and kissed Elana's shoulder. She was probably right. And if Alexandra's soldiers had even less experience with Blue Sights than their commander, it wouldn't take much for them to be spooked by an angry student. "Let's just hope this is over before it comes to that."

"Yes. We can hope."

Elana fell silent and Diana hoped she was falling asleep. As Elana's breathing became more even and her body grew warm and limp in her arms, Diana finally started to fall asleep herself.

Her dreams were haunting and full of shadow. She chased Elana through a forest at midnight, the trees nothing but inky black silhouettes against the night sky. Elana seemed to shift in and out of the darkness. Diana could only catch a glimpse here or there, a shift of her hair, a snap of a twig under her foot.

Elana didn't seem to want to be caught, but Diana couldn't slow. She knew something was desperately wrong. Elana was in danger. She had to help. Why was Elana running away?

"I don't want to go. Don't make me go."

Elana's words spoken out of her dream the night before continued echoing in Diana's mind. Her heart was torn between dreams of Elana on Yemaya, Elana and their children, Elana and the Sheas and the knowledge that she could never force Elana to do anything she didn't want to do. She couldn't force her off world. And if she left Aggar without Elana, their lifebond would quickly kill Elana.

If Elana wouldn't go, Diana wouldn't either.

Diana cried as she continued chasing her fleeing bondmate, searching for anything that would make her understand. That would make her stop. Anything that would bring her soroi back to her.

Diana woke as Elana pulled away from her. She was trembling, having just come out of another nightmare. She hadn't made a sound.

Diana reached out to her in the darkness, her hand falling against her the smooth skin of her back, but Elana didn't respond. After a long moment of silence, when her trembling finally calmed, Elana stood. "I need to go for a walk."

Her voice was hollow and distant, almost as if it were echoing from far away. She hadn't talked like that since Diana had rescued her from the Maltar and Diana instantly knew what she was dreaming about again.

"Elana?"

"Please. Just let me go."

The words stunned Diana to silence. She watched as her mate dressed in the darkness and disappeared out the door, blending into the shadows exactly as she'd done in Diana's dream.

Diana leaned back against the pillows, unsure of what to do. Despite her age, Diana hadn't been in many relationships. Certainly not with anyone like Elana. And the situation certainly didn't help her confidence.

She grunted in annoyance. She also wasn't used to feeling

useless. If Elana wasn't so dear to her...

Diana frowned. Why was she acting any differently with Elana than she would someone else she cared about?

She heard the clack of horse hooves outside in the courtyard. Diana stood and glanced out the window. Elana was galloping out of the stables. Diana could feel the increasing distance between them through their lifestone bond.

Diana was instantly spurred to action. Elana's mood didn't matter anymore: if she was leaving the Keep, she wasn't doing it alone. With assassins flitting through the forests, most of whom Elana wouldn't be able to sense, Diana didn't trust her bondmate to return home safely.

Diana threw on her riding clothes and cloak. She raced out into the Keep, her long legs taking the stairs three at a time and carrying her quickly out into the courtyard. Kaing was already anxious as she ran into the stable. It seemed he was used to riding with Leggings enough to notice her absence.

“It's all right,” Diana assured him as she saddled him and rode him out into the courtyard. “Come on.”

She galloped across the grounds for the bridge that marked the entrance to the Keep's lands. She caught sight of Elana in the distance on a hill just past the bridge, no longer galloping. Whatever had spurred her to flee from the Keep as fast as she could had calmed. Diana let out a breath of relief. If Elana had continued racing into the forest, she would have been nearly impossible to find.

Elana turned as Diana crossed the long bridge over the ravine that separated the Keep from the rest of the forest. Diana's heart stilled as Elana tensed. Her sudden impulse to run away again was obvious. She was on edge, like a frightened eitteh crouching in the trees.

“Elana!” she called out. “Please don't leave.” Elana stayed. Diana leapt down from Kaing as she approached. “What's going on? It's dangerous out here alone.”

“I needed to get out of the Keep. The energy is just...” Elana shook her head, unable to find the words she wanted. “It's heavy, Di'Nay. Dark. Tense. It makes me sick. It's messing with my head.”

Diana walked up to Leggings and reached up to Elana. “Come down. Please.”

Elana hesitated. “I just want to ride.”

"We don't have to go back right now. But please. Come be with me. Don't run away."

After a moment's hesitation, Elana reached down and slid into Diana's arms. "I wasn't running away from you," she whispered against Diana's chest. "Just running."

"I know. But next time, bring me with you."

"I haven't faced something like this with someone else before."

Diana chuckled softly. "Neither have I. But it's about time we learned. I'm not going to abandon you, Elana. You don't have to be alone anymore."

"What if I want to be alone?" Elana's tone held a hint of teasing, just enough for Diana to know she was all right.

Diana kissed her head. "Then you can take time alone. Just not in a potentially assassin-ridden forest."

"You're no fun."

"Hardly ever."

"Thank you for coming for me."

They held each other in silence for a long moment. Finally, Diana spoke. "We haven't been talking much."

"No, we haven't."

"Why not?"

Elana glanced up at Diana, her blue eyes like sapphires in the darkness. "Because we're both afraid of what the other will say."

Diana's breath caught in her throat. She was so easy to read for Elana. "Yes."

"Why are we afraid?"

"Because we're just starting to get to know each other after a mission. Because we don't know what the other will do."

"I've been dreaming of the Maltar again." The confession was an invitation. A need to break down barriers no matter how hard it would be.

Diana brushed the hair from Elana's eyes. "I know. I'm so sorry you have those memories."

"It's not really the Maltar I'm dreaming of. I feel helpless. Broken. All I had was the power of my Sight. Now that puts me at risk. Puts the people I love at risk."

"I understand. I feel helpless myself. Your world is so new to me. I don't have any powers. I don't understand everything you're feeling or going through. All I am is a sword."

"You're an ambassador with the Terrans. Do you think we'd be able to work together at all without you?"

"I worry that wasn't a wise decision."

"We won't know until this is over," Elana conceded. Diana's heart warmed as Elana dropped her pride in her honesty. "There's still something you're not telling me. I can feel it. Something you've bee worrying about for a while."

Diana clenched her jaw. How was she supposed to ask? Was this the time? Would It ever be the time?

"Elana... Soroi... Everything between us has been so different lately. I'm starting to realize –"

"You're starting to realize I'm not the woman you thought I was."

The words sounded harsh and sharp coming out of Elana's mouth. Diana quickly shook her head. "No, no, not that."

"Exactly that," Elana insisted.

"I'm not second-guessing you or us. But you're right that I've never seen these sides of you. Your anger. Your sadness."

"My vengeance."

Diana could only nod in response. "I don't know what to do for you. I don't know how to bring you out of that darkness."

"You don't have to do anything. Just be with me."

"I'm scared of what this will do to you."

"Diana, I've always been angry. I've always been solitary and protective. You've just never seen it before. Finding you – bonding with you – has helped so much. I have never been so happy in my entire life. But I can't promise I'll ever change. Does it bother you?"

"I just worry about you."

"I can guarantee that will never change." They both smiled. "Like our future children, sae?"

Diana trembled and her cheeks flushed. "You keep using my language against me."

"It's a powerful weapon, soroi."

"You're fighting me now?"

"Only trying to break down our barriers." Diana pressed her lips into a straight line. Elana cocked her head to the side, reading her face with concern. "There's something you're still not telling me. Asking me?"

Diana forced a false half-smile. "Can't you read my mind, Blue Sight?"

"I can't read your mind, my love. You know that. But I can tell something is still weighing on your mind."

"Elana, I --"

Diana paused. Something suddenly didn't feel right. She glanced around the hillside.

"Di'Nay? What is it?"

"You don't feel anything?"

Elana looked around nervously, her breathing coming in short bursts. "No. I don't feel anything."

A sharp rustle in the trees was their only warning. More than a dozen men, their mouths and noses covered with black scarves, ran out of the trees. Elana screamed as they were grabbed. Diana tried to fight her way free, knocking out a couple of them before she was pinned to the ground, her arms and legs secured by different men.

Elana fought desperately to free herself, but it was clear she was more of a target. Six men wrestled her to the ground as she screamed. She bit and clawed like a wild animal but it did no good.

Diana watched in terror as they went after the horses, but Kaing and Leggings were used to combat. They kicked and bucked at their attackers and galloped back toward the Keep.

"Leave them!" a deep, masculine voice called. "Cover her eyes." A man with a red face scarf walked out of the trees. One of Elana's captors bound a black scarf over her eyes. Her skin was a sickly sepia in her terror. She trembled violently.

"Di'Nay? Di'Nay!" she cried Diana's name over and over as she lost all sense of her surroundings, her eyes covered and the amulets worn by their captors making them all but invisible to her.

Diana's heart nearly pounded out of her chest. Not again. She wouldn't let Elana be at the mercy of a mob of captors again. Not after what happened to her at the hands of the Maltar. Diana fought harder than ever, but she couldn't free herself.

"Let us go!" she demanded of the man with the red scarf.

He only shot her an incredulous look. He crept over to Elana and grabbed her hair, forcing her to face him despite being blind. "You shouldn't have crossed the bridge. Don't you know it's dangerous after dark?"

Elana pulled away from him and he released her, but his skin was darkening with pleasure. Diana grit her teeth, her eyes flitting quickly around the clearing looking for any kind of weapon or chance at escape.

"Don't bother, Amazon. You'll never escape us. And even if you did, we'd find you again."

"Touch her and I'll kill you," Diana seethed.

The man grunted. "We wouldn't touch a demon. And we won't kill her yet. We know who she is. We know what she's worth at the Keep. And we know you need to live to keep her alive."

"But you promised us their eyes!" one of the Order shouted, his voice disgruntled and sharp. "And the lifestones!"

Diana tensed. They seemed to know a lot more about them than she expected.

"In time. Just... not yet."

Elana didn't make a sound. She was folding in on herself, retreating away from reality like she had when she was last imprisoned. Diana wanted to call out to her. To reach for her. But she couldn't. And she wouldn't rob Elana of her defense mechanism just to soothe her conscious.

"Which camp should we take them to?" one of Diana's captors questioned.

The leader eyed Diana for a moment before turning to the man standing at her head. "We don't need her hearing us, do we?"

With a swift, violent motion the man punched Diana in the back of the head and she was instantly unconscious.

PART THREE

ALLIES

CHAPTER ONE

Elana came-to slowly. She'd been dragged through the forest, until her fear and Sight gave way to terror and she fell completely inside herself. At some point she must have passed out. Or perhaps she had just retreated so far into herself she'd just lost sense of her surroundings.

She was still blindfolded. The fabric was too thick to make out anything, not even light. She could feel the amarin of the soil beneath her and the tree behind her. She knew it was day as she felt the flowers near her reaching their petals up to the sun for sustenance.

She felt the ropes around her wrists, waist, and ankles. She let out a sharp gasp of relief as she felt Di'Nay. Her amarin was gentle, as if she was sleeping, but she was alive.

Elana could hear people around her. She could hear their feet on pine needles and their voices in the distance, but she couldn't feel anyone but Di'Nay. She was completely blind. Alone in the darkness. Alone except for Di'Nay.

She grabbed at the ropes that bound her hands and tried to free herself, but they were knotted tight. As she pulled the fibers cut into her skin until they burned.

She bowed her head, unsure of what to do. For all she knew, she was surrounded by her captors, hiding their laughs behind their hands as they watched her try to escape. Any moment they could attack. They could blind her. They could kill her. They could hurt Di'Nay and she wouldn't be able to save her. She was alone. She was broken.

She drew deep, calming breaths. At least she wasn't alone. At least she was outside, not entombed in stone. At least Di'Nay was alive and near.

"Elana?"

Di'Nay's voice, heavy with pain and groggy from unconsciousness, called out to her. "I'm here," Elana whispered, instantly reaching for her only source of comfort. She felt new pain and blossoming across Di'Nay's amarin like blood rising to the surface. "You're hurt!"

"They hit me. Knocked me out. It hurts."

"Do you feel nauseous? Can you focus?"

"I don't think it's a concussion," Di'Nay promised, reading through Elana's questions. "But it'll take me a while to be at full strength."

"Are you bleeding?"

Diana chuckled softly. "Do you really want to know, Soroi? Or do you just want to trust that I'm alive?"

"Di'Nay." Elana's voice shook with the tears she was holding back, a cascade created by memories of captivity and abuse. Her terror at losing her Sight. Her fear of what was to come and how it would affect Di'Nay.

Elana heard a rustle and a shift, and then the faintest touch of Di'Nay's fingers reaching out to her hand. They were barely able to hold each other's fingertips. "I'm here. I promise."

"I feel you."

"We're tied to a tree. Bound around the trunk at our waists and wrists. There's a camp in the distance and a path nearby. I think we might be between guards. There's signs of a post just ahead."

"I heard someone walking when I woke," Elana confirmed. I thought we were surrounded."

"No. I think most of them are afraid of you."

"We guessed that," Elana retreated to logic. "That most of them are backwoods grunts led by a few more malicious conspirators."

"That lines up with what I saw when we were captured. Why would they keep us together?"

"I remember them talking about lifestones. They know I'll die if you die. They may even know I'll die if you're too far away. They may not know how far we can be from each other to stay healthy."

"They seem to have a very selective knowledge of the workings of the Keep."

Elana clenched her jaw. "They know too much."

"If we find out where they're ignorant, we can exploit it,"

Di'Nay reasoned.

"How... how many are there?" Elana wasn't sure she wanted to know the answer.

Diana hesitated. "A lot more than we thought. And before they knocked me out I heard there's more than one camp."

"How many, Di'Nay?"

"I would estimate nearly a hundred."

Elana was stunned to silence. The Keep could defend against a hundred, but they had been preparing for a dozen at most. They were wholly unprepared for what would happen next.

"We'll escape, Elana. I won't let them hurt you. I can be your eyes, "Di'Nay fought to reassure her. "We're together this time."

"I trust you."

The sound of steps approaching and Di'Nay's fingers retreated. Elana fell silent.

"You're awake." A man's voice Elana had never heard before. He sounded uncomfortable, his voice a bit distant, as if he wouldn't walk any closer to them. "I wouldn't have taken this shift if I knew you were awake."

Di'Nay didn't respond. Elana fought the urge to flinch, constantly feeling as if someone were standing just a breath away from her.

The guard fell silent as well. No one spoke or moved for hours, the stillness only broken by the occasional passerby and a woman who came to bring the guard dinner. Elana was shocked to hear a woman's voice. She assumed the Order would be loathe to include women, as most men of Aggar saw them as wives or slaves. The woman, while bringing a meal, didn't sound subservient and the guard didn't give her any orders. Was the Order traveling with women companions? Had their hatred of the Keep – of the seers and Blue Sights – outweigh their sexism?

The thought turned Elana's stomach. How could so many hate them so much? She nothing more than an object. A demon. She was nothing. Aggar was her home and she was nothing.

Elana fought her growing depression as she felt the sun begin to sink, the plants and animals of the forest preparing for nightfall. She retreated into what she could feel through her Sight. She communed with the trees, escaping into their web of connection, of peace. They were standing long before her troubles and they would stand long after she was dust. They were unaffected by hate. By pain. They weren't even affected when one of them were cut down. They were a unit. A whole. And they would always stand.

After a time, there was a shuffle and rise as the guard stood and, after a moment, Di'Nay reached out to her again.

"He's gone. I think they have to fetch each other between shifts. We have a few moments."

"They must not be very organized," Elana observed. "What if we tried to escape?"

"They'd see us. We're in clear view of the camp. But I don't think they can hear us if we speak softly."

"Do you see anything that could help us escape?"

"Nothing yet. Can you feel anything with your Sight? Anything natural? Anyone coming from the Keep? Kaing and Leggings must have returned. They should know we're missing."

"I feel trees and flowers and foliage. A few small animals. I can't feel the Keep at all."

"That's because you're not near the Keep anymore."

Elana tensed. She recognized the voice of the leader of the men who had kidnapped her. She turned right and left, trying to hear where he might be. Di'Nay didn't release her fingers.

Someone snapped beside Elana's right ear and she jumped, turning to face the sound. She heard feet walking across the fallen pine needles and then a soft exhale as the man crouched down beside the tree.

"What do you want?" Di'Nay demanded.

"Just checking in. Hungry? I assume you aren't tired. You've been out so long."

"So you're just here to try to make us angry," Di'Nay countered. "Fine."

Elana felt Di'Nay retreat from the conversation and heard a rustle as she turned away. The sound was louder than it normally would be. She was telegraphing her movements for Elana.

Another shuffle of pine needles and Elana pressed tighter against the trunk of the tree behind her. She could feel him getting closer, invading her space. "You really can't feel anything, can you?"

"Leave her alone." Di'Nay's voice was acidic. She strained against her bonds, but she never released Elana's fingers.

"I wonder if you'll feel it when we destroy the Keep. Does the amarin of hundreds of deaths expand? Can you feel the terror of a seer stronger than the terror of a Blue Sight? Or a Shadow?"

"You'll never take the Keep." Elana's words shot through her clenched teeth, her fear turning to rage. "You think you can invade a seer's vault? Your men don't even want to guard us when we're bound to a tree."

"You're so sure? You don't seem to know anything about our capabilities."

"And you don't know the strength of the Council."

The man laughed, low and confident. He patted Elana's head like a child and she shrank back from the sudden touch. "We'll see what happens."

The man shifted and Elana heard him stand and take a few steps away. She relaxed as she felt him move away from her.

"Don't look at me like that, Amazon," the man groused. "I told you no one will touch her. Not until the Keep falls. And even then... well, we have to keep a few of them alive if we're ever to find out where they get their powers."

Elana's stomach turned at the implications in his words.

"You'll die first." Di'Nay's threat was vicious and sure. Elana had never heard such venom.

"I expected you to say as much. I know all about your... unnatural union. I know the reputation of your people. But for all your bravado, I don't see you capable of doing much while tied to a tree."

Elana felt Di'Nay's anger rising. She was taking his bait in her need to protect Elana. Elana squeezed her fingers hard, begging her through their lifebond, through the desperation in her grip, to be calm. If she antagonized the Order enough, they might blindfold her as well or worse, take her away. There were a lot of ways they could hurt both of them without breaking their lifebond.

Di'Nay seemed to sense Elana's fear. She swallowed her frustration and fell silent. The man chuckled softly. "Like rats in a trap." The shift of pine needles as the man's steps drifted away. "The Order of Blindness sees more than you expect. And with our tools, you don't see anything at all. Tell me if you feel anything from the Keep. It will be valuable. For science."

"Monster," Di'Nay hissed and Elana knew he was gone. "The least he could do is show his face when he's threatening us."

"We can't let him bait us," Elana announced. "I don't want him to hurt you."

"I won't let him near you," Di'Nay argued.

"He won't do anything to me. Not yet. And most of his men seem to be afraid to approach us alone. Why else would there be such long breaks between guards and only one guard at a time? He must be having a hard time convincing his people I'm not dangerous. They wouldn't risk attacking me."

"What If they do?"

"They'd be more likely to do something to me without you at my side. Please. I don't want to be alone. I can't escape without you."

Di'Nay sighed. "Okay. I'll stay calm." Di'Nay drew a breath as if to speak again, but she stopped herself. The tension between them – the feeling that something was going unsaid, settled between them once more.

"There's something you want to say."

Di'Nay hesitated. Her grip on Elana's fingers went slack, but she didn't release her. Elana strained against her bonds, wanting nothing more than to see her love. "Yes."

"Something you wanted to say before?"

"Yes."

"Please tell me. This isn't the time for secrets."

"We're going to be fine. We're going to get out of here."

Elana strengthened her grip on Di'Nay's fingers, not allowing her lover to pull away. "And if we don't, I want to know there's nothing between us."

"Elana... soroi... There's nothing between us. I just want to take you away from this. I want you to be safe."

"You've been thinking this since before we were captured," Elana rebutted.

"I don't mean take you away from this camp."

Elana paused, finally understanding. "You mean take me away from Aggar."

"This planet isn't safe for you. They don't appreciate you. But on Yemaya you would be valued. Treasured."

"I already promised to go with you. Why are you afraid to talk to me?"

Di'Nay's voice was strained, her words flowing together as she spoke before she could stop herself. "Because I don't think you want to come with me. And I don't want to force you."

Elana felt a rush of relief in her bondmate at finally speaking mingling with fear at Elana's response. Elana's mind spun as she tried to understand the implications of Di'Nay's fear without the use of her Sight or the ability to reach out to her.

"Why would you think I don't want to go?" Elana's words sounded hollow even as she spoke them.

"You say you don't want to go when you sleep. You're obsessed with saving the Keep and avenging the Mistress. You talk like you don't consider yourself a Sister and you don't trust anyone born off Aggar. Would you be able to stop worrying about the Keep? Will you ever consider Yemaya your home? Would you truly consider yourself a Sister?"

Elana didn't know how to respond. Di'Nay was right. She'd been pushing it away for so long it was shocking to hear her bondmate say it aloud. "I... I feel torn, Di'Nay."

"Don't. Please. I don't blame you. This is your home. This is where your family is. Your responsibilities. I shouldn't have thought you'd be ready to leave it all behind just because I'm scared for you and I want you with me."

"I want to be with you. I want to see your world. And I want you to be able to go home."

"I dedicated my life to traveling to other worlds. You didn't. If either of us is going to live away from home, it's me."

"We aren't so different. I didn't have the choice to leave Aggar, but I did leave my home for adventure. I left my family. I became a shadow. I bonded with you and I couldn't have had a better companion. My bonds with this world go against everything I was ever trained to be."

"But it's part of your nature. Making a decision like changing your homeworld shouldn't hinge on what you think you're supposed to be instead of what you are. You care about Aggar."

"I care about you."

"I'll stay with you. I'll keep you safe."

"Di'Nay –"

"Hush." Di'Nay's voice was full of warning. A moment later Elana heard the crunch of boots on the ground and a new guard settled in for the night.

Elana leaned back against the tree and closed her eyes despite her blindfold. She was exhausted. Emotionally drained. But she couldn't sleep.

Di'Nay's words raced through her mind. Did Di'Nay really

think it was her duty to stay with Elana despite her obvious desire to go home? The fact that Di'Nay would make such a sacrifice without even discussing it didn't sit well with her.

Elana didn't know what she wanted. She didn't know where her responsibilities and allegiances should lay. But she knew she would stay with Di'Nay for the rest of her life.

Elana's wrists and legs cramped. She wanted to move, to curl in on herself. She was suddenly hyper-aware of her bonds, her thirst, her hunger. She had to get out. She had to free herself and Di'Nay.

"I know you can hear me," Elana called to her guard. Di'Nay rustled in surprise.

"Be quiet."

"You think your amulet will protect you, but it won't. I can still feel you. I can still get into your mind."

"Impossible. I know the amulets work. And you're blindfolded."

Elana smiled at the quiver in his voice. He sounded young. Unsure. It seemed the Order really was having trouble convincing people to watch over her. "You don't know what kind of powers a Blue Sight has, do you?"

"Filthy demons, possessing our children and invading our minds. I would never underestimate you."

"And you think an amulet will stop me? You know my name. You've heard my story. Perhaps a little bit of metal stopped weaker Blue Sights before, but me?"

"I saw you pinned to the ground. I saw you beg. I saw you broken!"

"You saw me act. How else could I get to the center of your camp without drawing unwanted attention?"

The young guard hesitated and Di'Nay reached out to her, grabbing her hand, encouraging her. Elana was getting to him.

"You're lying. All demons lie."

"Then you know I can control you with my voice. I can make your life a living nightmare. I can haunt you long after you've destroyed this body."

"You've never seen my face."

"I know your smell."

Elana could feel Di'Nay's amusement through their connection. She didn't try to hide her smile. Her amusement seemed to terrify the guard even more.

"Stop it. I'm not listening to you anymore."

"You can't stop her. She'll always get her way," Di'Nay took up the game. "You don't know what she's done to me. What she'll do to you."

"You're her bondmate."

"I'm her slave. I'm only able to speak freely because you bond her eyes."

"I knew it worked."

"It does. She can't do anything to you with her Sight. The amulets keep her at bay. But she can still speak. You need to bind her mouth with an amul –"

"Silence," Elana commanded and Di'Nay fell quiet. "You won't speak anymore."

Di'Nay fell quiet. Elana wished she could see her bondmate's acting skills, but she could feel Di'Nay shifting against the ropes and the terror in the guard's voice grew to a more fevered pitch.

"With an amulet? That will keep her contained."

"You will do nothing," Elana commanded.

"I'm not listening to you. You can't control me."

Elana heard the shuffle of the guard's feet on the foliage and she fought not to smile. Just a little closer. "You'll regret this," her voice was even and menacing. She felt the pull on the ropes around her waist that signified Di'Nay was moving, silently goading the guard on.

Elana could feel him stop right in front of her. She felt the cold press of metal against her lips as the guard pressed the amulet against her mouth. She pretended to fight, just enough to encourage him to continue. The feel of the amulet made her head light and her stomach twist in vicious knots. Her sense of Sight was distorted, every imprint fainter and tangled around each other, but she could still feel. She could still effect the world.

And as her captor wrapped the amulet chain around her head, affixing the pendant over her lips, and took a step away, Elana could feel him, too.

The sound of walking. "Can you talk now?" the guard asked Di'Nay.

Elana reached out with all her strength, finding his Amarin, and flooded his senses with the strength of her Sight. He didn't make a sound as he fell unconscious.

"Elana, you goddess!" Di'Nay cheered. Elana heard her

struggling to

Di'Nay grunted as the guard collapsed on top of her. Elana shook her head, trying to dislodge the amulet, but it only slid down over her neck.

"He has a knife," Di'Nay announced as she pulled on their ropes. I just have to reach it."

"Di'Nay..." Elana's voice was weak.

Di'Nay paused, her voice hesitant. "What is it?"

"The amulet."

Di'Nay moved faster, her motions sharp and abrupt. "I have it. Now to just free my hands."

The ropes jerked and Di'Nay hissed with pain. "Di'Nay?"

"Just a cut. But my right hand is free."

A few more jerks to the ropes and Elana felt the ropes at her waist go slack and heard Di'Nay push the guard off herself. She crept around the back of the tree, obviously trying to avoid being seen in the camp. How long did they have until the guards were changed?

Elana almost wept as Di'Nay removed the amulet and threw it aside. Amarin rushed back, filling her senses and wiping away her headache. Di'Nay removed the blindfold. Even the dim light of the waning moons seemed bright as the sun. Elana blinked a dozen times before her eyes adjusted. The trees rose high overhead, the camp in the distance a cluster of lanterns and tents.

"Are you all right?" Di'Nay questioned, her thumb wiping blood from beneath Elana's nose.

Elana focused on her lover. Dried blood was matted in her hair and dark bruises blossomed around her wrists and cheek. "Di'Nay!" she exclaimed in concern.

Di'Nay shook her head and went to work severing Elana's bonds. "It's nothing, Soroi. I barely feel it. I promise. We need to get back to the Keep. Do you think you can run?"

"I only felt sick when the amulet touched me. I'm fine now," Elana promised. "It's so good to see you again."

Di'Nay smiled softly and laid a tender kiss across Elana's lips as the last of the ropes around her ankle fell free."Come."

Elana struggled to her feet, her muscles sore and tight from so long without moving. She was suddenly very aware of how hungry she was, how thirsty. She had barely noticed in the pain of captivity, but now that she was free, she realized what a bad position they were in.

"We can't be too far from the Keep. Their leader wanted to know if I felt anyone die. If we were too far away, he'd know that wouldn't be a possibility," Elana concluded as Di'Nay took her hand and they rushed into the forest.

Di'Nay looked up as she ran, trying to study the stars. "I think we're going the right direction. We need to get far enough away that we can safely make a plan. Forage for some food."

"What about scouts? Guards?" Elana questioned.

"I'm watching for them. And at least I now have a knife and my fists to protect us."

"What about horses? Did you see any? Could they catch up with us?"

"I saw a couple horses in the camp," Di'Nay confirmed. "But they'd be stupid to use them. You'd feel them coming by feeling their horses."

"Unless they have amulets affixed to their horses," Elana interjected.

Di'Nay pursed her lips in frustration. "I suppose."

Elana held her hand tighter. It was so good to have so much closeness when the most they had for the last couple days was the touch of their fingertips.

They ran until the sun started to rise. Elana couldn't trust their luck that they hadn't encountered any scouts or guards. Were they being followed? Toyed with?

Di'Nay came to a stop in a particularly thick cluster of trees. She bent forward, holding her stomach as she was suddenly overcome with weakness.

"We should stop. Rest," Elana suggested. "Find something. I can forage."

"We need to stay together," Di'Nay insisted as she straightened. "I'm fine."

"Neither of us will be fine until we get back to the Keep."

"True. Do you feel anything at all? Anything from the trees?"

Elana drew a sharp breath. She tried to commune with the trees, to use their web of amarin to more fully sense her surroundings. She let out a slow breath, the tension in her muscles starting to ease out of her consciousness. The trees were so comforting. So stable. So safe. She could feel their leaves stretching to the sky, greeting the rising sun after a long night's sleep. She could feel various creatures waking, rustling out of their nests and burrows while the nocturnal creatures were nestling down for the day.

Elana felt her fears and cares condense down to finding food, raising children, defending her burrow, and absorbing sunlight into her leaves. It was so tempting to just fall into their world. To leave herself behind. But she wasn't that disconnected from her body, nor was she ready to willing to leave Di'Nay behind in the world she was so tempted to abandon.

She focused, using the trees to extend her Sight. She looked for anything familiar, a valley she recognized or a Terran scout from Commander Turner's unit. Anything that could signify they were closer to home. But there was nothing. Only more forest.

She was about to give up when she hesitated. She felt a disturbance, a new creature stepping into her web. A creature the forest recognized and didn't see as a threat, but something the forest rejected as a part of the usual web.

"Di'Nay!" Elana let her deep connection to the forest fade into the back of her mind. For the first time in a long time she beamed a genuine smile of joy. "It's Kaing!"

Di'Nay took Elana's arm. "Kaing?"

"Not far from here, wandering the forest. He must be looking for you."

Di'Nay's shoulders sagged but her smile was radiant. "He was always a good horse."

Elana took her hand once more. "Follow me. He'll be able to take us home."

Di'Nay kept pace with Elana. "I can't wait for a big meal. A bath. Something to drink."

"We need to tell the Council about the eminent attacks," Elana reminded her.

Di'Nay nodded. "Of course. But then we can bathe and eat and collapse into a bed of furs and quilts."

The fantasy Di'Nay spun was tempting, but Elana knew she wouldn't be able to pull herself away from the Council meetings that would accompany such a warning – or the private meeting with the Mistress her superior would want to have after escaping capture. The Council would probably even want to speak with Di'Nay as she was the one who'd had use of her eyes the entire time.

"Soon," Elana assured her. "Once we know everyone is safe."

"And then we'll make a plan to destroy the Order before they can hurt anyone else," Di'Nay growled.

Elana clenched her jaw and her eyes flashed, but her rage was now tainted with a strain of fear. She could feel something coming. Something dark and threaded with loss. Something she wasn't sure she was ready to face, but she had to be. "Yes. Soon it will be over."

CHAPTER TWO

Diana sat at the Council table, her chin resting in one hand, her eyes darting between the Council members. Elana sat beside the Mistress, now strong enough to move around the Keep once more and sit at the Council table with her peers. The Master and poisoned Council members had also been released by the hospital, their health nearly back to what it had been before the attacks. But the empty chair Karis had once occupied was a stark reminder that not everyone had survived the Order. And they weren't safe yet.

The Council had been in a panic when they returned on Kaing. The Mistress swore she could still feel Elana alive, but Terran scouts had found blood and signs of a struggle. Many believed they were dead. Their return had brought hope to many in the Keep. Terran scouts had been immediately dispatched to try to find the Order camps. But Elana and Diana's story had dampened things.

Elana and Diana had barely had time to eat, drink, and change their clothes before they were called into meetings to share their stories.

"There are so many more than we thought," the Master whispered. "And they're stronger, too."

"Not necessarily stronger. The average member was fairly simple. Foolish even. But their leader seemed dangerous," Elana offered. "And even the weakest member of their order is a danger to anyone with the Sight – and especially to the seers. If any of the seers saw this coming, it's no wonder they cloistered themselves."

"They must have. They still won't let their caretakers in, and they've started screaming when they're guarded by Terrans," a councilman announced. He tugged at a soft white beard as he considered their situation.

"Perhaps they see something about the Terrans we don't," another counselor suggested, her brown eyes sharp and suspicious. "The Order knew much about Elana and her bond. They have spies in the Keep."

Diana tensed. "Only one guard was a Terran. The rest, including the leader, were of Aggar. A spy is more likely to be among the trainees than the soldiers."

"You think one of our students is working against us?" The Mistress's voice was cold.

Diana shook her head. "I don't know what to think or to expect. I just mean that everything we're learning about the Order points to the Terrans being random accomplices, not main conspirators. Elana and I bonded well before there were Terrans in the Keep. They have information from another source."

"I can't believe there are that many of our people who would want to kill us enough to actually attack the Keep," a councilman remarked.

"There are." Elana's voice was sharp. "Many of them. They were only kept in check by fear. They're still scared of our power, but not enough to stay away."

"That's a jaded way of looking at things," a councilwoman Diana had seen teaching young trainees chided. "We do a lot of good for Aggar."

"They're scared of us," Elana argued. "And some of them no longer see our value. In the grand scheme of things, we're vastly outnumbered. And if they have the ability to hide from our Sight, we no longer have an advantage outside of the natural fortifications of the Keep."

Two more members of the Council opened their mouths to speak but the Mistress held up her hand. "We've all known for a long time that the people of Aggar often don't support us. We see it in the children we bring into the Keep. We see it in the politics of the world. They don't trust us, not our power or the abilities of our Shadows. But to say the majority hate us is false. Many appreciate what we do. We've been attacked in the past. We'll be attacked again. We just have to put this particular threat down."

Diana leaned forward as Elana glanced away from the Mistress and clenched her jaw, the muscles in her cheeks trembling. The Mistress glanced at her and Diana couldn't tell if she was silently entreating her to remain silent or if she was worried about her granddaughter. If Diana hadn't seen the Mistress's distress when they first returned to the Keep, Diana would wonder if the woman realized what Elana had been through over the past couple days.

"We still need to know where the Order is getting their information about the Keep. If there are any informants in the Keep, we need to weed them out or find what they know," a councilman announced.

"We need to avoid paranoia," the Mistress commanded.

The professor councilwoman shook her head. "The students are already walking a razor's edge between anger and fear. I'm afraid they'll eventually act on that fear, especially once it spreads that Elana and Di'Nay were kidnapped. We've been telling them they were on another mission to Markessa."

"We have to keep them calm. The Terrans are our guests, but they don't have much experience against Shadows, Blue Sights, or seers. We don't want to scare them and we don't want too many of our practices and abilities drawing the attention of the Empire," the Mistress announced.

"We've already shared too much with them," a councilman groused.

"That kind of attitude won't help us," the Mistress chided. "We have to set the example for the children."

A shrill shriek echoed through the hallways. Elana leapt to her feet, followed shortly by the rest of the Council. They ran for the door as another scream rang through the corridors.

They raced down to the lecture hall where a cluster of students stood around a young Shadow and a Terran soldier collapsed on the ground.

"Dasha!" the Mistress cried.

The student spun around, her green eyes narrowed in fury. Elana grabbed Diana's arm. "Something's wrong," she hissed.

Diana furrowed her brow. "What–"

"He had an amulet!" Dasha cried, holding out an Order of Blindness pendant in her right hand.

The hall exploded in chaos. Diana couldn't make out any individual voice in the throng, but she could feel the heat of their fear and anger. She took a step back. She had to get to Alexandra.

Elana clenched her arm with both hands, her fear a palpable wave surging through Diana's lifestone. "Soroi?"

Elana pulled her back away from the crowd as two of the Council members pushed through the students and secured the Terran offender. "I have to get away from here."

"We need to talk to Alexandra. We have to stop this," Diana insisted.

Elana shook her head hard. "They'll imprison him. The Mistress with send for Commander Turner. I can't be here."

Diana laid her free hand over Elana's grasping hands, her touch gentle and reassuring. "Of course."

Diana and Elana rushed away from the madness, climbing up a nearby stairwell and making their way to their room. Once they had returned, the door locked behind them, Elana finally released her.

"Thank you."

Diana watched her lover in concern as she sat on the bed, her arms crossed over her chest as she hugged her shoulders. She was so closed off. Elana glanced at her and smiled softly, the expression forced and weak. "I'll be fine. I promise. There's just... there's so much anger. So much hate. I could barely breathe. I'm so tired of being surrounded by so much fury."

"They'll tear each other apart over this," Diana agreed. "Commander Turner's people may even have to leave."

Elana shook her head. "No. The Council knows they need the Terrans, even if they wish they didn't. They'll start a massive search. They'll root out anyone with amulets and imprison them."

"That would be a good thing, sae?"

"I think so."

"But you aren't sure?"

"Something feels off, Di'Nay. There's something no one is seeing."

"Do you have any idea what it might be?"

"I wouldn't put anything past the Order anymore."

"Do you think the Mistress will be able to keep everyone under control?"

Elana closed her eyes and shook her head. "I don't know. I just don't know."

Diana slowly sat beside her and Elana leaned back against her chest. Diana folded her in her arms and laid soft kisses in her hair.

"I don't want to talk about it right now," Elana confessed.

"We don't have to. You're safe. You're home. Let them deal

with this. Just be here with me."

"I'm so tired."

Diana held her tighter. "Then rest. You're not Eldest Prepared anymore. The Council can handle this. You owe yourself the time to heal after what you've been through. They should understand."

"I hate this," Elana muttered, her eyes still closed, her weight heavy against Diana's chest.

"Then do it for me," Diana begged. "We both need to sleep. To recover. And I don't want you far from my side until this is over."

Elana was already drifting into sleep. "Anything for you."

Diana laid back, not even bothering to undo her boots, and Elana tucked against her like a child. Whatever was happening in the Keep could wait. Whatever challenges were coming were still in the future. For now, there was only the two of them. Finally safe. Finally free. Still alive. Still together. And to Diana, that was all that mattered.

When Diana woke it was already dark outside. The twin moons were high in the sky. Elana was still in a deep sleep, resting her head on Diana's shoulder, her hands tucked against her chest. Diana couldn't remember waking more comfortably, Elana's weight and warmth soothing away the last of her fear.

Diana glanced out the window at the night sky. They'd certainly slept longer than they intended to, but the Keep was still standing and she couldn't hear any screaming. Obviously nothing too terrible had happened while they rested.

Diana closed her eyes and imagined herself far away from the Keep, sleeping on a warm summer day in the hills with Elana by her side. She only had a few moments of imagining before Elana started to shift. She rustled and finally sat up, one arm stretching out across Diana's waist.

"It's night."

"We needed the rest," Diana muttered without opening her eyes. "Do you feel better?"

Diana braced herself for Elana's frustration at sleeping too long, but Elana only sighed and laid her head back on Diana's chest. "A little."

Diana opened her eyes and ran a hand over Elana's shoulders. "I'm glad."

Elana's brow furrowed as she leaned up on her elbow. Her hair fell past her shoulders, framing her face in a thick swath of ebony. "You're surprised?"

"I thought you would be more upset about sleeping so long."

Elana laid back down on Diana's chest. It seemed whatever energy she'd regained in sleep was suddenly sapped away. "I'm not mad."

Diana glanced down at her bondmate curiously. Her tone was so different from the vengeful Shadow she'd been since the first attack. She was softer. Weaker. Sadder. "Did you have another nightmare?"

Elana shook her head. "No. I didn't dream at all."

"They would have sent for us if there were more problems," Diana pointed out. "Everything feels peaceful."

"It's not," Elana argued. "I can feel the energy in the Keep. Anger. Fear. Dissent. I wouldn't be surprised if more amulets were found. The Mistress just didn't want to wake us."

Diana clenched her teeth. "I'm sorry. That shouldn't be the first thing you feel when you wake."

"It's just a part of the Keep now. Something I can't escape."

"It'll be over soon. We'll capture the leaders of the Order. Everyone will be safe. We know they're nearby and closing in. Soon they won't be hard to find. Our information will help the scouts and soldiers find our enemies. They may have protections against seers and Blue Sights, but not empire weaponry and Shadow senses. They can't beat the Keep. Everything will go back to normal." Elana didn't respond. Diana ran her fingers through her hair, trying desperately to give her any comfort. "Do you believe that?"

Elana laid silent for a moment before finally rising up and kissing Diana, her touch gentle and protective. "I believe in this. In us."

"You didn't answer my question," Diana whispered.

"No, I didn't."

Elana climbed out of bed and started undressing. Diana raised an eyebrow. "What are you doing?"

"Getting ready for bed."

"You don't want to find out what's going on?"

"I want to sleep until someone calls for me."

"You're still tired?"

Elana kicked her boots across the room and left her clothes in a pile on the floor. "I'm exhausted, Di'Nay." Elana climbed back into bed, slipping beneath the quilts. "Are you going to stay with me?"

"Are you sure everything is safe out there?"

Elana's eyes narrowed. "I'm tired. I want to be alone or just with you. But a real problem would outweigh all of that. I'm not totally irresponsible. If the Keep was in danger, I'd go."

Diana shook her head. "No, I didn't mean that. If there's something that needs to be seen to, I'll do it so you can rest."

Elana pulled a quilt over her head and burrowed down deep into the covers. "They'll get us when they need us. Or we'll be attacked. Either way, there's nothing we can do about it. So we might as well spend the time in each other's arms."

Diana wasn't sure if she should argue or just allow Elana to heal. She only knew what she wanted to do. "You're right."

Diana stripped out of her clothes as well, leaving them in the piles Elana had begun. She climbed into bed after her bondmate and slipped under the covers with her, the blankets creating a pocket for them – a soft border between their personal world and the outside.

"I'll be fine in the morning." Elana muttered against her shoulder. "I'm not broken."

"I never thought you were."

"I know. But I wanted to say it anyway. Give me time."

"As much as you need. Just don't pull away from me."

"Not anymore. I promise."

For a moment the spark returned to Elana's eyes, untainted by sadness or anger. For a moment she was the woman she'd been when they first fell in love. When they first journeyed together. She was still there. She could still be happy.

Diana held onto that look, treasuring it. Elana smiled and kissed her again before they curled around each other and drifted back to sleep.

A pounding knock on the door drew Elana and Diana out of their dreams. Diana squeezed Elana's shoulders and slipped out of bed. The sunlight was almost blinding after sleeping in the dark cocoon of blankets and the cold was a sharp contrast after the heat and softness of Elana's skin.

She opened the door a crack and angled her head out. Telias stood on the other side. The young woman blushed honey brown.

"I'm sorry to disturb you, but is Elana awake?"

"She's not feeling well," Diana announced.

"I'm sorry, but I'm afraid I must speak with her. It's urgent."

Diana heard Elana slide out of bed and pull a nightshirt from her trunk. "What is it, Telias?" she questioned as she came to the door, freeing Diana to dress for the day.

"Three more amulets were found among the Terrans overnight. Then another this morning. In the Keep."

Elana tensed. "Among the students?"

"No. An adept. Frisk." Diana paused in recognition and Elana cocked her head to the side. "So you have met him."

"A couple times and in passing," Elana admitted. "He didn't seem to be with the Order."

"It's confusing some of the Council as well. Frisk was always a trusted member of the Keep and one of the most skilled Shadows. But it's no doubt the amulet was his. And he has the skills to attempt assassinations."

"We're shadows. We all have the skill to attempt an assassination," Elana rebutted.

"Then you do doubt his guilt."

"I have concerns, yes."

Diana finished lacing her boots and came to the door as well.

Telias squared her shoulders. "He's asking for you, Elana. Says he won't speak to anyone else. Do you know why that would be?"

Elana hesitated, her eyes narrowing as she read the younger woman. "Are you suspicious of me, Telias?"

"I'm suspicious of everyone. It isn't personal."

"I don't know why Frisk would be asking for me. Again, we've barely met. But He did safely deliver a seer child and an adult seer back to the Keep after an Order attack and he sent for Diana and I after the second round of attacks and we safely arrived at the Keep. He had many chances to betray us and he never did."

"Perhaps his orders were not to draw suspicion."

Elana crossed her arms over her chest. "I never took you for paranoid."

In this world where there's no way to tell who is speaking truth, where the seers won't communicate with us and our Blue Sights are blind, only a fool isn't paranoid."

"If you keep thinking like that, we'll fall to the Order," Elana warned.

"Is that a vision?"

"Just common sense." Elana glanced back at Diana, her weakness from the night before vanishing in the heat of necessity. "I'll dress and then Di'Nay and I will go to Frisk. Where is he being held?"

"All prisoners are being held in the dungeons."

"The Keep has dungeons?" Diana questioned.

"We haven't needed them in generations. But yes," Telias informed her.

"We'll be there in moments," Elana informed her, then shut the door. "This is getting out of hand," Elana huffed as she dressed for the day.

"You really have that much faith in Frisk's innocence?" Diana questioned.

"I don't mean Frisk. Telias has always had a level head. Now she's spiraling. If she's that scared, many others will be far more unstable."

"I never thought the Keep would become so volatile. Everyone always seemed so logical. Even divorced from their emotions."

Elana finished lacing her boots and began braiding back her hair, her slender fingers moving with a practiced ease. "It's easy to be confident when you have access to powers and abilities the rest of the world doesn't. It's easy to be cold and talk about divorcing from emotion when you feel secure. But many of the members of the Keep come from broken pasts and we no longer can trust our special abilities. The fact that we could be captured and held for so long out in the forest proves that to even the most skeptical adept – unless they come to think we faked it. They feel powerless again. I suspect we'll see a wide array of coping techniques before this is over."

Diana folded her arms across her chest. "Will being with me hurt your reputation? Will they be more suspicious of you? I'm an off-worlder."

Elana stood and kissed her, her blue eyes even and fierce. "I don't care what they come to think of you or us. And if we can stop this chaos before it grows too out of hand, it won't matter."

Diana smiled. "I'm glad to see you strong again, Soroi."

"I'm always strong, Di'Nay. Sometimes I just don't want to be."

Elana swept out of the room and Diana rushed to stay at her side. They descended into the depths of the Keep, following a maze of stairwells and hallways Diana had never traversed. As they reached the entrance to the dungeon, Diana held back a snort of laughter. Stacks of cauldrons, crates of supplies, extra mattresses and various other furniture and storage were stacked along the walls, bleeding out into the halls. It was clear the dungeon, so long out of use, had been used for storage.

A cluster of Shadows stood guard beside a row of doors. An older man with a long, graying beard rushed forward in relief. "Elana, I'm glad you could come. He won't talk to anyone else. He just demands to speak with you."

"How is he?"

"Focused. He doesn't seem scared. It... isn't helping his case around here." The man glanced anxiously over his shoulder. "I've known Frisk since he was a boy. I've been his teacher since before he was allowed to begin lessons. He's incredibly loyal. He wouldn't turn on the Keep. I know it."

"I heard we know for a fact he was in possession of an amulet," Elana countered.

"It was found in his bag as he carried it, yes. And he hasn't denied it's his. But he wasn't wearing it. And the bearer must make direct contact with it for it to work, yes?"

"I thought so," Elana admitted. "I don't think any of us know what all the amulet can do."

"Frisk isn't a member of the Order of Blindness. I'd stake my entire reputation on it."

"You probably have," Elana remarked. "But I'll talk to him."

"Thank you."

The man led Elana and Diana toward Frisk's door on the end of the row. He opened the door slowly. Frisk sat in the corner of a small stone room, his arms resting on his knees and his eyes turned to the ground.

Elana and Diana stepped into the room, but Frisk looked up sharply as another guard tried to follow. "No one but Elana and her bondmate."

"We have to protect them," one of the guards groused.

"I won't attack anyone," Frisk groused as he raised his hands to show once more he was unarmed.

"I can protect her," Diana countered, not wanting another fight.

The guard and Diana exchanged glances, but the guard finally nodded. "Fine. But we'll be right outside if you need us."

"Thank you."

The prison door closed behind them. Elana crouched down in front of Frisk, her face unreadable. "What did you want to talk to me about?" Frisk glanced at the door, his face tense. Elana cocked her head to the side. "You don't really have the luxury of not being overheard. We're as alone as possible."

"I'm not a danger to you."

"You had an amulet."

"Yes."

"Was it yours?"

"Yes."

Elana hesitated. Diana raised an eyebrow. She'd expected him to deny it, or at least have an excuse for it.

"You're a member of the Order of Blindness?"

"No."

"For someone who was demanding to speak with me, you're not particularly communicative." Frisk glanced at the door again. Elana glared. Diana turned to the door in shock as she heard a shambling shuffle and then the sound of boots walking away.

"What did you do?" Frisk questioned.

"Those susceptible to my Sight have walked away. The rest won't hear anything we say."

"Is that wise?" Diana questioned. "What if we need their help?"

"His intentions aren't dark," Elana informed her. "And I want to know what he has to say."

"They really can't hear us?"

"Either you trust me or you don't," Elana countered.

Frisk sat up straighter, firming his chin as he made up his mind. "I had an amulet because I was studying it. It was sent to me from Markessa."

"Who in Markessa is sending you amulets?" Diana questioned.

Elana stood, looking down at Frisk with a glare. "You're with the Royal Marshals."

"Yes."

"You're a Shadow of the Keep," Elana argued.

"They aren't mutually exclusive."

There was something about the way he spoke that seemed familiar to Diana. She sucked in a sharp breath. "You're related to Tristan."

Frisk curled his lips in an unreadable look of frustration. “I left those family ties behind when I became a Shadow. But in another life, yes, he was my brother.”

“You're not a Shadow. You don't belong to the Keep. You're Tristan's informant, aren't you? How long have you been working for them?”

Frisk's eyes were alight with anger, but he didn't lose his temper. He didn't so much as tense in his relaxed seated position. “I'm not a traitor. I want to keep the Ramains safe. It's important to maintaining peace in Aggar. So yes, I joined the Marshals. And yes, I keep them informed of necessary information about the Keep. But I don't tell them everything, and I respect our privacy. It's a fine line to walk, but I've never betrayed anyone. I've been trying to help.”

“Tristan did seem to want to help us,” Diana reminded her.

“Have I ever been anything but loyal to the Keep?” Frisk demanded. “If I had wanted you dead, I could have killed you many times over. I've done more for the Keep than I ever have for the Marshals. I chose this life and I've dedicated myself to it more fully than most. And whether you agree with my decisions or not, you know I'm telling the truth. You know my motives are pure.”

Elana and Diana exchanged glances. “I'm inclined to believe him,” Diana commented, her voice hesitant.

“Why?” Elana's question was sincere.

Diana considered. “He was... gentle with the seer child. He didn't seem scared or hateful.”

Diana's response gave Elana pause. Frisk sent her a thankful glance. After a long moment, Elana turned back to Frisk. “What do you expect me to do?”

“You need to get me out of prison. I'm no help to anyone here. And the Marshals have been doing more than you know.”

“Then you need to convince the Mistress you aren't a threat. Tell her about the Marshals.”

Frisk shook his head. “The Marshals can't act effectively if too many people know about us. Especially someone as powerful as the leader of the Keep. My trustworthiness would be compromised. I'd lose my place as a Shadow and a Marshal. Tristan took an enormous risk even telling the two of you.”

“How am I supposed to get you out without telling anyone the truth?”

"You have to think of something. You're the only one I can trust."

"It might take me a while," Elana confessed.

"You'll want to move quickly. Tristan expects me to regularly report. If I stop, he'll know something's wrong and he may send people for me."

"You told me the Marshals are allies of the Keep," Elana countered.

"The Marshals protect the Ramains. As long as their goals align with yours, then you're safe. But if you ever diverge, the Marshals will protect their country above all."

"I'm not afraid of them," Elana growled.

"You should be. If you think the Order and their amulets are frightening, you don't want to go up against the resources of the Marshals."

"Is that a threat?" Diana questioned.

"Not at all. It's a friendly warning. If Tristan thinks I'm in trouble, he'll see me freed. Trust me it would be better for everyone if you help me before he finds out."

"If the Marshals go against the Keep, which side will you align with?" Elana questioned.

Frisk drew a sharp breath. "I'd rather it not come to that."

"Do you know anything about the Order of the amulets that you aren't telling us?" Diana demanded.

"Not about the amulets. But we're closing in on the identities of the leaders of the Order. The strategists. Tristan believes they're a group of nobles from the Ramains."

"They're? More than one?" Elana questioned.

"Most definitely. There's no way one person could pull something like this off. They may have a single leader, and they certainly have a mob of ignorant muscle, but there are more than a few truly dangerous leaders among the Order."

"If you know so much about the Order and you have so many resources, why aren't you and the other Marshals finding the assassins for us?"

"We'll step in when we're truly needed."

"One of our Councilmen have already been killed. When will you judge this situation dire enough to act?"

"I'm afraid counselor Karis's death, while unfortunate, wasn't deemed a large enough threat to the nation." Elana reared up in fury, but Frisk raised his hands inoffensively. “I didn't agree with them. I petitioned for help. But I couldn't sway them. They have to weigh the severity of the threat to the potential for exposure. For what it's worth, I've been doing everything I can on my own. And I'll continue petitioning for help until they either agree or the threat is neutralized.”

Elana grunted. “I'll talk to the Mistress. I'll do what I can to help. But you can tell Tristan I don't appreciate the way he's playing with our lives. And if I ever find you've turned your back on the Keep –”

“With all respect, Elana, I've been living this life since I was a child. I know what's expected of me. And I know how to balance my loyalties. There's nothing more important to me than my Keep. And there's nothing more important than my country. I truly believe they depend on each other. And I'll do everything I can, until my last breath, to ensure the safety of both.”

Elana nodded sharply and the sound of boots echoed through the halls again. “I expect a lot from you, Frisk. Now that I know your resources, I'll expect you to use them to keep us safe.”

Frisk leaned back against the wall again. “Thank you. For everything.”

Elana opened the prison door and Diana followed her back into the hall. The guards seemed dazed, barely aware of the two women as they walked away. Diana studied them in awe, then looked at her goddess of a lover. Just when she thought Elana couldn't surprise her with her power anymore...

“I'm going to speak with the Mistress,” Elana announced. “Do you want to come with me?”

“Don't expect me to leave you alone until this is over, Soroi,” Diana returned. “You're going to get sick of me. But neither of us will be kidnapped without the other.”

Elana smiled at her. “I could never be sick of you, Di'Nay.”

“Give it a couple decades,” Diana returned.

Elana took her hand. “I'd be happy to.”

CHAPTER THREE

Elana stared into the distance, her arms crossed over her chest. The sun was sinking, casting the sky in a fiery swath of color that reminded Elana of her father's forge and the molten colors of her mother's glassworks. She'd heard so many describe fire as destructive. As dangerous. But on quiet evenings she couldn't help but see it as creative and bonding. Refining.

It stood in stark contrast to chaos in the air and her growing tension about the Order's threats. Any moment, an assassin could strike or a party of raiders could attack the Keep and the threats from inside the Keep seemed even more hazardous. She'd never felt so blind.

"There you are."

Di'Nay stepped up beside her and leaned back against the wall, facing Elana. Despite all the sleep they'd gotten the night before, she looked exhausted.

"There haven't been any more amulets found, but everyone's in a panic. I stopped three fights today myself. Everyone's on edge."

"Word has finally spread about what happened to us," Elana agreed. "They're scared. Maybe we should evacuate."

"I don't think we could navigate a successful evacuation. Not with tempers this high," Di'Nay stated. "The Keep is well fortified. More so than anywhere else we could go."

Elana sighed. "You're right. Sometimes I just wonder if it would be easier for us to hide. The seers seem to have the right idea."

"They finally made contact with their guards. Asking for food. Once they were given supplies, they locked themselves in again."

"Like I said. They're the only ones making sense right now."

Di'Nay smiled softly, but it didn't reach her eyes. “I thought you'd be in meetings with the Council.”

“I wasn't invited. Not after I spoke with the Mistress about Frisk. I think they're discussing what to do with him. Or perhaps they don't trust me enough to be involved in making decisions anymore.”

“Why wouldn't they trust you?”

“Most of them don't buy my confidence that Frisk is innocent. It's not much of a logical leap to go from wondering why I'd try to get Frisk freed to considering that I'm involved with the Order.”

“What?” Di'Nay's rage was like a blast of sunlight against Elana's skin. Sudden and hot, but comforting. “After everything you went through? How dare they?”

“They're just as scared as everyone else. Perhaps more since they're used to having multiple ways to get information. We weren't ready for something like this.”

“Do you think they'll be ready when the Order attacks? I'd think they'd move faster once they realized we escaped.”

“I've thought about that every moment since we got back. We're more unorganized than ever.”

Elana flinched as she felt a sudden spike of anger and rage, followed closely by the sound at least three people crying out. Di'Nay spun around to look out the window. Another fight already broke out. Di'Nay moved to run down the stairs, but a small cluster of Alexandra's soldiers rushed to do it instead.

“Those were all students,” Di'Nay observed.

“I noticed,” Elana responded, her voice heavy and sad. “No one trusts anyone anymore.”

“Another reason they can't travel.”

Elana considered Di'Nay, letting her mind wander over their options. “They can't travel, but we can.”

“What do you mean?”

“I don't want to sit here and wait for the Keep to fall to pieces or the Order to attack. I don't want to sit here while I'm second guessed and suspected. I want to go on the offensive.”

“How?”

“We need more information. We need to know how many members of the Order are out there and if they're moving in on us. If possible, I want to capture one of their people. Learn more about their plans and capabilities. I want to to turn the tables.”

"You don't mean..."

"I want to go out after them."

Di'Nay pushed off from the wall, her face lined with confusion and concern. "Is that wise? We just escaped. You've been having nightmares. I can see how traumatic capture was for you."

"I'm having nightmares and feel violated because I feel like my power has been taken away. And not just my Sight," Elana insisted. "I never want to be tied up again. I never want to be under their control again. But sitting here worrying and wallowing is just as effective as ropes and chains. And I'm tired of it. I may not be able to sense them with my Sight, but I'm still a Shadow of the Keep. As far as we know, they don't have any particular way of tracking Blue Sights, just blocking us from sensing them. I know they're out there. I can get what I need. What we all need."

Di'Nay studied her, obviously trying to choose her words carefully. "Are you all right with leaving the Council?"

"I'm not protecting them much now. And half of them are starting to suspect I'm a traitor."

"Are you sure?"

"Yes." The word was precise and sharp, clipped by Elana's determination.

"You've obviously made up your mind. Tell me what you want me to do. I'm with you."

Elana took Di'Nay's hand. "We should change into something more mobile. We'll leave once darkness falls."

Elana knew the forests around the Keep like the palm of her own hand. She'd grown up in these woods. She'd learned to be a Shadow in its pools of darkness. She knew its amarin like a friend. Like a pet. It was gentle and supportive. But now it was tainted.

The trees were still whispering their distress to each other. They could sense the corruption creeping through their forest. They felt just as confused and violated as Elana. Their energies resonated together, connecting them even when Elana wasn't specifically concentrating on them.

Elana wondered if the Order knew how connected she was to nature – how much she could use the anger of the trees to find them. She doubted they knew anything. They were so scared she was a demon bent on controlling or possessing them that they didn't understand the real nature of her abilities – she was connected to Aggar. She was made to See and understand the ways the planet interconnected with every living thing she supported and grew. Blue Sights weren't born to control people. They were born to be conduits for Aggar herself.

It was that basic understanding of her nature that would be the Order's downfall. Unless they trapped her in a stone cell, devoid of any life or contact with living things, they couldn't truly blind her. They could only increase their chances of hiding.

"Do you feel anything?" Di'Nay requested. She crept closer to Elana, her sleek black pants and shirt didn't even rustle as she moved.

"Not yet, but the trees are angry and complaining. We can't be far."

Elana turned as she felt a new presence. An eitteh, its silver-white paws standing out in the darkness, landed hard on the ground. Elana's brow creased in concern as the creature limped forward.

"Poor thing," Elana cooed as she slowly approached the winged-cat. It mewed as she attempted to scoop it into her arms and flinched. Elana back away a step, her hand outstretched. After a moment, the eitteh allowed her to pet between its ears, its fur soft and downy.

"What happened?" Di'Nay questioned.

"Someone tried to shoot her. Probably from the Order. She hit her back legs trying to flee," Elana explained. "At least she avoided the arrow."

"Are they broken?"

Elana shook her head. "No. Just bruised."

"Why would they shoot at an eitteh?"

"Who knows? Meat. Annoyance. Some people think eitteh have the Sight. It could have been an attack out of anger."

The eitteh finally curled up in Elana's arms and started to purr. Its voice was deep and rumbling. Elana smiled as she felt the winged-cat's appreciation. "Where were you hurt, Little One?" Elana muttered as the cat closed her eyes and pressed her head into her hand.

Elana tried to comfort the eitteh as she studied its amarin for clues of where the Order members who attacked it were camping. She could see flashes of trees and soil. She heard voices through the eitteh's thoughts. They had to be nearby. The memories were still so clear.

Elana ran her hands gently over the eitteh's bruised hips and willed as much comfort and health into her as she could. Her Sight couldn't heal, but she could give some relief. "Thank you."

She shifted her weight and eased the cat onto a soft bed of clover and fern, the foliage spongy and thick. She could rest until she felt strong enough to fly again.

"Did you See anything?" Di'Nay questioned.

"They're nearby. At least a few of them. Enough for now."

Elana crept through the forest again, sliding from shadow to shadow. Di'Nay stayed close enough to defend her, but far enough away to both assess their surroundings and not draw attention with her heavier footfalls.

Elana fought to focus, trying to find a good balance between using her Sight and knowing she couldn't rely on her Sight alone. She had to use her eyes. It felt mundane. Almost disorienting. Primitive. But part of her was thankful life had revealed a new weakness to her.

She wondered once again what her life would be like if she lost her Sight upon leaving Aggar. She pushed it out of her mind. It wasn't the time to dwell on the future.

Elana crouched low beside the massive trunk of an ancient tree. The rough bark beneath her hands both centered her in the present and appealed to her Sight. She could feel the slow pulse of the sap just under the bark, keeping time with the tree's amarin.

A cluster of members of the Order of Blindness crouched around a fire, warming their hands. Seeing them was comforting despite the fact that she couldn't feel them. She could feel Di'Nay at her back, keeping her safe. She was finally the hunter.

The Order didn't wear the face scarves they had when capturing Elana. She memorized all of their faces; every scar, line, peak and curve. No matter what happened tonight, these three would never escape her vengeance.

Elana glanced back at Di'Nay, her lover crouched low, one hand on a sword at her waist. Elana drew a knife from her belt. They nodded to each other and tensed to charge when a new voice called out of the trees.

"You have reports from Terrol's camp?"

"They're closing in along the northern border. You came alone?"

"I'm not afraid like the rest of you," the Leader hissed.

Elana's breath caught in her throat. She recognized the voice. The leader of the Order stepped into the clearing, his face lit by the fire and the moonlight. Di'Nay moved closer, grabbing Elana's hand, but Elana was beyond feeling. Di'Nay was worried she'd feel threatened. That she'd be scared. But that was the last thing on Elana's mind.

"He's mine," Elana hissed.

"And the others?"

"Liabilities. They made their choice before they ever came to the Keep."

Di'Nay studied her face for a moment, but finally nodded. "Now?"

Elana and Di'Nay leapt out of the trees. The Order turned in shock but they hardly had time to react. Di'Nay ran one through and Elana stabbed the other. Di'Nay was making quick work of the third as the leader of the Order drew his sword and parried Elana's blow. He held both women off for a time – Elana knew immediately he had to have been trained in either the military or court – but he couldn't last long.

Within a few strikes, Di'Nay knocked him to the ground and leveled her sword at his back.

Elana crouched beside him and kicked his knife away. He looked up at her, his eyes alight with rage. "You came back."

Elana didn't respond. She didn't need to. She grabbed the chain of his amulet, clenching her teeth against the pain as she removed it and threw it into the fire.

In an instant his amarin was open to her. In his panic his thoughts and emotions came in fits and starts. She felt his fear, his anger, and his crushed pride all at once. She looked directly into his eyes, holding him captive as she sifted through his amarin in a way she never had in her adult life. She didn't care if she hurt him. She wanted to know what he was hiding, who he was. She needed to know how to save her family. And she wasn't too proud to admit to herself that she wanted to see him suffer.

His nose started to bleed and he trembled hard enough Di'Nay moved her sword so as not to accidentally impale him.

"Elana, that's enough for now," Di'Nay warned.

Elana didn't let up. She felt hints at everything rushing through his mind. Everything he most desperately didn't want her to See, his shame and fear bringing those things to the front of his mind. He thought she could read his thoughts. She smiled, feral and wicked.

"Elana!" Di'Nay gasped, her voice full of shock and pleading.

Elana glanced at away, breaking her bond with the man. She didn't want to scare Di'Nay. She used the last of their connection to knock him unconscious, then she retreated entirely.

She stood and took a step back as Di'Nay heaved his unconscious body up. Elana dug through the camp supplies and tossed Di'Nay a length of rope. Di'Nay tied him to a nearby tree then moved to stand beside Elana as she used her Sight to wake their captive.

The leader rustled. He glanced around, his eyes clouded as he slowly became aware of his surroundings. He flexed against his bonds, but Di'Nay had secured him well.

"My scouts will find me," he muttered, his voice thick and heavy as he tried to wake from semi-consciousness. Elana grinned at the realization that he was more susceptible than most to the effects of the Sight.

"You'll be dead first," Elana threatened. "I just need you alive long enough to study your thoughts."

"You wouldn't kill me here. You'll take me back to your dungeon," he countered.

"You underestimate my cruelty or you overestimate my kindness," Elana warned. "You also seem to think you have some power here. You don't."

He started to panic. Elana could feel his heart racing, the pound a ripple in the amarin around her that beat against her skin.

"What's your name?" Di'Nay demanded.

The man glared up at her, his jaw clenched in defiance.

"I don't care what his name is," Elana countered. "He's nothing. He's weak without his amulet. I want to know what he's planning for the Keep. When are you attacking us?"

"Why don't you read my mind?" he demanded. "You can't, can you? I've trained for this."

Elana sneered as she grabbed his hair, yanking his head back and forcing him to meet her eyes. Their connection was too intense. A trickle of blood ran from his nose and his breath came in sharp bursts. Elana broke their connection right before he passed out.

"I can do whatever I want to you. But I want to hear it from your mouth. You know you can't fight me. You're brave when you can cripple me with an amulet – when you can tie me up and taunt me and threaten to experiment on me. But you can't challenge me directly. You're smarter than that, aren't you? Some rich bigot who decided to puff his own ego leading a band of idiots on a crusade. You're just a good actor. Educated, but weak. Nothing else."

"You don't know anything about me!" he shot back, but Elana could feel she'd struck a chord.

Elana leaned back. "You're no threat. Not really. And you'll tell me what you have planned or I'll kill you now for being completely worthless."

He trembled with fear, his eyes darting around the clearing as he tried to avoid Elana.

"He's not going to tell us anything," Di'Nay sighed.

"Yes he will." Elana drew her knife and pressed it against his throat. He closed his eyes, breathing heavily, sweat pouring down his forehead. "I will rip your mind to pieces. I won't even kill you. You'll just stay here, a shriveled, brainless husk. And you won't even have a way to end it."

"Please... please don't..." his please were barely audible, but Elana smiled.

"After what you did to me?"

"I'm sorry."

"You're not. You're sorry you're here. But I don't need your apology. I need what you know. Tell me."

He let out a bursting sob, his breath exploding out of him in a single sound of pain and defeat. "We aren't."

"Aren't what?"

"We aren't attacking you."

Elana hesitated. "What?"

"There aren't enough of us. More and more abandon the cause every day. We never could have stormed the Keep."

"He's lying," Di'Nay accused. "We saw how widespread the Order is!"

"I'm not!" he shouted. "Yes, the Order is large. And many supported us when we were poisoning and sending in assassins, but they wouldn't come with us to the Keep."

Elana removed her knife. His amarin didn't show a hint of deception. "Then what are you doing here?"

"We're sowing distrust. Fear. Paranoia. Our operatives among the Terrans have been hiding amulets. We poisoned who we could. We killed one of the Counselors. We wanted to scare you."

"What good would that do? Just scare us? Put us on edge? Why?"

"Because you're the most powerful people on Aggar. No one can take the Keep while its people are united. But if we could divide you..."

"You were hoping they'd turn on each other," Di'Nay accused.

"Or disband. Or splinter. Then we could attack."

Elana glanced up at Di'Nay in shock. All this time, all the energy she'd spent being afraid was for this? This pathetic man? This plan that should have been, at worst, an annoyance? This is what had nearly undone her?

Elana stood. "If you're lying to me..."

"I'm not," he swore.

"The Council will want to see him," Di'Nay announced. "It will clear you of any doubt."

Elana could feel her unspoken message. She was afraid Elana would really kill him. "You're right. We'll take him to the Keep."

He went into a panic, struggling against the ropes, his eyes wild. "Don't take me there."

"Be thankful you're not laying in a pool of your own blood. Or worse," Di'Nay grunted as she untied his ropes. "If you try to flee, Elana will knock you out again."

He didn't fight. Di'Nay tied his hands behind his back and then to his waist, creating a leash he couldn't pull against.

"When you disappear, the rest of your followers will, too, won't they?"

"Probably."

"You aren't fooling anyone," Elana groused.

"What do you mean?"

"You're trying to make your organization sound weak. Like it isn't a threat."

"It's not."

"It is. Those amulets aren't trinkets from the Markessa marketplace. We've been warned how widespread your organization is. How powerful in local circles. Wide enough that you can't be its ringleader. Maybe the others didn't support your campaign here, but that doesn't make them benign."

He fell silent, no longer knowing what to say or how to handle his situation. Elana was grateful. She was sick of his voice. She was tired of this siege. More than anything, she wanted to stop the darkness in the Keep before it spread out of control.

CHAPTER FOUR

The rope in Diana's hand dug into her skin as she pulled the Order of Blindness leader through the forest. He wasn't fighting her, his spirit was already broken, but Diana couldn't seem to loosen her grip. She wasn't going to risk him escaping. The rope felt like a lifeline. With the leader of the Order in custody, they would be able to find the rest of the camps. The Terrans – those who weren't Order plants – would be able to sweep the forest. The innocent would be cleared. Perhaps they'd even learn more about the amulets.

Elana walked ahead of them, her steps even and swift. She wasn't hiding anymore. She wasn't scared. But she was still a complex patchwork of emotion Diana couldn't figure out on her own. Diana couldn't predict what she'd do next. But she liked seeing her more confident and less sad.

As they reached the ridge of the hillside that overlooked the Keep, Elana hesitated. "Di'Nay."

Diana moved forward. Elana sounded suddenly terrified. "What is it? What's –" Diana's question died on her lips as she caught sight of a dancing orange flame in the courtyard. It was too big to be a campfire.

"I can feel the Keep."

"The amarin? From here?"

Elana turned and met her eyes. Diana's breath caught in her throat as she felt a hint of what Elana did. An overwhelming wave of darkness and anger. She felt the heat of flames and could hear a cacophony of screaming and shouting. Somehow Diana knew it wasn't the Order causing the chaos.

"You can feel it this far away, then?" The leader of the Order took a step forward, a bit of his smugness returning at the look of horror on Elana's face. "I always wondered how close you'd have to be to feel them dying."

Elana turned to Diana, her eyes aflame. "Can you carry him?"

Diana nodded, already knowing what Elana would do. Her lover strode forward and grabbed the leader of the Order by his collar. A moment later he was unconscious.

"We have to get back to the Keep," Elana shouted.

Diana hoisted their prisoner into her arms and then over her back. Settling his weight, Diana raced after Elana toward the Keep.

A swell of heat billowed over them as they reached the entrance to the courtyard. Diana could hear the horses in the stables whinnying in terror and the pound of their hooves against their stalls. If they weren't calmed soon, some might die from fright. Diana silently prayed Kaing would be able to calm them. He was much more aware than the others and better under stress. Unless they were attacked directly, he would remain calm.

As they passed the stables, Diana could hear shouting. Smoke filled her lungs and mouth. The flames were coming from the Terran camp.

Elana ran faster, leaving her behind. Diana didn't call out. She knew what she had to do and Elana trusted her.

She ran for the Keep, heading for the dungeons. The entryway to the Keep was unnaturally empty. Everyone had to be out in the camp. The thought gave her an extra surge of adrenaline and she sprinted the rest of the way.

"What's going on?" she demanded of the only guard left in the prisons.

The Shadow gasped, stuttering over his words. "I – I don't know who started it. I just heard the screams. Then there was fire. They're going to kill each other."

Diana found an empty cell and shut the Order leader inside. "This man must be watched. He can't get away, do you understand? You need to stay here. Elana and I will sort this out."

The man nodded sharply, thankful for orders. "I will."

"Di'Nay!" Frisk shouted as he banged on his cell door. "Di'Nay, let me out!"

"Release him," Diana ordered.

"But –"

"We need his help."

The Shadow regarded her for a moment longer, then did as he was told. Frisk burst out of the room, his knuckles chaffed from pounding on the wooden door. "Thank you."

They raced out of the dungeon, Frisk staying a single stride behind her as she guided him toward the fight. The fire was dying down as they threw open the front doors of the Keep and raced toward the Terran camp. A cluster of Terran tents were reduced to ashes while two others collapsed. Diana silently prayed no one had been trapped sleeping inside.

Diana's heart raced as she spotted splatters of blood on the courtyard stones and spotted the first body – a Terran soldier slumped up against the castle wall. Diana didn't dare check if he was alive or not. She had to focus on the pockets of Shadows and soldiers brawling across the courtyard and gardens before the set everything ablaze.

"Stop it!" Diana could make out Elana's cries in the distance. She sprinted to her side as Elana grabbed a young Shadow by the arms and pulled her away as Alexandra held back a soldier.

"He's from the Order!" the Shadow shrieked.

"Blue-eyed demon attacked me!" the soldier countered.

Alexandra bashed her soldier over the head and he dropped, instantly unconscious.

"This is done," Elana hissed in the Shadow's ear. "We have the leader of the Order. We're not under attack."

"I'm supposed to believe you? Where have you been all night, Elana?"

"Use your Sight," Elana demanded.

"What if you have an amulet?"

"Think about what you just said. You can feel me. Tell me I'm lying."

The younger Blue Sight closed her eyes and slowly stopped fighting. "I'm sorry."

"Don't be sorry. Help me stop this fight. You have the Sight. Use it for good."

The Blue Sight raced to the nearest cluster of fighters.

"What happened?" Diana demanded of Alexandra.

"Another amulet was found. This one on a student. A student who had accused two of my men of being traitors. A brawl broke out, then it spread through my camp. I can't believe this got so out of control. That so many of my people would be involved in such a corrupt organization," Alexandra seethed as she stepped over her fallen soldier. "I thought I could trust them."

"They may not all be guilty. Some of the amulets were plants."

Alexandra's eyes flashed. "What?"

"We'll talk later. We need to get this under control now," Elana insisted. Her eyes were wild, her shoulders tense.

"What do you feel?" Diana questioned.

"They've moved into the Keep."

Alexandra nodded to her lieutenant. "Well take care of the rest out here. Go."

Elana and Diana raced for the Keep. The entryway was as empty as before, but Elana wasn't deterred. She led Diana up the stairs toward the lecture halls. The sounds of pounding feet and furniture shattering echoed through the halls.

"Stop!" Elana screamed as she reached the main lecture hall.

A cluster of Councilmen, soldiers, and students brawled. The bookshelves were torn down, books and pages scattered across the circular room. The benches were toppled and splintered. Half a dozen fighters were scattered and unconscious.

"Please! Stop!" an old councilwoman – a teacher – stood in the center of the room pleading for sanity. She spotted Elana and Diana as they entered and her eyes lit with hope. "Elana!"

Diana watched in awe as Diana tore through the room, grabbing every fighter and using her Sight to knock them all unconscious. She was a goddess of vengeance, her movements swift and merciless, but Diana couldn't help but notice how gently they all slipped away. How often she tried to break their fall. In a matter of moments everyone but the teacher were draped across the floor and whatever benches still stood.

"Thank you." The teacher held her face, her ancient, willowy hands trembling. "They destroyed my books. My classroom."

Elana held her shoulders, "It will be all right. The fighting is breaking up. We have it under control. And we have the leader of the Order prisoner. This is almost over. I promise."

"You have a prisoner?"

"Yes. Now get to your room. Lock the door until everything's quiet again."

"My classroom..."

"Can be fixed. Please. Keep yourself safe."

"I will. I promise."

Elana and Diana watched her go. "This is ridiculous," she hissed. "We played right into his plan!"

"It will be all right," Diana assured her.

Elana shook her head, adamant. "I feel something."

"Still?"

Elana nodded. "I just don't know what..."

Elana's voice faded as a massive blast rocked the Keep. Elana cried out in horror and, as the vibrations stilled, she was already running for the door. Diana watched her go in shock, dust and debris shaken loose from the mortar of the stone keep filled the air, leaving a salty, earthy taste in Diana's mouth. Her ears rang and her skin was cold from shock. She'd never met someone from Aggar who used bombs.

As her head cleared and the ringing in her ears dimmed, Diana took off after her lover. She reached the path that led to the front door as another blast rocked the building, nearly sending her pitching down a steep stairwell. More stone and mortar rained down over her head and shoulders and she glanced along the walls, searching or signs of cracks or instability. Despite being unsettled, the building seemed to be secure.

Elana's scream filled the air as Diana raced into the courtyard. She felt a burst of pain spread up her arm through their lifestone and she spun around wildly, looking for her bondmate.

"Elana!" she cried into the chaos, trying to trust her instincts to find Elana in the madness. Smoke filled the air as the last of the tents smoldered. The bombs must have detonated in the Terran camp.

The blasts had shaken those less-dedicated to fighting out of their madness. They raced through the crowds, pushing people apart and trying to protect the Keep from more explosions. Both Terran soldiers and Keep adepts worked together to put out the fires.

Elana screamed again, the sound a howl of misery. Diana grunted and held her arm as another surge of pain spread up her arm. It was getting stronger. Was Elana hurt? Wounded? Dying?

Diana grabbed Telias as she ran past, her cheeks smeared with soot and blood. Her robes were singed. "Where's Elana?" Diana demanded.

"T-there." Telias pointed at the entrance to a garden along the south wall of the Keep. The gate was stained with soot and fiery scars. The tops of the trees were scorched.

Diana released Telias and ran. Elana's cries grew louder as she reached the gate. A cluster of students and councilmen stood in a bunch. Diana's heart dropped. They had to be looking at something.

"Let me through," she grunted as she pushed her way to the center of the crowd. She froze in shock.

Elana was draped across the ground, weeping and wailing as she gathered the body of the Mistress into her arms. The elderly woman was singed and battered, her body spotted with bruises and burns. Diana caught a faint movement over her hand – she wasn't dead yet – but Diana knew she wouldn't survive her injuries.

She slowly approached Elana and her grandmother, her heart breaking in horror and from the overwhelming wave of Elana's grief. Everything they'd done to keep her safe – everything Elana had sacrificed – was made worthless by a single act of violence.

Diana knelt beside her lover, but Elana barely seemed to notice. She rocked her grandmother, weeping into her shoulder, willing her to live.

"Ona. Ona..." the Mistress whispered, her voice labored and fragile all at once. "Ona, listen to me."

"Diana will get you a healer. We can –"

The Mistress shook her head and Elana fell silent. "You already know I'm beyond healing."

Tears streamed down Elana's cheeks. "I worked so hard to save you."

"You can't linger with me, Ona. You have to stop the fighting. You have to save the Keep."

"I'm not leaving you," Elana insisted.

The Mistress raised one weathered hand and touched Elana's cheek. "I've lived a long time. This isn't a tragedy. It's the Mother finally calling me home."

"It's not. You were attacked. This was their fault! It –"

"Ona." the Mistress placed the last of her strength into the single, stern word. "Do not use the memory of my life to fuel your anger. Don't you dare."

Elana's face fell and she buried her head in the Mistress's shoulder, her anger instantly shattering into all-consuming sadness.

"Don't leave me."

"I have to. But Ona... Elana... listen to me. Please." Elana glanced up and the Mistress held her face, their eyes loving as a cloud started to form in the Mistress's gaze. "I spent my life dedicated to the Shadow. To putting my family aside. It lost me my husband and my daughter. But it always seemed worth it. Until now."

"Mistress?"

"You're my family, Elana. You always have been. And I want you to know... I want you to *know* before I die that I love you. I'm so proud of you. I have been since you were a little girl. My Ona. My Elana. My last connection with my daughter who disowned me."

"Grandmother?"

The Mistress lost the last of her strength, all her wait collapsed into Elana's arms. She looked up at the clouds and the upper towers of the Keep as she started to fade. "She named you for me, you know. My Rai. A curse if ever I heard one." The Mistress laughed once, the sound more like a tense exhale of breath than a cheer. "My Elana. My granddaughter."

"Named for you?" Elana whispered.

"Eliana. My name, before I left it behind. I was born Eliana."

The Mistress let out a final, tender breath, calm as a breeze through the tops of the evergreens surrounding the Keep, and her spirit fled her body.

Elana held tighter to her, feeling more than anyone else her grandmother's soul flee her body, melding once more into the amarin of Aggar. Diana held her tight as she wept uncontrollably, her last strong connection to her homeworld now just a hollow vessel.

"What are you doing?" Elana looked out at the crowd, her voice ragged and full of desperation, fury, and despair. "You're just going to stand here? Your Mistress is *dead*! By *our* hands! Stop this feud! Stop it right now! Go!"

The crowd started to filter away, many adepts looking on in shock grief as the leader of the Keep lay dead. Elana snarled ferociously, casting her Sight out through the crowd as a wave. No one dared challenge her. They raced back out to the courtyard and helped break up the last of the fighting.

"Elana..." Diana fought for something to say, but Elana only shook her head.

"Please. Don't say anything. Just be here with me."

Diana held her tighter and nodded. "Of course, Soroi. Always."

The flames rose high against the night sky, standing out starkly against the cloudless void of space. Elana stood still at Diana's side, her hands clasped behind her back, her face still and her eyes unblinking as she watched the Mistress's body, bound in perfumed and ornate folds of lace, disappear into the flames.

It wasn't the last funeral they'd have. It was the first of many: Terrans, students, and counselors had all been killed in the battle, most in the two explosions triggered when an ammunition supply tent caught fire. Elana hadn't even been aware the Terran soldiers were carrying guns, let alone ones that ran on gunpowder. The cheaper weapons were all the Empire had allowed the Terran base, as they weren't actively enveloped in the Empire's war.

Most of the members of the Keep and soldiers had left, mourning their own losses. The remaining counselors would meet in the morning to name the new members and a new Mistress. The Terrans would be leaving at dawn. But Elana was committed to watching the last of the Mistress's embers fade and Diana wouldn't leave her lover's side.

There was a soft shuffle of steps in the grass and a man walked up beside Elana, his eyes on the funeral pyre.

"You're not wearing an amulet." Elana's voice was ice-cold. "It's a long way from Markessa."

Diana gave the man a second look and tensed. Tristan adjusted the high collar of his jacket. "Colder up here."

Elana didn't take her eyes off her grandmother. "What are you doing at the Keep?"

"It came to my attention that you both helped release my brother from prison without giving away our secrets. Thank you."

"Your brother was nearly suspended from the Keep. I'm not entirely convinced he shouldn't be."

"I wouldn't be so quick to cast him aside if I were you. Frisk is dedicated to the Keep. Not even I can pry its secrets out of him. And, forced to choose, I'm not confident he would pick the Marshals."

Elana crossed her arms over her chest. "He's a liability to us both, then."

"Or an asset. I have more work for you both. Work that will help the Keep and keep something like this from happening again. Wouldn't you agree Frisk is the most natural liaison between the two of us if we want secrets to remain?"

"What do you want?" Diana demanded.

"There are still seers missing. Children. They're being held by the Order of Blindness."

"We have their leader. We'll know the truth about the seers soon as well."

"I have a regional leader. I've spoken to your Counsel and they've turned him over to me."

Diana spun around to face him. "What?"

Elana raised a single hand, touching Diana's stomach. "Not for the Marshals. For the Ramains."

"He's the son of one of our nobles. He should stand trial publicly. A warning for the more easily-swayed members of the Order to give up peacefully. Your counsel seems content they have all the answers they need from him. What's left of your counsel, anyway."

"If you're working so closely with the Counsel, why are you coming to us about this?"

"You think the Keep will be strong enough to act on anything for a while? Your new counsel will be built from ancient professors and new graduates – people who never expected to run the Keep, or expected to be much more experienced when they did. I need a small force. One that can move discreetly. One that knows about the Order and has defeated them before. You're the only two who make sense. And I suspect, after civil war like this one, that neither of you will have much of a connection to the Keep anymore."

Diana hesitated to answer. She suddenly felt it wasn't her place to reply – it was Elana's. This was her world. Her people. Her Keep. And while she'd spent entire nights weeping for the Mistress, Diana suspected the Mistress's last words had gotten to her granddaughter. She had no idea where Elana's heart lay anymore."

"We played right into their hands. They almost defeated us." The edge in Elana's voice had turned hollow.

"You did."

"I'm tired of Aggar. Diana and I are going to her world."

Diana glanced at Elana. It was the first time Diana had heard Elana speak so firmly about leaving.

"I don't think you will. Not yet."

Elana finally looked away from the Mistress at Tristan. "Why?"

"Because these missing seers are children. And while events have left you jaded about the Keep and the attitude of the average person of Aggar has scared you, you won't abandon helpless children. No Shadow would."

"I'm not scared," Elana rebutted. "I'm sad."

"I know."

"What's in it for you?" Diana questioned. "You help us save these missing seers... what do you get in return?"

"The Order of Blindness is more widespread and powerful than previously thought. You captured a regional leader. He's charismatic, but he has relatively little authority in the grand scheme of things. Undoubtedly he was seeking to gain power by taking the Keep. The Order is still strong without him. It's a threat to the Ramains. I want to see that threat neutralized."

"You want us to do your dirty work so your people aren't made public." Elana's words were an accusation.

Tristan was unaffected. "Yes. Exactly."

Elana and Diana stood in silence. Diana looked at Elana and took her hand. "The decision is yours. I'll take you back to my home if you like. Or I'll stand with you here."

Elana squeezed her hand. "I know."

"Our reports suggest up to a dozen children are missing. We don't know if they're alive. But we have leads. You'll have all the support of the Marshals at your disposal. And I'm sure the Keep would like to have its children back."

"How do we know to trust you?"

"Have I proven myself to be anything but honest with you?"

Elana considered his words. "No. You haven't."

"I won't force anything on you. If you reject my offer, I'll take it to your counsel. I suspect they'll come to the same conclusions I did and they'll ask you themselves. And if you deny them as well, we'll find another solution. I don't think I need to explain, however, the perils of sending young, untrained Shadows across the world after the Order. And a young adept is all the Keep will have to send after the Counsel is called and Shadows with a diplomatic flair are used to repair relations with the Terrans and seek aide from the Ramains."

Elana looked back at the funeral pyre, her brow knit as she stood deep in thought.

"What would she want?" Tristan indicated the pyre.

"Don't," Diana commanded, instantly silencing him.

"She would want them safe."

With that single sentence, Diana knew Elana had already made her decision. She steeled herself for one more adventure. One more quest on Aggar.

Elana turned to Tristan. "Where do we go first?"

The End of Book Five

DICTIONARY OF AGGAR TERMS

amarin: The amarin is the essence of life, the empathic imprint of animate existence which results in a cumulative pattern of feelings, thoughts and reflexes. It is one's aura.

basker jackal: a sleek, scavenger canine, native to the Ramains' plains and renowned for its blood lust; semi-domesticated by militia for chase and guard chores

black glass: a ceramic-glass compound of especially durable strength that hones to a sharp edge; commonly used in making knife blades

blackpine: A valuable hardwood conifer with a black, barkless trunk and green-black needles which is common to Maltar's lands.

Blue Sight: The Sight or Blue Gift is a sixth sense genetically linked to blue eyes; an awareness of and ability to manipulate life auras and amarin. The terms also refers to a person possessing the Blue Sight.

bondmate: any eitteh, human, or sandwolf who has been empathically bonded into a sandwolf's familial unit (see pack bond; sandwolf)

boko: A food native to the Ramains, boko is a vegetable-meat paste wrapped in boiled leaves.

braygoat: a short-horned goat native to Ramians' southern districts

brushberry: an evergreen bush with a sweet-tart berry; a Ramains wine

bunt: A tall, stemmed grain which yields red-brown seedlings and whose husks are often used for animal fodder. The term also applies to the grayish flour produced from the seedlings.

buntsow: a carnivorous, hooved mammal; a scavenger native to the northern forests; a non-venomous cousin of schefea

"By the Mother's Hand": (idiom) "Done with the Goddess' blessings."

Changlings: Sentient half-human, half-feline beasts native to the Northern Continent, Changlings are a race of people known for their amoral selling and reselling of information. They are also miners of lifestones.

Circle, The: The elite soldiers of the Core, bands of bandits and warriors who do the Twins' bidding

Clan, the: people of the Clan's Plateau; descendents of off-worlders who were stranded on Aggar at the fall of the Galactic Terran Empire; renowned for their weapons technology and raiding activities

Clan Lead: legislative representatives chosen by and from among the Clan folk; (plural) a governing assembly; civil servant

Clantown: the governing settlement and militia corp of the Clan's Plateau; a village in the ancient Terran Quadrant, located at the edge of the eastern plateau adjacent to the Ramains' Great Forests

commons: A Ramains' term for a tavern housed by an inn.

Core, The: The nation risen from the ruins of the Clan's settlement, once the Maltar's realm.

Council of Ten: A collection of ten Masters and Mistresses educated in the history and humanity of Aggar who are guardians of the planet's integrity.

Crowned Rule: the designated heir of the Ramains' Royal Family; usually chosen for skills of statescraft rather than warfare

cucarae: A small, extremely poisonous scavenger, this crustacean is found in the wastelands of both the Northern and Southern Continents.

cucarii: A group or nest of cucarae.

Desert Peoples: Also known as The Southerners, the Desert Peoples are loosely organized nomadic tribes native to the Southern Continent and renown for their distilled liquors and merchant ventures.

Diblum: a small Ramains' village southeast of Khirla

dracoon: A governing marshal appointed by the Ramains' King.

Dumauz: (plural: – en) a kind-hearted individual; a concerned friend

early moon: The first of the twin moons to rise on any given evening.

eitteh: A sentient feline native to the Northern Continent. The term eitteh usually refers to the winged females of the species as males are never seen. See also winged-cats and men-cats.

Eldest Prepared: These individuals are the best of the Shadow trainees at the Council's Keep and are the preferred choice for assignments and lifebonding. They also instruct the younger recruits.

Fates, the: The male deities of evil mischief, the Fates are mystical rulers of the dark underworld. Their primary figures include Malice and Ambition while their secondary figures include War, Ire, Greed and others.

Fates' Cellar: The legendary home of the Fates, Fates' Cellar is the mythical place where evil souls go after death to suffer in a punishing afterlife. Also known as hell.

Fates' Jest: (idiom) A malicious turn of events attributed to the Fates.

Firecaps: These intersecting, volcanic mountain ranges comprise the northeastern third of the Northern Continent. They are uninhabited and controlled by Seers in order to stabilize continental land masses.

grubber: A generic term for ground rodents in the Northern Continent. Grubber generally refers to smallish, nasty-tempered mammals.

harmon: a soul-spirit; self-image projected by a Blue Sight to another

honeywood: a deciduous hardwood with rough, red bark; yields a golden grain of decorative value; common to the southern Ramains

Jezebet: Usually given to a woman, this title is bestowed upon someone who is a resident of the Council's Keep and is trained in the arts of lifebonding Shadowmates.

jumier: a fowl native to the Ramains' northern districts

Karatan: a jungle region in the southern-most continent of Aggar

Khirla: Dracoon's capital in the Ramains' southeasterly district Khirlan

lexion: A domesticated fowl common to farms of the Northern Continent which is raised for its meat.

lifestone: An opal-like energy stone often found in limestone deposits in the Northern Continent and used by the Council in the practice of lifebonding Shadowmates.

mala': A female slave or bond-servant of the Ramains whose duties are restricted to the household and the bedroom.

Maltar: The ruling family of the northern half of the Northern Continent. The term may refer either to the ruling family member or the country itself.

men-cats: The male of the eitteh species, these cat-like savages inhabit the mountain ranges on the Northern Continent.

mesta: A thick-skinned, amber fruit with a tart, meaty pulp in the seed pods that is cultivated by farmers in the Northern Continent.

midnight moon: The second of the twin moons to rise on any given night.

Min: A generic title given to free-born women in the Ramains. It is comparable to the Terran term ma'am.

milkdeer: middle-sized, long necked mammal native to the Ramains; frequently domesticated for its milk

monarc: A standard calendar division, roughly equivalent to a Terran month, which is comprised of four, ten-day periods.

Mother, the: A nurturing female deity who is seen as the birthmother of the universe. Aggar's twin moons are associated with her watchful light.

mumut: a spice leaf grown chiefly in the lower districts of the Ramains

pack bond: empathic understanding of personal commitments; empathic bond of sandwolves used to define familial units (see sandwolf)

pripper: A small, tree-dwelling mammal known for its comical antics and bushy coat.

Purge, The: The last attack on Aggar by Terran forces that culminated in the use of biochemical warfare that massacred nearly every Blue Sight. The battle also destroyed the Council's Keep and Valley Bay, scattered the seers and Amazons.

Ramains: The southwestern third of the Northern Continent which is united beneath a liberal monarchy and shares a border with the Council's lands.

Royal Marshall: special emissaries of the Ramains' Royal Family; originally banded to protect travelers; duties expanded to provide districts with legal and military resolutions, to supply the Royal Court with information from outlying districts

sandwolf: sentient canine, originally native to the Southern Continent, which instinctively imprints at birth to one or more sentient others to provide an emotional, empathic bond in developing protective behaviors and communication skills (see pack bond)

schaefea: A hoofed scavenger of middle size native to the northern mountains. The schaefea has protruding tusks and venomous saliva glands.

Seers: Those individuals gifted with the Blue Sight who are bound to Aggar's lifecycles and no longer capable of individual thoughts or actions. They are directed by the Council of Ten and are the crafters of Aggar's landscapes. Sometimes referred to as mystics.

silverwood: A hardwood conifer with a smooth, silver-green bark and gray-green needles which is common to the Ramains foothills and mountain regions. Also called silverpine.

single moon: The night at the end of each monarc in which only one of the twin moons is visible. Term is synonymous with monarc.

Songs: the unseen force that allows the Choir to manipulate the minds of the people of Aggar; named for the mournful tune that drifts through the air whenever they're near

Tad: Generic title given to free-born men in the Ramains which is similar to the Terran term sir.

tinker-trade: a traveling merchant member of the Traders' Guild ten-day: A division of days within a monarc, roughly equivalent to a Terran week.

tenmoon season: A period of time roughly the same as two Terran years. The name comes from the fact that ten single moon nights will occur during the time it takes for Aggar to complete one orbit around its sun.

torin: An edible, broad-leafed fern commonly found in the wooded rangers of the Northern Continent.

Traders' Guild, the: a merchant union supported by membership dues that promotes the fair exchange of market goods; endorsed by the Desert Peoples, Ramains, Council and Valley Bay the union may provide arbitrators, bonded transport agents, and travel lodging to supplement regional resources

twin moons: Two planetoids orbiting around Aggar's globe. The term is also associated with the Mother's watchful care.

Twins: The tyrannical, magical rulers of the Core

Unseen Wall: An unidentified energy field which was ordered by the Council of Ten and is controlled by the Seers; the Unseen Wall comprises the border around the Terran Base Quadrant.

Valley Bay: the settlement of the Sisterhood; located near the White Isles, isolated from the Northern Continent by the Firecaps; governed by the Ring of Valley Bay and bound to the home world through the Blue Sighted gifts of the Ring's Binder.

waterferret: amphibious ferret with both scales and fur; often used to aide fisherman and common along coastal towns; very intelligent, but often sneaky and prone to theft.

White Isles of Fire, the: The group of volcanic islands off the eastern Firecaps of the Northern Continent. Sometimes called the Archipelago, it is the native homeland of the Council and the Seers.

Wine of Decisions: A spiced wine containing a natural drug which prompts the visions of the Blue Sight.

winged-cats: Generally used as another term for female eitteh.

DICTIONARY OF SORORIAN TERMS

Amazon: a Sister choosing to work/settle outside of the Sisterhood's jurisdiction

ann: (idiom) A word used to emphasize thoughts or ideas and function as a verbal exclamation point. Ann might also be translated as "Take note!" Other meanings include to be far away or distant.

be: far, distant

beasties: Large, hoofed mammals, these horned animals have copper-colored, wooly coats and are descended from the Highland Cattle of old Terra.

bin: A preposition meaning between. Sometimes means to or from.

Cee: A word that refers to the customs or ways of any given people.

cheroan: to make safe, to protect

Coramee: daughter

corean: A verb meaning to find precious, to treasure.

crone: a wise elder among healers n'Shea

dey: This word can be used as either an article as in "the" or a pronoun as in "we" or "our" and is meant to connote respect.

duen: to do kindly; to act with concern

Dumauz: (plural: —en) a kind-hearted individual; a concerned friend

Feast of Helen: This anniversary celebration of unity and independence marks the birth of the Sisterhood's firstborn child.

felan: A verb form meaning using, doing or creating.

Founding, the: the original planetary colonization of dey Sorormin under the Galactic Terran Empire; settlement of the home world

Helen: This name refers to the Red star of dey Sorormin's solar system, the firstborn of dey Sorormin's original settlement and the leader of n'Sappho during early negotiations to retain Sorormin independence. The word means "light."

Houses of dey Sorormin: surnames of Sisters, designating family and/or skills; six of Seven Houses recall ancient goddesses of Terran lore (n'Athena: guardians (Greek), n'Awehai: crafters (Iroquois), n'Hina: agricultural providers (Polynesian), n'Huitaca: artists (Chibcha), n'Minona: historians/teachers (Dahomey), n'Shea: healers (Irish); First House of dey Sorormin (n'Sappho: legislative leaders) recalls a Terran stateswoman of Greece

Kahmee: little daughter; a very young girl

kahn: A noun meaning sunrise or dawn.

kamak: A verb which indicates something is brought to completion or finished. It may also be used in place of is made.

kau: A pronoun referring to the second person singular (you).

ki: A word indicating possession (yours).

kumin: A verb meaning to join together.

m': A preposition denoting as or of (from).

m'Sormee: birth mother; (literally) from the woman's life

mae: A word indicating that something is dear or precious.

"Mae n'Pour": (idiom) An expression which means "Give me strength." This term is often used as a curse to express frustration or anger but can also be used as a genuine prayer to the Goddess.

mau: A noun meaning heart.

mauen: The plural form of mau (hearts).

mee: A noun which denotes life.

minmee: A word meaning birth, minmee also carries the connotation of the sacred connection of life-giving or creating.

n': This expression denotes possession. It is usually used to indicate an individual's House.

n'Athena: One of the Seven Houses of dey Sorormin, members of this house are traditionally the guardians of the Sisterhood. The term also recalls a Terran goddess from ancient Greek lore.

n'Awehai: One of the Seven Houses of dey Sorormin, members of this house are traditionally the builders and craftswomen of the Sisterhood. The term also recalls a Terran goddess of Iroquois (Native Northern American) lore.

n'Hina: One of the Seven Houses of dey Sorormin, members of this house are traditionally the agricultural providers of the Sisterhood. The term also recalls a Terran goddess of Polynesian lore.

n'Huitaca: One of the Seven Houses of dey Sorormin, members of this house are traditionally the treasurers of music and arts of the Sisterhood. The term also recalls a Terran goddess of Colombian Chibcha (Native Southern American) lore.

n'Minona: One of the Seven Houses of dey Sorormin, members of this house are traditionally the historians and teachers of the Sisterhood. The term also recalls a Terran goddess of African Dahomey lore.

n'Sappho: First House of the Seven Houses of dey Sorormin, members of this house traditionally make up the legislature and leadership of the Sisterhood. The term also recalls a Terran stateswoman of ancient Greek citizenship.

n'Shea: One of the Seven Houses of dey Sorormin, members of this house are traditionally the healers and earthwitches of the Sisterhood. The term also recalls a Terran woman-deity and/or the white witches of ancient Irish lore.

n'Sormee: parenting mother or guardian; (literally) of the woman's life

nehna: (idiom) A prompt for more information meaning and then, then it happened that or so then.

Niachero: Daughter of the Stars; descriptive of Sisters who genetically resemble those n'Athena who negotiated the settlement of Valley Bay; Amazons who led the space protectors to save Aggar during the fall of the Galactic Terran Empire

nor: An word that indicates an event happened in the past.

puor: An word meaning strength, stability or virtuousness.

quinn: A word denoting peace, tranquility or the absence of violence.

quitan: to nurture; to tend with compassion

ret: A word meaning cruelty or harm.

sae: Another term for please, this word denotes a request.

sak: This word means intelligence or cleverness.

shea: This noun refers to a healing witch from the House of n'Shea. A member of this house will frequently be one who is closely bound to nature. She may also be a mistress of love potions and possess the evil eye. See the term n'Shea.

sheaz: A noun meaning the earth or world, this term may also refer to the components of a nurturing Earthmother Creator.

Shekhina: The moon of Helen's second planet. This moon is home to Helen's high-tech base where diplomatic contacts between the dey Sorormin and the Galactic Terran Empire occur. It is also the home of the Immigration offices and the orientation/screening facilities for new Sisters. Historically, the term refers to an ancient Terran goddess of Judaic lore and sometimes connotes the divine image of a woman.

sor: The noun meaning woman.

soroe: The noun denoting friend or dear companion.

Soroi: loved one; lover; beloved

Sororian: The woman-made language of the Sisterhood. The term derives its root meaning from the ancient Terran word which refers to sisters.

Sorormin: A noun that is synonymous with the word Sisterhood.

Sorormin, dey: The word which represents the proper name of The Sisterhood. The term also refers generally to the culture of women who settled on Helen's second planet. dey Sorormin are recognized members of the Senate in the Third Galactic Terran Empire.

sueht: A past tense form of the verb to lose or to misplace.

tau: A pronoun denoting me.

ti: A word that indicates possession (my).

tizmar: A verb which means to remain, to settle or to unite and/or join together.

vu: A term meaning very little, a small amount.

z': A term indicating for or with.

"Z'ki Sak, Diana": (idiom) An expression of regret or disbelief which translates as "By your wits, Goddess."

www.ingramcontent.com/pod-product-compliance
Lightning Source LLC
Chambersburg PA
CBHW070524100726
47907CB00004B/970

* 9 7 8 1 5 9 0 9 2 9 3 2 2 *